Walking
with the
Angels

Walking with the Angels

The Valiant Papers
& The Philippian Fragment

Includes the short story "Ralph"

Calvin Miller

Baker Books

A Division of Baker Book House Co
Grand Rapids, Michigan 49516

Published by Baker Books
a division of Baker Book House Company
P.O. Box 6287, Grand Rapids, MI 49516-6287

Second printing, December 1994

Printed in the United States of America

Library of Congress Cataloging-in-Publication Data

Miller, Calvin.
    Walking with the angels / Calvin Miller.
        p.   cm.
    Contents: Ralph—The valiant papers—The Philippian fragment.
    ISBN 0-8010-6308-6
    1. Christian fiction, American. 2. Angels—Fiction. I. Title.
PS3563.I376A6   1994
813'.54—dc20   94-7402

The Valiant Papers was originally published in 1982 by Zondervan Publishing House.

The Philippian Fragment was originally published in 1982 by InterVarsity Press.

Contents

Ralph   7

The Valiant Papers   23

The Philippian Fragment   123

Ralph

I met Ralph in the smoking section of the bar in the Monteleone Hotel in New Orleans. It was late on Friday night, April 3, 1987. I was waiting for a single table in the main restaurant and was stirring a pinch of lime into a tumbler of tomato juice when I caught sight of him. The light was so dim that it seemed on the verge of going out completely in that section of the restaurant. My eyes first fell on Ralph when I became aware that something in the shadows cleared its throat. The hair rose on the nape of my neck. My vision fingered the darkness to see what was invisibly there. I stared hard at the dim emptiness and tentatively asked, "Is someone there?"

"I am," said Ralph.

The voice issued from nowhere.

I slitted my eyes now to laser focus and poked holes in the darkness to make any two molecules of substance gather themselves together in the aching absence.

"Shall I call you Calvin or Dr. Miller?" asked the voice from the void.

I pushed back my chair and stood to move to a section of the bar that was better lit.

"Move if you will," it said. "But I'd sit down if I were you, Dr. Miller."

"Calvin—please call me Calvin. I despise being formally addressed by ghosts and ghouls and things that go bump in the night."

"All right, Cal it is!"

"*Calvin* please, I don't like ghosts who get too familiar, either."

I sat back down, staring hard into the semi-darkness across the small table. It was then I saw a thin, milk-white hologram of a soul. It was opaque but so thinly visible that I could see a wall plug through its transparent body. It had a face.

"Yes, I have a face," he said. "Does it look familiar?"

I shuddered. The thing had my face! It was then that I realized it even talked like me!

"What's your name, Banquo?" I asked, hoping the infernal shade would appreciate my Shakespearean reference.

"Very funny," said the shadowy thing.

9

"My name is Raphael, but you can call me Ralph. I'm your guardian angel."

"Excuse me, but I'm fifty years old. Why have you waited till now to show up?"

"I've been around since you've been around. For five decades now I've never been more than a few feet from you. If you are just now seeing me, it's because you have never experienced .532 degree half-light. When that precise level of illumination occurs, guardians become visible, or mostly so. You see, my good Doctor, you mortals rarely experience this precise level of illumination, and only at this level can my realm visibly touch your realm. So gaze at me and see what may be seen. You will likely never see me again in your life, and yet for the rest of your life, I will be here."

"But, I hear you as well as see you. What does illumination have to do with hearing? Do sound waves also come in at .532 half-light?"

"At such moments as angels are visible, they are also audible. When we are seen we can also be heard."

"I am surprised," I said, "that we look so much alike!"

"Are you troubled about that? Believe me, it is far harder on angels to look like humans than vice versa. It would be much simpler for angelic egos, if you none-too-comely mortals would just agree to look like us. All angels are troubled about being ugly mortal look-alikes at first. Don't take this too personally, but balding and cellulite are not considered beautiful in either of our realms, I'm afraid."

"I find it hard to believe that I'm not hallucinating. The mind makes angels out of stomach acid. I had a friend who used to see whole hosts of angels when he was tripping out on LSD. If you're really my guardian, how much do I have in my checking account? A guardian would surely know things like that."

"Well, not enough this month," said Ralph.

"Don't try to weasel out of it, how much?"

"In your Nations Bank or your Bank America account?" asked Ralph.

"Forget it!" I said. It gave me the heebie-jeebies to know he knew. "You've been here the whole fifty years?" I asked.

"All of them. I can remember your life before you can remember it. You wanna know how much you weighed at birth? Seven pounds fourteen ounces. Now you weigh two hundred and seven pounds and would like to lose twenty, wouldn't you? I tried to stop you from eating that Snickers bar this afternoon."

Now I felt very uncomfortable. Being reminded of the candy and hearing my weight spoken "out loud" stirred me with guilt. "Okay, okay," I said.

"You remember when you fell on the water meter?" he asked.

"You know about that? My mother told me about it. I still have a scar on the back of my head."

"You really bled. The doctor stitched you up and I stood watch till you gradually began to feel better again."

"Thanks."

"Don't mention it. Do you remember the night of 1945 that you went to that tent revival in northern Oklahoma?"

"I sure do. I was only nine years old but I found Christ—that was a night the angels sang!"

"Yes, we did."

I suddenly began to have the feeling that Ralph knew more about me than I really wanted him to know. And not just about the spiritual things, either.

"Remember that book with all the pictures that Gene Hampstead circulated in the back of your sophomore geometry class? You were a Christian—rather vocal about it, too. But there you were reaching for pornography and posing as a geometry scholar. Remember how long you held the book inside your open textbook? Remember how long you stared?"

"Okay, okay! What's your point, Ralph?"

"I just want you to know how well I know about everything you've ever done."

"So, is that all you angels have to do—take notes on your victims over a lifetime and go around bringing up sins that God forgave long ago?"

"Not victims," Ralph paused. "You're our charges. The Boss puts us in charge to battle bad conscience and to do all we can to keep you alive and well till you've reached the fullest state of inner maturity that can be reached."

"How close am I to the goal?"

"Actually, to say that both the Boss and I are disappointed would be an understatement." Ralph seemed harsh for an angel. "It's your inner hypocrisy we find so intolerable. Here you are a professor in a seminary, wearing the mask of warm godliness and spirituality—but the things

11

that go through your mind! Frankly, your inner life is a little too Mr. Hyde for the Boss. You enjoy being called Doctor, don't you?"

I didn't answer. He knew I did.

"So did the Pharisees," he said. "You like wearing your academic regalia too, don't you?"

"I . . . I . . . I . . ." I stammered, trying to defend my academic career.

"Well, so did the Pharisees," he said.

"All right, just a cotton-picking minute. I resent your comparing me to the Pharisees. I'm not like them."

"Remember the day you prayed with that student who was toying with unbelief and exploring agnosticism?"

"Yes, I prayed with him—and I still believe I helped that student when I prayed with him."

"Yes, but remember that you left your office door open so the less godly people who passed down the hall could see you praying? That was a tad exhibitionist, don't you think?"

"Well, I . . . I . . . I . . ."

"Cal, don't you . . ."

"Calvin," I interrupted.

"Okay, Calvin, but we both know if I were one of your students you'd insist on Dr. Miller."

"Okay, Ralph, call me whatever you want to, but we both know that I am not like the Pharisees."

"Remember the bleeding Pharisees?" said Ralph. "Remember how they walked around with their eyes cast down, so that they would never be tempted to lust? Then they ran into things and bloodied their foreheads. That's why they were called bleeding Pharisees."

"Now just a cotton-picking minute! Most of the time I'm as pure as Billy Graham. I am not like those bleeding Pharisees!" I could feel myself growing angry. "Besides, lust is never there until we take the second look."

"You never take a second look, do you? No, not you. You don't have to take a second, do you? You just take that long first look. There's no one who would accuse you of looking down to avoid lust. You always just keep looking up."

"Okay, Ralph. Is there a good word from the other side?"

"Well, the Boss says you've made some progress. You're able to love fundamentalists, liberals, and people that have out-succeeded you, which nearly everybody has done."

I felt a little better for the moment. It was the kindest thing Ralph had said so far.

"Still, you seem to be a bit too proud of your humility and your academic status. Here's a special word from the other side: The Boss would like for you to work a little harder on your conformity to Christ."

"Okay, what's the recipe?"

"Well, to start off with you watch too many movies."

"The Boss doesn't like movies, does he?"

"Well, he does get wrathful at hearing his name wallowed around through the pigsty of movie scripts. He's noticed that while immorality in the cinema used to offend you, you've gotten to the point where you hardly notice. It once bothered you a great deal when actors used illicit anger and profaned holiness, didn't it?"

"Well, there is a lot of that kind of stuff in movies, but what am I supposed to do, stay home all the time? Does the Boss prefer naivete over cultural understanding?"

"You see how you defend yourself? Why not confess your seared conscience? Besides, you like the sex scenes that now comprise most movies."

"Look, Ralph, I never go to X-rated movies because I don't like sex scenes."

"Wrong, Dr. Miller, you never go to X-rated movies because you *do* like them. The Boss wants you to memorize Philippians 4:8: 'Finally, brethren, whatsoever things are true, whatsoever things are honest, whatsoever things are just, whatsoever things are pure, whatsoever things are lovely, whatsoever things are of good report . . .'"

"Okay, okay! I've been to seminary. I know what it says. Is it okay with the Boss if I watch the Disney channel?"

"Listen, Calvin, why watch anything at all? Why not return to the Bible? Why not try praying more? Why not act a little more like you're hungry for heaven and not so completely satisfied to be living an indulgent life on the planet? Your biggest problem is not caring about the things God cares about."

"Like?"

"Like human lostness. Like the sins of political and military aggrandizement. Take this morning, for instance. You looked at a child's picture on the milk carton and didn't care. Your conscience is so seared that you can pass automobile accidents and get angry that injured people have slowed you down and prevented you from keeping your appointments on time. You read about children burned up in an apartment fire in Milwaukee and you don't give a fig."

"I care. But those who live in a slaughterhouse cannot weep for all the dying!"

"Calvin, Calvin, can you not hear in your voice an attempt to justify your callous soul? Pardon me, but the Boss told me if ever I became visible I should tell you a story."

I moved back into the shadows and listened as Ralph went on uninterrupted.

"There was once a boy born shortly after the Great Depression had begun to recede. He was born in a large family whose poverty might have been eased, if the boy's father had not been such a terrible drunkard. Just before the outbreak of World War II, the father's drinking habit had become so severe that he was often thrown in jail for public misdemeanors and unruly drunkenness. Once when the father was jailed, the boy's mother obtained a legal separation and the father abandoned the boy's family.

"Without his father the small boy felt very afraid and was often disconsolate. During World War II, the boy's older sisters became the wives of American servicemen. This further increased the boy's feelings of loneliness. Often as a child his insecurities haunted him with bad dreams and engulfing depression. Then in 1945, the war was over and the boy became a believer in Christ."

"Ralph," I interrupted, "this story has a familiar ring to it."

"It's a story you may know well, but it is not your story." He was most insistent, so I grew quiet and let him continue.

"Well, this childhood commitment that had led him to know Christ was but the beginning of a long love affair. For reasons the boy could not explain, he was possessed of a desperate hunger to know Christ better and better. He was mad with joy. He sang the Sunday school songs and memorized Scriptures. He prayed, as children pray, with all his heart. It never occurred to the child that there were more things to believe in than he suspected. There were no other ways to see the world than he saw it. He looked at the world only briefly; gave it a side-glance and then returned his young eyes toward Jesus. Here and there the harsher world came into view. Once he was beaten up by a group of sidewalk ruffians, who seemed to have no motive for their assault except that they enjoyed the sport of their own hoodlummery.

"The boy cried all the way home, and when he reached home, his mother consoled him. It was strange that he really didn't seem to need her consolation. The trials of his childhood were not especially easy for him, but they did engender a furious need for God, and with each of them he seemed to develop a growing spiritual closeness.

"His adolescence was in some ways typical. He found himself walled in by growing feelings of a maturing sexuality. Sometimes the rise of these new feelings obliterated his best resolve, and his mental permissiveness caused him to wonder if he would ever be free enough of his fantasies to be of much use to God. But ordinarily he studied his books and found himself reasonable about most things."

"Stop, Ralph!" I was almost shouting. "I tell you this story is mine! I know its outcome and quite frankly, I'm bored!"

"Don't flatter yourself. The story is not yours. You never have been this story. Believe me, the story will all too soon be dissimilar from yours. Now . . . let's see, I was about to say that in his sixteenth year, the boy had a terrible nightmare. His quiet life was invaded one midnight by a demon named Gloria."

"A girl demon?" I was relieved. This was the first time in the relating of his narrative that the story did not seem to be my own.

"Yes! A girl demon or so it appeared, although the whole supernatural realm of demons and angels is essentially sexless. But demons may for deviant purposes appear any way they like, and while Gloria's real name was probably something Screwtapish, like Scabheart, as far as the boy could see, she was a woman.

"She was plenty seductive, too! Not in any sexual sort of a way, but in a way that seemed to say, 'Come hither, son, and I will make you wise.'

"'Get thee behind me Satan!' said the boy. So ordered, she left the room, but only for a moment or so. For after the boy had gone to sleep, he would wake up in the wee small hours of the morning to find her simply sitting in the corner of his room, smiling, waiting, and oddly beckoning to him with her finger crooked. Sometimes she slouched seductively in a chair and used her glistening body to lure the boy toward a kind of carnality that tempted him with such fantasies that it became increasingly harder for him to say, 'Get thee behind me, Gloria!' She drew upon his blossoming, adolescent sexuality far more seductively than any of the Sirens that vexed Ulysses and his men."

"So Gloria was one of those late puberty demons? No matter. This boy is no different from the rest of us. Which of us on waking up in puberty has not known Gloria? She is cheerleader, tight jeans, *femme fantasia*. She is that seductress of emerging masculinity, all staple-in-the-navel, *Playboy* centerfolds. All men have known Gloria, Ralph." Ralph ignored my interruption.

"Gloria always came to the boy with a condemning grin on her face as though she knew that, sooner or later, she would win over his reluctance. He never spoke to her, though she came and went in his room for over a year. Then one day he never saw her again."

"Not possible, Ralph! Gloria is there all our lives. Trust me on this. All you sexless angels and demons cannot possibly understand this one. Better leave it alone. Gloria hangs around us as surely as those little books that circulate in geometry classes. That's where we first meet Gloria. Who do you think poses for those porno pictorials? It's Gloria. And she is there as long as we live. So if you're trying to tell me that one day Gloria just walked out of the boy's life—I'm sorry, I'm just not buying your story. There was a seventy-nine-year-old professor at our seminary that once lectured on marital fidelity. At the conclusion of his lecture, one of the young married men in the class asked him, 'Sir, about what age do men quit looking at pretty girls?' The old man wryly answered, 'Well, sonny, I don't know for sure but I do know it's sometime after seventy-nine.' So you see, Ralph, Gloria hangs around the red-blooded men of this world all their lives. She runs the counters of every adult bookstore in this nation. She does the can-can at every Moulin Rouge in France, too." I was talking pretty straight with Ralph. But I knew that he really didn't understand Gloria. I thought it was time to set his inadequacies straight. "If you're ever invited to lecture on the male mystique, Ralph, turn it down. Okay?"

Again Ralph refused to pick up on my dialogue.

"The boy graduated from high school at seventeen. He determined that he would devote himself to the Boss. He loved God. He was singular about this. He couldn't stand the long intervals between Sundays, for he did so love to worship. Any thought that came from his mind which was not about Jesus was a thought wasted. He determined that he would become a foreign missionary and thus he started off to college. He was a natural student in many ways, and his grades were excellent. As a missionary in the making, he was determined to teach, rather than preach. He was not trying to be overly humble in selecting a teaching career over a pulpit ministry. He just never felt as though he was capable of so high a calling.

"It was during his sophomore year in college that two very different events were to impact his life. First, the Russians put up the first space satellite. The event caused an outcry that America was lagging behind the rest of the world in the teaching of the sciences. Since the boy was majoring . . ."

"Excuse me, did this boy have a name?" I interrupted.

"How about Clay?"

"Fine, Clay."

"Well, Clay was now assured that he was on the right track. He was majoring in science, in a world that needed scientists. He knew that God wanted him to teach science on some foreign mission field. Now he was settled. He studied hard to be worthy of what he believed was the highest calling of all. He would teach and help those who had never had a chance at education come to treasure learning. Furthermore, never did a day go by that he did not enter into prayer, so that his own devotional life would not just help him teach science, but would ensure that he would live in a growing bond with his Lord. He hungered to belong to Christ. At moments when there was a lull in his studies, he would worship Christ. He was a living, walking, breathing testament of grace. He practiced the presence of God. His soul longed for God as the deer longs after the water. He would walk alone in the darkness and meditate upon the glory of Christ and the richness of their relationship. He even applied to go on to seminary once his college days were ended. He had begun to look forward to that time of new spiritual growth. In seminary he would deepen his faith and ready himself to begin his service abroad. As much as he desired that glorious time of future study, he never hurried a moment. He believed that the only place one can meet Christ is in the moment. He rose in the morning to praise Christ, and Jesus was the last word on his tongue when he closed his eyes in sleep each night.

"The dream would have gone on forever, except that at the beginning of his junior year in college, Gloria came back."

"The demon?" Ralph looked annoyed at my interruption.

"Yes," he went on. "Yes, the demon. Only now she wasn't a demon any longer. Now, she was a real, live person."

"Aha, now we're getting down to it," I cried. "I told you, Ralph, they never go away!" I had gotten so loud in my rebuke of Ralph that two men looking at a street map of New Orleans both turned and looked across the bar in my direction. I made a note to let Ralph go on talking. He was quieter than I was. The two men looked back at the map and Ralph began again.

"Gloria took an immediate fancy to Clay. She grinned like the demon that had haunted his adolescence. Whenever she did this, it unnerved Clay, for he could not help but remember how fearful those early days had been. She was a beautiful girl and so alluring that merely walking her across campus on a moonlit evening would stir his libido to a near frenzy. Twice she invited him up to her room for drinks and the 'chance to get to know her better.' Twice he refused, but it was much harder the second time.

"Gloria was also rich, as was her father. She promised him that if things continued to work out between them, she could guarantee him that her father would give him a six-figure job and his own Corvette. She would often lure him from his studies on a beautiful afternoon. If Clay was utterly devoted to his studies, she would remind him that it was not 'what you know, but who you know in life, that causes you to win or lose.' Finally she talked Clay into leaving church on Sundays here and there so they could go to the lake or to the shopping malls of the city. She seemed to be luring him away from his spiritual value system to one that was not merely fun but gloriously secular.

"One beautiful Sunday, Gloria picked up Clay and they went for a drive. They had a leisurely dinner and continued driving far into the late afternoon. Gloria had stuck a card in her pocket. It was a plain white card but she had blotted her lipstick on it, folded it, and tucked it into her blouse. She had told her roommate that her intention was to 'wean Clay from his Victorian lifestyle.' Clay of course had no knowledge of her intentions and was so incapable of suspicion he went with Gloria to spend the day—captured by both her beauty and the overwhelming spell of a late summer afternoon.

"Their drive lasted a long time. Gloria always allowed Clay to do the driving though the car was hers. Both of them realized the kind of car that she could afford was beyond the means of a budding missionary.

At length Clay pulled her Mercedes to a stop and parked on a lonely country road. They both walked through the woods to a waterfall far from the road. Several times along the way they stopped, and Clay drew Gloria up to him and kissed her. The daylight had now spent itself, wasting its golden sunlight on yellow fields and on a thousand darkening landscapes. Evening began to fall as they moved farther through the woods toward the roaring cascade. Clay felt a surge of passion such as he had never felt before. At the beautiful pool, Gloria unbuttoned his shirt. He reciprocated by unbuttoning her blouse. He suddenly was so overcome with passion that he crushed her against himself and smothered her with kisses. As he held her against him, he suddenly felt something sticking him sharply in his chest. He reluctantly released his hold on Gloria and noticed something in the pocket of her blouse. It was a sharply creased card. He pulled it out of her pocket and unfolded it. The light was very dim in the heavy foliage by the waterfall—in fact, it was exactly .532 degree half-light."

"Don't tell me, Clay's guardian showed up and saved his chastity?" I wished I hadn't interrupted Ralph.

"Clay's guardian did in fact show up. As Clay held the card in his hand, the guardian said, 'Take and read.'"

"Listen Ralph. I've read Augustine, I know what the card said. It read: 'Let us walk honestly, as in the day; not in rioting and drunkenness, not in chambering and wantonness, not in strife and envying. But put ye on the Lord Jesus Christ, and make not provision for the flesh, to fulfil the lusts thereof.'

"But if there was nothing written on the card, where did those words from Romans 13:13–14 come from? How did the Scripture get on the card?"

"Some wonderful things happen in .532 degree half-light, son. You see, Augustine was right about irresistible grace. Sometimes the Boss saves people from themselves. Sodom and Gomorrah prove that we should never count on it. But Rahab proves that once in a while the Boss acts to spare us even when we are precipitously close to consenting to evil. Who can understand the Boss? His ways are inscrutable.

"Well no sooner was the Scripture out of his mouth than Gloria fell to the ground. There was laughter all around Clay in this primeval glen. The laughter was so shrill that it nearly blunted the lovely roar of the waterfall. Gloria was suddenly gone. Clay reached down to lift her blouse, which had fallen on the ground when she disappeared, and when he lifted it up there was nothing there but a snake. It didn't frighten him. He knew enough about snakes to know it wasn't poisonous. He thought of crushing it beneath his heel . . ."

"There's a verse of Scripture like that in Genesis," I said.

"But," Ralph went on, "It was somehow too connected with Gloria for him to step on. 'No,' mused Clay, 'I can't step on you, I just took you to dinner. I almost . . .' Clay realized that it was this 'almost' that had *almost* destroyed him. He was alone with his guardian who said to him, 'Come on, Clay, .532 degree half-light won't hold much longer. I've got to get you out of these woods before it gets too dark for you to see me, because then it will also be too dark for you to see the path out of here.' Clay could see even as he began to follow his guardian out of the woods that Gloria's clothes were being absorbed into the earth and soon all traces of her would be gone. As the snake watched him leave, Clay broke a chunk of bark off the tree where Gloria had so recently melted away."

"Why?" I asked.

"Clay's guardian said that as he walked away from the waterfall, he kept feeling the roughness of the tree bark in his hand and incessantly repeating these words from Genesis 3:3: 'But of the fruit of the tree which is in the midst of the garden, God hath said, Ye shall not eat of it, neither shall ye touch it, lest ye die.'

"Clay is an old man now and sometimes he will look wistfully into the distant horizon and say oddly to himself, 'of every tree but one . . .' Then he seems to see a better tree and he repeats Revelation 22:1–2 in low tones: 'And he shewed me a pure river of water of life, clear as crystal, proceeding out of the throne of God and of the Lamb . . . and on either side of the river, was there the tree of life.'"

"But what of the Mercedes?" I asked.

"Vanished!" said Ralph.

"So the coach at last turns back to a pumpkin, and Clay's purity paves his way to the foreign mission field? What is this—a kind of fairy tale for Christians? A marriage of Cinderella to missions and demonology?"

"Clay walked back to town that night along dark and lonely roads. He knew what Gloria was. She was not merely a temptress. She was a constant bid for an alternative to reality. She could have been Clay's, any night he called. She was appetite gratification. She was wealth. She was image and self-esteem. He knew that most missionaries and pastors also knew Gloria. They kept her in a room at the back of their minds. They had all been to the same tree. They had all been reminded by guardians huddling in half-light, that Romans 13:13 was to be reckoned with. But most of them went on keeping Gloria around. They permitted themselves a quasi-commitment to Christ that they could exhibit freely where they needed to bolster their spiritual image. But they liked housing Gloria in their hearts. They walked with Christ in public covenants, but away from their field of ministry they ran with Gloria. They drove hot cars and made six-digit salaries, all the time promising publicly to die for Christ in poverty and submission.

"But, as I said, Clay is an old man. He works in a village of thatched huts in one of the islands of Polynesia. He walks among the islanders teaching them of the very Christ he never seems to get enough of. He is up each morning just before the sun rises, for he has, on three separate occasions, in that split second of time experienced .532 degree half-light. He likes looking at his guardian every now and then just to remind himself that his world is not the only world that is. On a crude carved shelf in his hut, there reside two odd artifacts that create the only altar of remembrance that he permits himself: a piece of bark he broke from a tree near a waterfall, and a creased card. The card has nothing written on it most of the time, but at those few special moments of .532 degree half-light, a couple of verses from Romans clearly surface. Clay is the wealthiest man I know. He is rich with a love affair that so possesses him, he is ashamed that he nearly lost it all at an old tree. Someday, I suspect, Clay and Christ will be walking along in the constant conversation that absorbs his days and he will pass through the gates of his redemption so absorbed in his Redeemer he will not see them."

"Ralph, you are right! This is not my story."

"I know it is not your story. You have no chunk of bark on your low-altar shelf. You've made too many deals with Gloria. You've been tamed by a mouthy secular commitment that only talks about intimacy with Christ but never gets close to Clay's life of joy."

I thought of Jesus, and how I once had loved him. I thought of all that might have meant in my walk with Christ. I thought of all the love we might have shared. I thought of all the souls I might have taught to breathe his name. But Ralph was right, I had made too many side deals.

"No, this is not my story." I was weeping now.

"Ah, but it might have been," he said, "it might have been."

Suddenly a woman with a camera stepped toward us. She was one of those photographers who take pictures of people in the restaurants and bring them to the table just as you're finishing your dessert. "NO— DON'T DO IT!" I shouted, just as the flash went off. But it was too late, .532 degree half-light was eradicated by an explosion of blue-white incandescence. Ralph was gone. I have not seen him since. When the searing light had died and my eyes had adjusted, I found the woman with the camera. "Please, madam, while I won't be staying for dinner, I would like a copy of that picture you took."

"To be sure, sir. I'll have it in fifteen minutes at the cashier's stand."

In fifteen minutes, we met again. "You're not going to like this picture, sir. I didn't realize you were crying when I took it," she apologized. I slipped it from its envelope and studied it a moment. It was true. I was obviously crying in the picture. My face was streaked with grief. "It's perfect!" I said. "How much is it?"

"Ten dollars. But sir, you don't have to take this one. I can take another of you and have it ready in half an hour." It was then that I looked down and saw her hotel nametag. It read, "Gloria."

"I should have known," I said.

"Pardon me, sir. Have we ever met?"

"You'll never know how often." I could see that she was puzzled as I walked out of the hotel into the streets.

As I said, all that was back in 1987. In every instance of moral decision since that time, I have developed an odd habit of looking for Ralph in dimly-lit places. For I know when the light is just right I'll be able to see him. Furthermore, I have put up a small shelf in my home. There's nothing on that shelf, except a photograph of an old, none-too-saintly sinner, caught in the act of crying. Oh yes, I also keep a plain white card near that picture. I know Ralph is pleased, for we both know that at regular intervals of day and night, in that split second when the light is just right, some pretty important words come and go on the card. I delight often in the presence of Christ and wonder why I so long denied myself the fullness of his pleasure. I am content in Christ, but in my contentment are lingering question marks, and I always wonder what my story might have been.

The Valiant Papers

Foreword   27
To the Committee   31
The Summary   33
Friday, June 25   45
Monday, June 28   49
A Certain Wednesday in July   53
Of August and Two Television Episodes   55
The Trees   59
From a Bedroom on an Autumn Night   64
The Last of October   70
Snow   72
The Fire and Image   77
Of Love and Backslipping   81
A Muddyscuttle Fear   84
A Special Word to the Committee   87
January   89
Star Thoughts   92
The Rural Saint   94
A Silent Winter's Night   102
The Middle of the Year   104
The Month of the Logos   108
On the Way to the Conquest   112
The Triumph   116
In the Bus Terminal   120

Foreword

One Friday night in April, I was traveling through Cleveland, Ohio. I was to change buses after a short layover and continue to Buffalo, New York. As we pulled into the terminal, I noticed a chartered bus filled with men and women who appeared to be somewhat older than college age. Through the large windows of the bus I could see they were sitting in a random fashion, not in the customary heterosexual arrangement of young marrieds. I assumed, therefore, that they were singles departing on some lark. I could not immediately think of the nature of their outing since it was too late for the ski season and too early for summer vacations.

One couple near the back window of the bus was strumming guitars and singing. As a pastor I have seen a lot of guitars and young folk, and I suddenly realized it was a religious retreat in its formative stages.

Our buses passed slowly. The one on which I rode pulled into the gate that the charter had vacated. This turned out to be the most timely of departures and arrivals. I was shortly to make an amazing discovery.

I found myself sitting in the terminal with my briefcase under my seat. I leaned back against the sweater that I had removed. I was uncomfortably warm and feeling a touch of nausea which I attributed to the irregular motion of the bus in the heavy city traffic.

While waiting for the bus to Buffalo, I sat absent-mindedly running my hand over the empty seat next to the one I occupied. In this distracted activity my fingers fell upon a sticky surface. I thought it to be cola accidentally spilled by a clumsy child probably as impatient as I to board a bus.

I instinctively recoiled. Something from the seat clung to my fingertips. The stickiness was not a beverage slick as I had thought, but a piece of semi-adhesive cellophane the size of typing paper, except much thinner. When I held the transparency to the light, I could see that it was not entirely clear. It contained some characters nearly impossible to read. The tiny "glyphs" appeared to be a faded form of handwriting. I squinted in a vain attempt to make the queer etchings yield words, or even a singe recognizable letter. They would not.

As I placed my hand upon the empty seat again, the sticky sensation recurred. Once more I drew back, and just as surely had lifted a second piece of this clear film bearing the same faint, unintelligible characters. I placed this second transparency behind the first and reached again to the empty seat. Another sheet adhered. Some thirty times I repeated the procedure until I had lifted and stacked everything that the seat contained. I arranged the sheets in exactly the order that I had retrieved them. When my hand finally fell on naked wood, I felt somehow cheated that the strange adventure was over.

My next activity must have appeared strange to others in the terminal. I rose and checked my own seat to be sure there were no sheets there. I moved along the row of empty chairs until I came to one occupied by a rather portly gentleman. He peered at me over the top of his newspaper in a way that unnerved me and halted my search.

I did not fold the sheets, but put them directly into my attaché case, planning to examine them later. As I placed them in the case, I took two aspirin from it and swallowed them, hoping to alleviate a headache that had grown to a dull throb during my stay in the terminal.

My bus was called at last. I grabbed my sweater and attaché case and walked to the gate. I boarded the bus still feeling nauseous. My condition worsened. I began to feel alternately chills and fever. The long ride to Buffalo became one of the most arduous trips of my life.

Several times on the bus I fell asleep in a deep slumber that resembled a coma. In brief moments of consciousness I feared that I might be experiencing some sort of seizures. In spasms of unconsciousness it seemed I heard the wing beats of some very large bird. In conscious moments I attributed these strange flutterings to the delirium of my fever.

I prayed to be free of the sickness. But neither aspirin nor prayer offered deliverance. Several times I thought of asking the driver to stop to see if he might arrange my transportation to the nearest hospital. But usually, by breathing deeply, I could feel some relief. In these better moments I felt embarrassed that I had thought myself to be sick at all.

Finally I arrived in Buffalo, took a cab to my hotel, and checked in. Once in my room, I turned down my bed. I wanted to collapse immediately into deep healing sleep. However, my mind turned again to those mysterious sheets in my briefcase. My curiosity was greater than my weariness, so I unsnapped the latches.

The sticky sheets were still there. While they had not grown thicker, they were becoming more opaque. I was delighted to see that the characters that had been too dim to read had grown more distinct as the papers lost their transparency. Most of all, I was relieved to see that they were written in English. I could now actually make out words and sentences. I knew if their legibility continued to improve, they would be quite readable by morning.

But again illness and fatigue overwhelmed me. I put the sheets back in the case and went to sleep. During the night I experienced more spells of fever accompanied by the sensation of audible but invisible flutterings.

By morning the illness was gone. I awoke with a start when the events of the previous day flooded into my consciousness. Suddenly and brilliantly the sun invaded my room.

I leaped from bed and grabbed my case. Eagerly I tore it open and discovered the strange sheets were still there. The crisp English sentences were bright, sharp, and exquisitely written on a kind of gossamer stationery.

I do not need to comment on the contents of the strange papers, for they formed the document that has become this book. I sensed in my first hurried reading that the material was in the process of decay even as I set about the task of copying it. What I thought I had, I now knew I was about to lose. I grabbed a pad and a pen and began the transcription in a race against time. I was determined that it be a race I would not lose.

I neared the end of my work twenty-four hours later. As I copied the last few pages, they were hard to read, and some of the text was obscure. The characters faded. The sheets grew again transparent and soon were invisible. Shortly even the desk where I had last laid them would not yield a tactile smudge. It was as though they had been absorbed into the wood and were gone.

All that remains from those curious pages is my handwritten copy. It is my hope that the reality of the elusive original will affirm the existence of a world which parallels our own.

The material herein contained was not intended for publication—at least on this planet. I believe I have acted properly, however, in releasing this manuscript. If not, I alone bear the responsibility. I have changed the names of the mortals involved. The other names appear exactly as I found them.

Calvin Miller

To the Committee

I still find it hard to believe that of all the places on earth that I might have desired, I have managed to arrive in Cleveland. I was in Japan the last time I came here, and I cannot say that I liked it any better than America. Either place is difficult once you have known the great dwellings of our realm. My exploits in Ohio cannot be of much interest to anyone in Upperton. Still, gentlemen, it will be your duty to explore these pages. They contain the tale of Mr. J. B. Considine. In his latter years—though he did not live to be very old—he worked as a junior executive of a firm called International Investors.

He was a baby when we first met. Aren't they all? I did not then suppose his life would be of much interest to me. Yet, for the twenty-six years I knew him I was torn between compassion and revulsion. It was his value system that bothered me most. Vices, not virtues, claimed his interest. His friends were like him, having his same erstwhile appetites and lifestyle. They have a saying in Cleveland that birds of a feather flock together. In J. B.'s case, his feathers matched the flock.

Throughout his brief years, he seldom spoke of God and when he did, it was never in a complimentary fashion. He didn't even dream clean. He was a Narcissus, I'm afraid. His priority was himself. Only near the end of his years did his life turn toward real truth. Unfortunately, he died shortly afterwards. The events of his final months are all recorded in this report. I must not leave you with any notion that I did not love him. I doted on him for twenty-six years. But loving him as I did, I could never motivate him to love truth supremely.

My short years here in Cleveland have taught me many things. The last time I came to earth, my client was an atheist who read much and drank little. J. B. Considine has completely reversed these values. I have found that atheists sometimes live far more thoughtfully than petty believers who drift between cocktail lounges and small amusements.

J. B. has taught me that persons who never formally reject Christ can still live an indulgent life that leaves no place for him.

If you are prone to be critical of my penchant for summarizing, believe me, it is best. There is little of interest in his first twenty-five years. However, I have dealt in detail with his last year of life. I have recorded those events in the present tense just as they happened.

Frankly, I'm tired! If it is at all possible, I would like a bit of a rest before my next assignment. My last two came a bit close together. Is it wise? Should anyone be asked to endure the dull illumination of places like Cleveland and Tokyo too frequently?

I am sure that you will find this report satisfactory. If I may be of help in clarifying any matter, you can reach me in Cogdill where I will soon be residing. I am completing these pages from the bus station in Cleveland.

Were I human, I would be troubled with the diesel odor from the huge buses. As it is, the odor is not so offensive as the delay. I am comforted but confounded. I shall have to leave the planet by way of a common bus. Since the time is at hand, I will not be negative. Still, I would have preferred to finish writing this report somewhere other than my lap.

Life is such
A shallow night
It trembles in the
Face of light.

Alleluia,
Valiant

The Summary

I smile now when I think of how loudly I once protested this assignment.

I am wistful now at his passing for it is our parting. I remember how I once longed to be the guardian of a minister of religion. I foolishly thought a Catholic monk would have been a posh assignment. I imagined myself following a soft-sandaled Franciscan around a quiet, sinless monastery. But an American businessman! They have an interesting piece of office equipment here on Muddyscuttle (a name I sometimes apply to this planet). The machine is called a Xerox copier and must have been invented by an American businessman desperate to clone his race.

J. B. Considine is but a Xerox of all his corporate acquaintances. How sad! The brilliant career he had planned will soon be taken up by yet another carbon of himself. If he had any idea he was about to die and leave this corporation, he would be terribly troubled. While his business is small, he imagines it strategic. He sees himself as most necessary to life here on earth. How overdone is most self-importance.

I hope I do not appear too negative. I know heaven still looks down on grumbling angels. Rest assured, I have not forgotten that Daystar began his Great Insurrection by frowning and skipping his morning Alleluias. I know that hell always grows out of paradise gone sour. I know also that fallen angels were once frowning angels who lived in joyous light without smiling.

So I smile, forcing it a little sometimes, watching J. B. dream his aggressive, selfish dreams. He constantly imagines himself as the president of his company. He flits in high self-esteem through a universe of secretaries who worship him, fight to take his dictation, carry his coffee mug, light his cigars, and make over his ideas at the quiet lunches he holds on the edge of his none-too-large desk. Like Nero in a Kuppen-

33

heimer suit, he strokes his chin and dictates volumes of letters and memos. J. B. is a winsome bachelor whose beautiful fans applaud his executive future.

His future will be neither as executive nor as long as he now thinks. That's the problem with most businessmen. They are forever planning to succeed without any real understanding of what heaven calls success.

I cannot quote our Christ and beloved Logos exactly, but his best advice to my charge would probably be, "What shall it profit any company climber if he gains the corporation and loses himself?" How sad that J. B.'s dreams were but reflections in a comic mirror; his own ego was but a distorted image of his self-importance.

So you can see why I am glad that my sojourn on Muddyscuttle is nearly done. My youthful charge has now boarded the bus to begin the trip from which he cannot return. He will go much further tonight than he supposes. We entered Muddyscuttle together and we shall make our exit together. He will "die," as they say in Cleveland, and others will mark his passing with a satin-box ritual. They will peer at him through flowers and go home to speak of how natural he looked.

Why do they speak of naturalness at a time like this? They pack their departed in roses and whisper above the organ music, "how very natural." Fortunately, neither he nor I will have to be here for the memorial services. At his funeral they will call to memory the life and works of J. B. Considine, the "dear departed." In this case, the "dear departed" has not done much that is worthy, so there will be precious little to call to mind. Even so, they will sigh above the flowery finale that he was always a "good egg." Who's to deny it? Eggs are sold by the dozen and are indistinguishable from others around them. They are easily scrambled, and once broken, they are never collectible again.

He did, however, just recently achieve something . . . ah, but wait! Let me take the events of his mundane life in order without jamming the end against the first. I will try to avoid my random wanderings as I summarize his first twenty-five years.

I remember my first abrupt meeting with him. I faced Cleveland with reluctance. Atmosphere always takes some getting used to. Air is a kind of thick resistance that clots the vision and sticks to spirit. It is as invisible as we are, only thick and gummy. You feel as though you are always pushing against it. I felt awkward in it, much as these earthlings would feel if they were suddenly forced to live submerged in water.

So from the light, clean freedom of Cogdill, I found myself in atmosphere, squirming to adjust to materiality. At the same instant, I heard an infant cry! Both the baby and I wriggled to adjust to new life. We both disliked it, but he (being immature) screamed and kicked and wept.

Wept, I say.

Crying is common in this world. It does little good to ask the reason for it. Muddyscuttle is what one might call a weeping planet. Laughter can be heard here and there, but by and large, crying is more common. As people grow up, both the sound and reason for their crying changes, but it never stops. Infants do it everywhere—even in public. But by adulthood, most crying is done alone and in the dark.

J. B.—though he wasn't called that when he first got here—wailed bitterly. He shrieked, really. But they were glad for his wail. For weeping is a sign of health here on earth. Isn't that a chilling omen? Not laughter, but *tears* is the life sign. It makes *weeping* and *being* synonyms. And this is how it was the night our twenty-six-year relationship began.

Still, when first I saw the weeping infant, I was immediately possessive. He was wet with life fluids, ruddy and umbilical, yet I knew instantly he was mine. I resented the nurse who handled him too roughly. She scrubbed him up while he continued his infernal—if I may use such a word—wailing. In but a few moments I found my first repugnance at his materiality dissipating. I determined then and there to be the best of all guardians.

It was three days before he was named. During those days I stood in the nursery of the hospital, never leaving his crib. "It's a boy!" they said. His father passed out cigars, which were smoked to celebrate his nativity. I did not altogether understand this smoky ritual of birth. Neither did they, but they puffed and billowed with gusto. (I no longer feel it necessary to delve into the reasons behind human antics. I have discovered that most of their nuances are irrational even to themselves.)

When they finally named him, he was called Johnnie Bertram Considine. While I did not find his name particularly lovely, I could not stem the flow of affection that I felt for him personally. I was anxious lest the slightest harm should come to him. Mine was the same unmanageable, furious love as came from Christ himself during his time on the planet.

It was not as though I did not love other mortals, for I felt attracted to them all. But Johnnie Bertram was the eye of my affection.

While he was a baby, I was often troubled. I ached the night he put his hand too quickly in his father's coffee. It hurt him dreadfully, and I found myself angry that his own father had been so haphazard in caring for him. I wanted him never to go hungry. While I know we are never allowed to resent any humans, I often found gaps in my good will. His mother too often let him cry at night merely because she wished he wouldn't. And, there was a touch of hypocrisy in her motherhood. She put on good shows of affection in public, but when J. B.'s 2 A.M. feeding annoyed her, she would show her irritation by handling J. B. too roughly.

I discovered that I was the very first to be able to communicate with Johnnie. While my spirituality could not form audible words such as humans can, I could make Johnnie smile by warm suggestions to his tiny inner person. Smiling is ever welcome on a crying planet. And when Johnnie smiled, they would gather about his crib and "tickle" him beneath his chin. They would marvel at his grin as though they had created it. But I knew, and hoped that in time Johnnie's own experience level would tell him subliminally, that I was really the one who brought his broadest smiles.

J. B. was his name, but during his first year his father began to call him "Googul," for what reason I will never be sure. During his second year they called him "Bubby." By his third it was "Sonny." But when he started to school they had settled on "J. B.," a name that stuck to him for the remainder of his twenty-six years.

Muddyscuttlers, at least in Ohio, all begin their education as kindergartners. This is a term of German extraction that I believe means "children's garden," though I am not sure. It was about then that I began feeling Johnnie's first attempts to shut me out. Some influence I brought to bear upon him was shrugged aside. He was mischievous, and his parents were permissive. They were disciples of the new psychology that sees all forms of spanking as barbaric. Spanking—if the term be unknown to the Committee—is the procedure of inverting children and flailing their fleshy posteriors in the interest of their futures. His parents were affording him too little direction, and I began to find it hard to get through to him myself.

His parents also gave him very little spiritual direction. We guardians know the better world. But there is only one place on earth where our world is ever discussed, and that is church. The Considines never went. I should say almost never. They did take little Johnnie there at the first of his "Googul" existence. It was the season when humans baptize their little ones into the faith. Into what faith I was never sure, since the elder Considines had no faith of their own and little esteem for anyone else's. There is a popular cliché down here that rails against "pie in the sky," and Johnnie's father had long ago decided against spoon-feeding his son "sky pie." This unfortunate attitude cut Johnnie off from any background of hope.

During Johnnie's seventh year, his father had a business problem that cost him his job. He became remote and irritable. During this time he began to drink more heavily than he "ought to." He was fond of saying it just this way, though he never seemed to make it clear how heavily one "ought to." Alcohol abuse and additional financial pressures caused the marriage to begin crumbling. The arguments of his parents were often so intense that little Johnnie cried himself to sleep at night.

At such moments I hovered close to my small charge, finding my intangible angelic nature so useless. Johnnie needed the comfort of touch. Angels cannot do it—let the Committee remember this weakness. It is for this reason that Christ became a man. During those long and lonely nights with my little charge I learned this truth: We cannot save what we cannot touch. It was skin that clothed Christ's eternal nature. The same flesh that made Christ touchable could also be crucified. So God in skin was sure to die. . . . Yet those who know Christ down here praise him for coming in the flesh.

What a blessing is in simple skin! What confirmation these mortals find in touching each other. Where there is touching, men grow secure and lovers delight themselves. Where there is too little touching, frightened children weep at night, and the race grieves. I can tell you when Johnnie was a little baby, I longed for one square centimeter of skin to set firmly on Johnnie's own! Without it I hovered, useless through his crying nights.

His parents' marriage crumbled. Johnnie's father began to shatter all his marriage vows. The pall of his father's restive sexual appetites seemed to stretch over Johnnie's own mind. When he was only nine he wrote a dreadful word on the sidewalk in yellow chalk. I pleaded with him to think of higher words, for men too soon become their thoughts. But Daystar had his way with Johnnie far more often than I did. As he grew older, Johnnie, like his father, craved more and more all his mind imagined.

The problems in his home increased over the next few years. They were never worse than at Christmas. Mrs. Considine overspent and Mister overdrank. The result was disastrous. On Christmas morning, both of them suffered from the results of their indulgences. Christmas brought little joy to Johnnie's world. He clung to the plastic toys they bought him, hungry for any kind of love.

Johnnie was still getting no exposure at all to the church. He had rarely gone since his baptism. With nothing bigger to believe in, he was compelled to believe in himself. Middle-class Americans either learn of Christ or they learn to survive without him. Survival is a kind of coping where men play hero to themselves. They bulldoze their way to meaning, worshipping only what they hope to become.

There is a local hero in this hemisphere who wears blue tights and a red cape and flies faster than a guardian angel—though they would say "speeding bullet." This super Scuttler is the ego extension of the man who makes it on his own. He is a great positivist who leaps tall buildings at a single bound. Most children, including Johnnie, know more about this muscled messiah than they do our Logos. He is the icon of human ego, caped and competent and cowering only before Kryptonite.

The years tumbled over one another. In spite of plodding loneliness, J. B. struggled on with homemade hope. His childish fears turned in time to teenage bravado. He was not vicious as a teenager, but he was a prankster.

Through all his early years there was only one touch of spiritual hope for the boy . . . Aunt Ida, his father's sister. Ida came often to visit. In her absence the older Considines referred to her as a fanatic, but Johnnie loved her nonetheless. Whereas his father read him fairy tales, Ida read him stories from the Bible. In his early years Johnnie mixed the stories so badly, he could never remember if Rapunzel or Rebekah was Isaac's wife. He was sure that Hansel and Gretel and Jonathan and David all played together in the Dark Forest. For J. B., life was special when his auntie was there. He always wanted her to stay longer than she did.

Ida was a Kentuckian and not so sophisticated as the Considines. But she was devout. Her whole personality was warmed by her affection for Christ, whom she knew, loved, and talked about in her own way. She was not able to bring about any real spiritual advances in Johnnie's parents, but Johnnie was able to discover in her a God that had enough skin to be credible. In fact, as J. B. could understand God at all, he attached the entire definition to Aunt Ida.

For his fourteenth birthday, she gave Johnnie a little Bible, but he could make no sense of it. Desiring to please her, he set out at once to read it, but became mired in the genealogies of Genesis and laid the book aside. He was never quite able to understand how a book so heavy with long names had ever managed to become the favorite of someone as lovable and touchable as Aunt Ida.

As he neared his sixteenth year, the course of his life was to change radically. His mother's and father's guardians met me in the hall one night in the month of February. They were ready to return to Upperton. Knowing they were about to leave Muddyscuttle, I had already braced myself for what shortly transpired. On that ill-fated night, the house was ominously quiet.

I must say that I have rarely seen such glum guardians. The Logos during his sojourn here referred to humans without hope as "the lost." The term fits in so many ways. It seems to me that during their lifetimes Johnnie's parents were lost. Lost to all they were . . . to all they might have been. They were psychologically lost . . . lost to love . . . lost to destiny. But worst of all, they were lost to Christ. Having all their lives known only his absence, they were soon to discover that the very composition of their destiny was absence.

But let me not interrupt my story. I suddenly realized that the hallway was filling with smoke. Knowing that humans can stand very little of the vaporous substance, I ran to Johnnie's room and moved into his conscience. He was instantly awake. I led. Unseeing, he never knew why he followed, but follow he did, till he was safely outside. By the time he reached the front lawn he could see that the house was ablaze. The fire had begun in his parents' bedroom, so there was little hope of their rescue. Johnnie tried to rush back into the house to drag them to safety, but the flames were too intense.

Firemen found him wandering aimlessly on the front lawn of the burning house. Though he was in his teens, he was clutching tightly to a teddy bear that Aunt Ida had given him on a long-forgotten Christmas. For some reason his hands, flailing in the darkness, had touched the stuffed animal, and he had dragged it from his home, which was soon after incinerated. The bear never left his bedroom for the remainder of his life. He did have some trouble explaining it to his college fraternity, but he kept

it anyway. It was to him a strong symbol of survival. It may sound strange in Upperton, but the bear became to him a kind of idol. The Bible Aunt Ida had given him perished in the fire, but the bear she once gave him had not. It seemed to J. B. that the bear had drawn him to life.

Grief in adolescence is a folding of the soul. Never have I seen a mortal grieve as he did. Never have I wanted anything more than to have the power of touch. But my shortcoming was soon redeemed by the kind Kentuckian. Ida was there and held him through the many hours that he waited for his parents' satin-box rituals.

Johnnie had little to move since everything was lost in the fire. He went back to Kentucky with Aunt Ida and Uncle Harvey. Uncle Harvey will need no special reference. He was not well and died shortly after J. B. arrived. He left his widow with a kind of ache which J. B. in his own grief helped to heal.

J. B. thought to attend church with Aunt Ida, but the sermons were too long and the music too slow. He openly declared after a couple of months that church, like the Bible, was all right for Aunt Ida but not for him. My hopes for J. B.'s conversion degenerated rapidly over the next few years. I still did my best to encourage him toward morality and straight thinking, but such items were not high on his priorities any more. His years in the college fraternity further loosened his idealism. From college he "knocked about" for a couple of years before he finished his master's degree in business. It was a mundane but typical course of university study.

Well, the preamble is concluded! I hope the Committee will not think this summary too terse. I feel I have given these years more time and detail than they deserve. So let us proceed directly to the beginning of J. B.'s twenty-fifth year. While I have summarized his early years, I am leaving my notes on the final year of his life exactly as I recorded them.

I know it sounds odd in Upperton to speak of his final year, for there are no final years.

> *Tell all the mighty ones, truth does not lie*
> *Where trumpets have sounded the news.*
> *He who is Love rules in the sky,*
> *Yet weeps before men without shoes.*

Alleluia,
Valiant

Friday, June 25

Because J. B. is new to the firm, International Investors held a dinner in his honor tonight. Now, I am afraid, he is drunk! What a non-angelic word for a non-angelic state! In my eternal life I have never worked as hard at keeping anyone straight as I worked with J. B. tonight. Even before dinner I realized that he had already had too much to drink. Temperance has never appealed to J. B.; the ghost of his father lives on, I'm afraid. Every time J. B. went back to the bar, I urged him away. It was useless. His social aggression grew with every martini. By nine o'clock he had a fearsome chemical courage toward everyone of the opposite sex.

Three times he tried to set up a "comfy session" at his apartment after dinner. Thankfully, none of those whom he propositioned were open to his suggestions. While his intentions were not honorable, they are customary in Cleveland. The base things he held in mind would beggar the fallen angels. All evening I rehearsed my lost dream of being guardian to a monk!

Here is a little list of his misdemeanors for a mere two hours:

6:00 P.M.—He purchased an unsavory magazine from a newsstand. I'm not sure even the Lord High Command knows of this one!

6:15 P.M.—He used the name of the Lord High Command in a Muddy-scuttle phrase.

6:20 P.M.—He lusted after a girl at a crosswalk while I tried to get his mind on a business proposition. Perhaps the Committee will object that I did not try to get his mind directly on Christ. Such a proposition is now so remote for my client that it would not be possible.

7:00 P.M.—He lusted after a picture of a girl who appeared in the magazine he bought at six o'clock. I tried to get him to read *Popular Mechanics* instead.

8:00 P.M.—He lusted after one of the secretaries at the dinner held in his honor.

This brief catalogue of his sins will illustrate for you my worst forebodings. J. B.'s all-consuming interest is my greatest fear. He is preoccupied with sex. What a three-letter spoiler is this word *sex*. It fills his mind constantly with images of full indulgence. He has but to view a strand of hair or a free ankle and he can build intense intrigues and fiery fantasies.

These fantasies did not begin at the party, I assure you. In the summary I could have mentioned that by the time he was fourteen he had an imagination that was adequate to spark an inferno. His wanton madness has grown ever since. He might curtail it some by taking charge of his mind. But he seldom does and so these storms of unrequited desire come only to a calm after his appetite has fed.

Usually he lives between longing and guilt. He seeks to cool the fever of his longing with sex. After his indulgence, his guilt is so grievous he can barely be cordial to those who afford him the pleasure.

And how does guilt stalk him? His fiery sexual visions are immediately replaced by a vision of Aunt Ida holding her Bible, wagging her head and shaking her finger furiously at him. At such moments he cannot even stand to look at the teddy bear he still keeps in his bedroom.

His ecstasy and guilt are born in one seething—full, yet empty—moment. To think that this reckless fiery force was given so that Adam and his mate might not be too casual in populating the empty planet! J. B. wants all of Adam's ecstasy and none of his responsibility. He has never considered sex as the work of the divine Creator for anything as practical as "replenishing the earth." Sex is for himself. So much so that most of his consorts are not persons but commodities.

I wonder how long he can go on using women before he loves one. Will he ever come to that place where a caring love replaces the rapture of transaction? There is always a "useable" woman there, but all sex is for himself; the geography, the time, the great orchestras that play through the muted speakers of his plush apartment, the flowers, the wine, the perfume, the softness and violence; these all serve nothing but his eager nervous system.

J. B. calls this "tea for two." But he is after the whole teapot, to consume it all for himself. At the height of his indulgence there are not two. There is only he—Narcissus, fondling his own manhood, breathing heavily over his own desirability. Pretending to be sharing the ecstasy with his sexual consorts, he uses women only to gratify himself; he grabs all delight and crams it into his own knapsack.

His behavior at the party was consistent with his life as a whole. I felt a comradeship in watching the other guardians there. The whole lot of us were scurrying about in an attempt to keep sin to a minimum, but it was a maximum night.

The only guardian I envied was Cloudsong. His charge is a posh assignment: a certain John MacDonald who is a teetotaling fundamentalist. Cloudsong was a little arrogant about his client's exemplary behavior. He was the only angel who had time to sit in the corner and catch up on his report. MacDonald left at 10:30—hardly the hour that the "red-blooded" depart—and probably both he and Cloudsong were at rest before midnight. The boss confided to J. B. that MacDonald was a "Seven-Up sipper" and hence is called a fuddy-duddy throughout the company.

But whatever his reputation at International Investors, MacDonald has left Cloudsong the envy of the angels. I am about to change my mind about clerics being the easy ones. I think I would rather have a fundamentalist fuddy-duddy—especially a married fuddy-duddy. Mrs. MacDonald has a certain pinched look that must have been of some assistance to Cloudsong. Even sin needs some spark of warmth to catch fire. Though the fundamentalist MacDonald might desire to defy his guardian, he might not have the courage to go against a countenance like hers.

J. B. is across the gamut from John MacDonald. J. B. neither resists nor struggles against booze or lust. Sex and liquor can both be indulged in and form for him a beckoning image of what is real and good.

I am not sure that things are as they appear with John MacDonald. I know his guardian well. We once served in earth's Eastern Hemisphere together. Cloudsong knows that MacDonald is what our Logos called a hypocrite during the painful years he spent in these wallows. MacDonald's prayers have only an eighty-foot radius. His low-wattage prayer communication is as infrequent as it is weak. Religion is all theatrics with him.

Cloudsong told me MacDonald's only prayer ever to make it all the way to Human Petitions was the one he uttered one night when he lost control of his Pontiac on a mountain road. His prayer was urgently answered by God. Even as he plunged over a barricade, his bumper caught a tree stump, and Upperton has not heard from him since. Cloudsong probably has no fewer problems than other guardians—they are only different in nature.

Seeing Cloudsong with his charge has left me in a quandary. I can't decide whether I would rather guard a lecher or a hypocrite. MacDonald is full of God-talk when it is convenient and when it is not. He has invited J. B. to church with him this weekend, and I can only hope J. B. will go. J. B. finds a kind of Aunt Ida fascination with MacDonald's "Holy-Roller mentality." So there is some possibility he will go, especially if he thinks he might catch sight of some "religious chickie." With this term, J. B. refers to those women Mr. MacDonald reverently calls his sisters in Jesus.

I would not leave the impression with the Committee that I believe that there are only two sins, drunkenness and lust. The great sins of every era are sociological, to be sure. Man's inhumanity to man are the great sins of genocide, racism, and unbridled power. How often has the church crusaded against booze and loose women, and never mentioned the great woes that leave humanity as refugees from hope? Still, J. B. is not so wide a thinker as to see these larger sins. His is a near-sighted hedonism that might be called the "Whiskey and Women" syndrome.

Now the party is over and I am trying not to dwell on the length of my assignment. I am taking it one day at a time. Methuselah's old guardian, Featherdraggle, used to say that no matter how tough it gets in the material realm, be grateful that God has put a limit on human existence. The whole thing will be over in seventy years. At least this is the average. I take heart in remembering that what Featherdraggle had to endure for centuries will soon be over for me.

> *All splendor and praise to our Lord High Command*
> *With nova-blue starfire encircling his head.*
> *He holds constellations with wounds in those hands,*
> *Now breaking the light-years—once breaking the bread.*

Alleluia,
Valiant

Monday, June 28

Things are sweet and sour at once.

What could be better than a Muddyscuttle summer day?

Considine did go to church yesterday, but he told a friend in his car-pool this morning, "I don't think I want in on this religious jag." Church offended him. Having lived through it with him, I think J. B. may be on the side of the angels.

I have been to church so seldom that I had forgotten the obscenity of some Muddyscuttle worship. I was stunned at the starkness of human praise in this particular service. The singing was more "Hallelujah, brother!" than "Alleluia, Father!" In one hymn Upperton became "up yonder."

The service went like this: Humans called ushers met the guests at the door to help them find a seat. I couldn't understand this, since so many were empty that no one would have had the slightest difficulty finding one. These ushers also gave worshipers a bulletin. This paper had the order of worship all printed out along with the church softball and bowling schedules for the week. It was a most unusual document. It also contained advice to pray for the sick so they could soon be back in worship. I could not escape the feeling that the sick may not want back in.

The service began as the choir entered and sang. I have heard few human choirs since I left Upperton, but I was shocked at what tonsils and adenoids do to praise. J. B., unaccustomed to anything finer, was not offended at this. After the choir sang, there was a period of general singing called "congregational hymns." J. B. had some trouble with this. They sang a hymn called "Come Thou Fount." He was a little embarrassed that he had no idea what a "fount" was, but he assumed it was because he was so rarely at church. The second verse had an entreaty to "raise an Ebenezer." J. B. felt it must be at least as hard to sing about Ebenezers as it would be to raise one.

John MacDonald seemed to enjoy everything, but not so his guardian. My assessment of MacDonald is correct. Cloudsong continually urged MacDonald to lower the volume of his singing, for he was always louder than the rest. During the sermon Cloudsong could not keep his charge awake. The poor guardian spent the entire service seeking either to silence or to rouse his client.

During the offering J. B. put two dollars in the plate and smiled at his generosity. I tried to keep him from feeling self-righteous, but he grew smug. His religious arrogance lasted only until the man down the pew put in twenty. Then J. B. looked away and was clearly glad when the offering was over.

They had a special soloist who was listed in the bulletin as "Gloria and her Gospel Guitar." She strummed and sang the most unusual piece of music I have ever heard. The song was called "I'm Just a Jesus Cowgirl on that Trail Ride to the Sky." I thought her song was satire and was really enjoying it until I noticed several around me crying from the emotional impact. *Gloria* is a favorite word in Upperton anthems, so I was expecting something a little more *in excelsis deo,* but this Gloria was not in the *excelsis* category. Brother Buford, a good Kentuckian, got up to preach. His congregation listened intently, but his dialect never translated. Nor did his message.

I'm afraid it may take a good deal of effort to get J. B. back to any church again. I was troubled by the quality of worship in that church. I do not berate the sincere. Still, I wonder how some of these poor mortals will ever stand the transition to eternity. How shall these who worship with this sort of praise ever adjust?

When the long sermon and service had ended, the choir sang "God Be with You till We Meet Again." The implication of this chummy anthem was that he had been there all through the service.

I managed to talk with Cloudsong after the experience. He agreed that there had to be something more effective to motivate J. B. toward conversion. Cloudsong told me that there is to be a gospel telecast on Thursday. Unfortunately, it is across the network from a baseball game. There is not much chance that J. B. will miss that game . . . it is a big game. He's been talking about it and "laying money" on it for weeks.

There is a new man at work named Beau Ridley. J. B. has noticed him praying in the cafeteria before his meals. To J. B. this is an offensive and eccentric custom. Ridley has taken a position in the Corporate Investment Division of International Investors. While J. B. has already mentally labeled him a Christian of MacDonald's ilk, I earnestly hope that Ridley knows our Logos. His guardian is a certain Joymore, who appears to be consistently calm. His emotional balance is a posi-

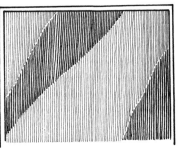

tive quality that may appeal to J. B. Oh that J. B. would unclamp his senses and let God in!

My desire to see J. B. "saved," as MacDonald would say, is not based upon his moral condition alone. There are many noble things about J. B.'s world view. He loves children and is even considering giving some of his Saturday time to working in a boys' organization in a deprived section of inner Cleveland. He is courteous to a fault. He goes out of his way to show little courtesies to all he meets. He is generous in most every expression of his life. As I said earlier, he doesn't think much about the great injustices of the planet. But were he to discover them, I assure you, he would grieve over every inhumanity to man. He just hasn't looked beyond the narrow limits of his current world.

Still, he must be reclaimed, for Daystar's chamber is forever. I love J. B. too much to let him slip beyond the glorious destiny I have in mind for him.

> *Come gallant in time, you couriers of love.*
> *Stir up in your zeal his mighty attack.*
> *Stand mute for the day that he entered in time.*
> *Shout songs for the day he came back.*

Alleluia,
Valiant

A Certain Wednesday in July

I must hurry J. B. down the pathway to encounter. He is so confident of time that he assumes it is endless. People do not manage time; time is the manager of most people. Life is short on Muddyscuttle. I knew an old star clerk in Cogdill who used to say, "It seems that I barely get the file folder out of the birth box before I put it back in the death box. There is nothing after that but to put it on hold for the Termination Event."

The most dreadful aspect of life on earth is its brevity. Sometimes when the wind blows across this planet, you can hear the wail of dying souls, weeping as they terminate. Only guardians hear it. Yet, it must float to the very foundations of heaven. Life is so temporary and diminished here.

How opposite it is to life in Upperton. There beings ever grow and spirits densify and enlarge. How can we guardians ever really understand pain or the curse of decaying materiality? But to consider this littleness is the real tragedy of human thinking. I constantly think of nothing else except J. B.'s need for eternal life.

Even as I squint in the dim illumination of this world—the lighting is always bad here—I carry for J. B. a more brilliant hope than he can imagine.

Please, as you read this report, understand that darkness always retreats from true knowledge. Knowledge cancels darkness. It amazes me how earthlings are prone to think they know it all, yet live on this dingy planet quarreling over trifles. It is ignorance that makes the planet dark. They know so little of the truth that really matters. This certainly is true of J. B.

As their minds are dark, so are their appetites. They desire all the wrong things. Their dark love of things must ultimately be set against the incandescence of God's reality. Consider this: They spend their years squinting over bankbooks and investments to gain but a little of the gold that paves our streets in Upperton. The treasures of kings are but cobblestones in higher worlds. The prisons here are filled with those who stole only little nuggets of what is heaven's cobblestones. J. B., like all the rest, is captive. His appetite for things does not compare in fervor with his lust for sex. Still, he seeks to sate both of these glistening enticements.

Let me not rail too severely on human value systems. Sexuality, unabused, is noble. I still remember my tour here in the late seventeen hundreds. There was sexual abuse and materialism then, too. But in the interim I have seen these appetites swell to a fever. Idealism has so degenerated in the race that every man is a bargain-hunter seeking great treasure at little expense. It all reminds me of what Wordsworth once wrote:

> *The world is too much with us; late and soon,*
> *Getting and spending, we lay waste our powers.*

Getting for mortals is a one-word definition of life. Having and loving is the two-word definition of what goes on down here. Oh, that life might enlarge for J. B. Once free of shopping and the bedroom, he would live in better light. While his hungers are so earthbound, he can only content himself with darkness. The light is always better when our appetites break their purely human tethers.

> *The Logos was life but they murdered him there*
> *On this planet of crosses and graves.*
> *There is treasure and light above this dark air*
> *Where life treasures trifles and raves.*

Alleluia,
Valiant

Of August and
Two Television Episodes

A kind of hope occupies my attention.

On an August Sunday, J. B. woke up to listen to Carlton Classie, a phenomenon in the "video church." Dr. Classie preaches with distinct diction and is always very positive about life. This Sunday he delivered a sermon entitled "The Winner." "You can be a winner if you think you are a winner," cried Dr. Classie. J. B. really liked the sermon. His eyes were glued to the TV screen. He moved only once and then in a mummified fashion to the refrigerator to get himself a can of beer.

"Remember," said Classie, "your mentality is your vitality. You can win if your mind doesn't sin. Think high, young man. Your career will soar only where your mind has already flown. God is a flags-down-throttles-open God. Low thinking will never let your career lift off the runway."

Classie went on uninterrupted. "God wants winners in this world. No loser ever honored God. God's mind is so glorious the entire universe proceeded from it. He is the Master Thinker. If you want to learn to think like God, you must think big! Take those difficulties that threaten you with defeat and wrap them in victory and give them all back to the Master Mind. Remember the airliner that flies too low is in danger—it is only safe at the heights. Most airline tragedies are not *air* tragedies. They occur on the ground. They are runway failures. Lift into the pure, clear air. There you are alone with perspective. All your little difficulties will dwindle as you gain elevation. Break the grind with a godly mind. Soar! Unchain your soul and take control. Soar . . . soar . . . soar!"

All too soon Dr. Classie's sermon was over. It was the first one J. B. has ever heard to its conclusion. He belched—like a common runway failure. He reached for his toothbrush just as Dr. Classie swelled gallantly and moved in close to the screen, "This is Dr. Carlton Classie reminding you to turn your pain to gain. *You* can win if you think you can." The music swelled, and there were some nature photographs. J. B. belched again and turned off the set.

Television is new since my last tour. It is the monumental preoccupation of the bored. Americans watch an endless parade of video dramas until a million pointless plots have fused. They seem to have so little use for talk, so they watch—and become obesity with eyeballs. They eat, drink, and make merry all before the blue-dull video glare. They show little emotion unless there is a power failure. While the device is the god of secular thralldom, Dr. Classie's program is one that at least hints at Upperton.

But even TV can hold moments of glory! On Thursday, J. B. actually watched a gospel telecast. He had intended to watch a sporting event, but as it happened, there was a great deal of video "fuzz" on channel three, so baseball was out of the question. J. B. tried to eliminate the blur. He twisted the various knobs in anger. He grew angry as he tried to make the screen clearer. But clarity was not to be his. Finally in utter frustration he spun the channel selector, feeling it to be better to watch something you don't like than not to watch at all—such is the power TV has over most Americans.

At length J. B. left the stubborn, blaring television, walked to the bar, and fixed himself a highball. Channel six, where the hapless device became fixed, was coming in loud and clear. As he sat down, J. B. faced a stadium filled with people who had come to listen to a man named Frankie Williams. Before he spoke, the Conquest Choir was singing melodies about sin and eternal life. I know I am now adjusting to the planet. Perhaps I am overadjusting. I suddenly found myself listening to Frankie Williams just as if I needed what he was saying.

My enthusiasm must have been catching because J. B. actually listened to me. When he was about to mix himself a second drink, I suggested that he couldn't afford a moment away from the set. He shrugged off my initial suggestion, until I reminded him that his Aunt Ida had always admired him and would be embarrassed to know he was drinking in front of a man of God.

Williams was preaching on the second coming of the Logos. He preached on human drunkenness and gluttony that would exist at the end of time. At the mention of these intemperances, J. B. sucked in his stomach, covered the candy dish, and pushed his empty cocktail glass out of sight. He fidgeted in his chair. He tried to think about his Aunt Ida. Her image was more accessible for him than the abstract God that Frankie Williams preached.

Then Williams talked about the millions of businessmen in American corporations who were living for themselves. "These men," he said,

"have never really considered making Christ the Lord of their lives." J. B. was actually smitten when the Conquest Choir began singing the entreaty. He was choked with emotion. I thought for a moment he was going to respond, but he suddenly turned off the television, sat down, and sighed in relief that the telecast was over.

I prodded him to read the Bible that his Aunt Ida had given him at high school graduation to replace the one that had burned. He lifted it from the bookshelf, turned it over in his hand, and cautiously opened it. Haplessly he thumbed the pages to Matthew 1. Why do all beginning Bible readers feel they must begin either in Matthew 1 or Genesis 1? "No!" I screamed to his subconscious. "A thousand times no! You'll be right back in the 'begats' again." Soon he was reading, "Zorababel begat Abiud; and Abiud begat Eliakim."

"I must read on just like Frankie Williams said," he thought. Fighting the urge to quit, he went forward: "Eliakim begat Azor," said Aunt Ida's great gift.

"I wonder why Auntie considered this such a hot gift," he said. "She always said it would bring me comfort in a time of grief. 'Azor begat Sadoc, and Sadoc begat Achim.' And what could she mean that I would find great peace in my conflict? 'Eliud begat Eleazar; and Eleazar begat Matthan,'" he stopped and folded the volume.

I urged him to go forward just a little, but he would have none of it. He was utterly bewildered that Aunt Ida and Dr. Classie and Frankie Williams all found such comfort in a book so filled with "begats." He concluded them all to be a kind of third sex.

Exhausted at his attempt to read the Bible, he lay down for his nap. He might have fallen right off to sleep, but I prevented it by filling his mind with images. I kept playing pictures of his Aunt Ida at prayer across the inner screen of his thoughts. He seemed to be envisioning a change for himself. He was experiencing a destitution—the kind that might actually precede the human phenomenon of repentance. Surely his reclamation will be forthcoming.

The heart can kindle scarlet fire
When men grow wiser than desire.

Alleluia,
Valiant

The Trees

The trees are lovely. I am captive to the planet. This bondage fell upon me as I walked with J. B. in the park today. He sat beneath an oak tree and wondered over all the years it took to make the plant. I marveled that it grew so quickly. Oaks are somehow marvels in this topsy-turvy world where trees outlive men.

But the grove *is* grand and I have heard that in the West there are trees that were already tall when our beloved Logos walked this earth. I see increasingly why God loved this planet so! Here the eyes may feast on nature, beholding geese set against the incendiary skies of summer evenings. There are gray mushrooms tufted in ochre grass. J. B. studied a ladybug that walked a spotted-amber promenade upon a linden twig. Does it seem incongruous that angelic eyes would gaze upon an orange insect in admiration for the jewel-like precision of God's meticulous detail?

I'm glad J. B. does love nature. But I wonder that he cares so little about nature's Maker. J. B. is evidence that creation may stop men short of the Creator. They fondle the art, content never to know the Artist. They see a tree and marvel at its beauty, but never go on to ask about the Maker of trees.

So J. B. does not suspect that his awe is only pantheism. He clings so desperately to this world, it blinds him to the world to come. His love for verdant towers and leafy shrines keeps his worship low. This leaves both his life and destiny earthbound.

Life for J. B. is all sensual. If he cannot see it, smell it, or touch it, it holds no value for him. He walks by all extrasensual reality never suspecting its existence. This leaves his world immediate and ours remote. The martyrs could not afford the luxury of J. B.'s pantheism. They longed for Upperton, for they were about to lose this present world. But in Ohio there are few dangers, so people adore creation without giving the Creator a thought.

But I am fickle.

Just when I want to criticize J. B.'s intrigue with the out-of-doors, I become fascinated with a swan moving silently across a pond. September is magnificent and must deserve some little Alleluia. Lest you think

I have been distracted from my task by nature, let me assure you my motives are unchanged. I spend every hour now in hope of my client's conversion.

It is true that I did not fare well in getting him to read his Bible, but I am learning to take one step at a time. I regret that it is forbidden for guardians to have the knowledge of when or if reclamation will occur. Without this information, I remain troubled by the certain event of his termination, which date I do know. There are only a few more months till his satin-box ritual.

I sometimes rebuke myself, feeling that I have become too familiar with Considine. I need to remember that I am his guardian, not his "chum." I realized too late that I almost considered our trip to church or our carpool conversations as outings for the both of us. Today our aloneness with the trees was almost rapturous. I was prone to view the telecast with J. B. as a sort of "lovely evening at home." I know I am not on Muddyscuttle upon some sort of interplanetary lark. Time itself concerns me only when I remember it is of utmost importance to him. I have all the time in the world, but J. B. will shortly run out of it. I must force myself to remember Raphael's Code, to which I first subscribed my allegiance to Upperton:

> I, Valiant, in the name and authority of the Lord High Command do swear to the beloved Logos, Ruler of Spirit and Matter, this twofold commission of his Majesty, the only true Sovereign and Source of Being. First, I shall do all within my power to work with human willfulness so that no unclaimed spirit ever shall be lost in Daystar's prison house of fire. Second, I will guard the physical life of my charge so he may acquire unending life and come with all Upperton to adore the Logos.

It is an unfortunate tendency of most guardians to seek friendship with their clients. While I am generally doing the right things, I wonder if I am always doing them for the right reasons.

I am spellbound by Frankie Williams. He certainly seems a good ambassador of heaven. With every Conquest service, thousands more come to know Christ. But the Logos never liberates by thousands. He always liberates one person at a time. May J. B. see that eternal life—however it looks on telecasts—is an individual affair.

I no longer feel any envy over Cloudsong's assignment. MacDonald

speaks of Christ, but he seems so much in love with himself and his need for recognition. How easily religion may sour! For MacDonald, the church is a miracle show where one may speak of God, yet glory in his own importance. MacDonald really thinks God has joined *his* team, content for MacDonald to be the lucky captain.

MacDonald grieves because J. B. is "unsaved," and yet Cloudsong grieves because MacDonald is "too much saved." MacDonald's view of the Logos makes God a great "grinch" who lords it over humankind for the sheer joy of slapping hands.

It is such a long way between what J. B. is and what MacDonald would like him to become. MacDonald would like for J. B. to be a Christian rather like himself, since he considers his own faith to be the standard of the planet. If MacDonald could only get one glimpse of J. B. sitting in his underclothes with a can of beer in his hand, smoking cigarettes, he would think it impossible for J. B. ever to attain the same level of sainthood which he himself has achieved. As MacDonald sees it, God will drub a man to hell for parlor games, tobacco, or wine.

MacDonald has been in constant misery since his reclamation. He suffers from either the guilt of sins which he's committed or the gnawing fear that he may soon fall into a major sin of some sort. Guilt is a violence that obscures God with an egotistic inner focus that produces nothing of value. Guilt steeps the soul in passionate self-concern.

Joymore, an old acquaintance of mine, is the guardian of Beau Ridley, the new man in the company. Ridley is pleasant and forceful, and J. B. is drawn to his charm and wit. J. B. has now come to know him and is no longer as critical of Beau as he once was. Most of J. B.'s judgments are *a priori* and therefore, much of the time, wrong. Except for Beau's habit of saying grace in the company cafeteria, which still offends J. B., he seems both comfortable and authentic.

As J. B. is drawn to Beau, I also am drawn to his guardian. I only hope that J. B. and Beau might become friends. This would permit Joymore and me to deepen our acquaintance. I used to visit with him regularly several anguria before the humanization of the Logos. A new friendship with someone from home might permit me to escape the earth fever that has captured me of late.

I am an angel in doubt. Maybe it's because my time is short, but my fascination with this planet pervades my whole worldview. I must be honest. I do love the world where I serve. I sometimes grieve that it is all destined for fiery erasure at Operation Clockstop. I must redouble my efforts at protecting my charge, lest the ancient fire fall upon him unaware.

> *He is glorious evermore*
> *Who holds both love and fire in store.*

Alleluia,
Valiant

From a Bedroom
on an Autumn Night

J. B.'s security is my passion. How shall I really protect my client in such an unpredictable world? There are many things over which I have too little control. The air tragedy on Thursday last is one example of what I mean. What if J. B. had been on that plane? All 119 Muddyscuttlers were "lost," as they say down here. On the same plane there were 119 guardians, never mentioned by the press. It is just as well. None of the guardians could do a thing to avert the disaster.

The fault lies in protoplasm, which is hardly worth its carbon formula. If human flesh warms over a mere 108 degrees, it succumbs to fever, the mind fries, and life is gone. If the temperature lowers to 90 degrees, the body chills and dies. Mine is the task of keeping my fragile human client between these stingy temperatures until he can be reclaimed. I must make his every tragedy a triumph. In every mishap, J. B. must be a "survivor." His hope of Upperton means he must remain in the flesh. Flesh? What is it? Nothing more than the sinew of dust! What can be said for it? Weather stings it. Sharp objects puncture it. Disease infects it. Old age alone will crack and consume it. Wars liquidate it.

Human beings seem to willfully complicate our work—it is as if they are eager to kill themselves. They assassinate, murder, and declare war. How can we possibly help them stay safe while they dream up a ghastly arsenal of ideas to kill themselves? They dare to set flesh against gunpowder and nuclear fission and war. Nineteen million men die every century from such scourges.

I often think of the way all life hurries toward death here. Twenty thousand died in an earthquake, and the number of small disasters is manifold. I could go on to speak of such human foibles as the Hindenburg or the Titanic. Specific instances matter not. The point is that again and again, Muddyscuttlers perish by the score while a host of guardians watch and weep. Our power over human safety seems an unending and fruitless vigil.

Even when protoplasm survives, it still says little about the quality of life. It is here I suffer my worst feelings of unrequited hope. How I wish J. B., who has little left in the quantity of his life, might yet discover a real quality of life.

Has his life any quality? What I must now report will be displeasing. I have suffered a setback. While J. B. was "having a few" at the Mayflower Lounge last night, he met Cassie, a youthful and coquettish human.

Cassie's guardian is an old angel named Alphalite who first served as a guardian of the Hittite princess before the Lord High Command ever initiated the writing of the Bible. Alphalite knows Featherdraggle and said they once roomed together in Upperton before the humanization of our Logos. Alphalite's Cassie is as independent as my client. She, too, pursues her own desires. They both see themselves as liberated, but it is a liberation that is about to destroy them. All of J. B.'s outer offenses proceed from his inner self. His mind is the real culprit in his physical gluttony. J. B.'s actual indulgence is but the performance his prior thoughts rehearse. As goes the gray matter, so goes the man. If he would only think higher, he could live higher.

Alphalite seems less concerned about Cassie than I do about J. B. Since he was once the guardian of a Hittite princess, Cassie must seem tame to him. Oh, if I were as old and wise as he! I know I am suffering from a lack of experience.

I know that my client's behavior with Cassie is much the product of something that angels never can understand—procreation. We guardians came directly from the foundries of the Spirit. Adam and Eve were the first humans to arrive directly as beings. Since them, people have been participating in the process of making people. I know, too, that lust is the mechanism that drives this human part of the divine plan. Thus for humanity to survive, the High Command had to endow it with the forces of sexuality. If I did not know how perfect the Creator is, I might believe he overdid it all. Well, let me get on with the story!

It pains me to have to tell you that J. B. brought Cassie to his apartment . . . and the whole episode was most embarrassing to Alphalite and myself. Two humans making love and two angels looking away, wishing for them better value systems. Not that I haven't suffered through this with J. B. a hundred times before. But I felt he was making such good progress.

Nevertheless, nothing would dissuade him. I tried to help him think of the Frankie Williams telecast. His intentions rushed forward. Even my suggestions of Aunt Ida's broken faith in him would not avail. Had they been man and wife, Alphalite and I would have found the situation a fond and close expression of noble eros. But what is to be said? We must regard the whole affair as but a gluttony of glands: a bogus offering of soul.

What shall I do? The same sentiment my client calls love, the Bible labels lust. If J. B. and Cassie could know real love, they would be slow to label their appetites with such grand words. I grieved to give the night to Daystar, but his will became their burning fever once again. Reason is on God's side while the voltage of human experience remains on the side of evil.

The planet is crazy about this phenomenon of sex. *Sex* is so short a word, it scarcely makes three letters. SEX, SEX, SEX. It must be said three times to make three syllables. Yet, this silent, screaming, inner drive drives all! The entire course of history pivots on this passion.

The entire planet celebrates one common appetite. The admen make every possible use of this omnipresent urge. Sex sells soap and autos, hand cream and clothing. From highway billboards half-naked forms, gargantuan in size, gaze out over eighteen lanes of traffic. The titan nudes smile down in bronze skin to sell the products they espouse. Seductive mouths smile with an intrigue across the void, begging tourists to lust, if only for an instant, as they hurtle down the freeways.

J. B. and Cassie are like their world. It is natural to the both of them to "make love," as they say. They make nothing really but tangled psychologies they shall spend the rest of their lives unraveling. What they experience was created in Eden by a lavish Artist, who thought in all his creativity to give the race the gift of intimacy. So to Adam and Eve was given the grand donation—the simple pleasure of skin. It was a tiny ecstasy compared with that great cosmic love the angels know firsthand. But those who never know the best will exalt the least. This great tactile pleasure is the planetary preoccupation.

What shallow occupations Daystar gives the globe! They follow their passions until the fever in their systems leaves them powerless to control the firestorms of their indulgence. The megavoltage of their eros burns hot till passion electrocutes itself and slumps in weak relief. Then they lie quietly, contented in the smoldering aftermath and speak of it as "love" which they are "in" or, indeed, have "made."

Their strange and fiery ritual was over in a furious quarter hour.

J. B. had a certain inner knowledge that ecstasy wasn't his by right. But neither of them speak of rightness or wrongness in their relationship. They boast of their liberation from the older, other times. They even then turn on the lights to show how liberated they are. They smoke in bed and speak of their enlightened innocence. They marvel that they feel joy without shame. "We are Aquarian," they said when they had finished. They are strange Aquarians who refresh themselves from fetid jars, yet call the water clean.

I will not have the Committee think that I believe that their illicit pastime is the greatest of all sins. No, the world bleeds from much greater kinds of moral and social wounds than J. B. and Cassie create. But their own indulgence blinds them to any greater purpose for themselves. Furthermore, they confuse their pursuit of pleasure with the pursuit of happiness.

Oh, that they knew what Alphalite and I have dreamed for them! If they could only see the Christ reaching in wounds to receive them, they would cry for honest love. They need the wisdom of Christ to understand what it really means to be liberated. Christ cried during his humanization that people should not call liberty by lesser names, for self-denial is the only pier upon which real love rests. Commitment is the only basis of true love. Love that will not commit itself is at last only lust. J. B. calls his lust love, for it allows him to gratify his flesh without obligating himself. J. B. and Cassie are not lovers, only lusters. They misuse each other and name the misuse love.

Human intimacy is not wrong. It is the very gift of the High Command to all who dwell upon this planet. But even when it is right, chief of virtues it can never be. The highest love does not seek sweating starbursts. Neither J. B. nor Cassie can admit this without their self-respect crumbling. Inwardly they know that there must be a higher love that does not come wrapped only in petty ecstasy. The best love still comes back from hilltops with wounded hands, forgiving its assassins.

I remember well the day Christ died. The vultures circled the gallows, but he would not leave the world. He hung there just as if he had to do it. He would not abandon those puny nails and come home. Finally his heart broke, and they laid his body firm against his mother's coarse-cloth garment. She cried. All Upperton agreed in anguish.

We waited through the hours with drawn swords, but he would not give the word. We knew he wouldn't. God's Beloved was in love! Christ was IN LOVE with a fallen planet, whose answer to love was the gallows.

How shall I communicate such excellence to J. B., whose definition of love is only penny-ante?

Call dying love.
Call flesh pretense.
Call human ecstasy a fault.
Call heaven's love, all moral sense.

Alleluia,
Valiant

The Last of October

The lovers have now spent two weekends together and seem to be settling into a lifestyle. I was wrong about Alphalite: He feels that the Hittite princess was chaste compared with Cassie. The princess, he says, always sacrificed doves to atone for her promiscuity. Cassie feels no such religious duty.

J. B. and Cassie have a pattern of behavior that is predictable. After work on Friday they begin drinking to loosen up. They are usually quite loose before they leave the lounge. Once they begin these sessions, it is most difficult to bring angelic influence to bear. I even feel sorry for them. Their naiveté contains a nobility of spirit, but one that is tightly chained to their frailties.

Once J. B. brandies his brain, I have trouble communicating with him. As I said earlier, it is in his mind that J. B. loses the battle. He swims in fanciful fornication for an entire afternoon before his actual indulgence. I myself swim in his fantasies, shouting idealisms over the roar of his glandular cascade.

I am weary these days. My one refreshing thought is that I am spirit and never shall be subject to mortality. Homesickness—that's what it is! I've only a few months to go here and then I shall be home again. How much I would give to know that when I enter Upperton, J. B. will be with me.

J. B.'s favorite sins always grow in acceptance till at last he blesses them. He has split himself into two people. One is a monk and the other a seething bohemian. The two wear the very same wardrobe yet never meet, so there is never any conflict. It is a safe arrangement by which many here on earth manage a double life that appears single in each of its contexts.

I heard of a poor man in France who many years ago was compelled by the state to be an executioner. The first time that his trembling hands raised the bloody blade of the guillotine, he cried, trembled, and wept that he was man. He could not bear to hear the victim screaming and kicking in protest against those who dragged him forward and clamped his straining form in the braces. He closed his ears against the dull thump and turned from the tense neck that lay against gory steel. So it was with the first dozen. Soon, however, he freed himself to look. Then he gazed. At last he rose eagerly on those mornings when the executions were scheduled.

The mind will soon permit what it earlier abhorred. I remember the first time that J. B. indulged in illicit sexuality. He was morose for days. Images of Aunt Ida dogged his guilt. He could scarcely eat, he felt so bad. Soon he tolerated his sin. Then he enjoyed it.

My interest in J. B.'s ethics may too much enchant me. They may even paralyze my service to him. They have an old proverb here on Muddyscuttle. "Fools rush in where angels fear to tread." It is somewhat comforting to know that here at least they separate fools and angels. I must be careful that I do not bring the categories closer.

> *When moral love flows broad as seas*
> *Men too grow moral: straight as trees.*

Alleluia,
Valiant

Snow

I am reeling at the circumstances. The first snow of winter has left everything whiter than it was. Glory has fallen with the snow. During a long and gentle snowfall, J. B. met Cassie at Henry VIII. While this may sound like a historical museum, it is but a bar. I noticed that Alphalite was in a supreme state of elation. He was buzzing in and out of walls and making frequent Alleluias. It is good that we sing in other dimensions or the bar would have exploded with the volume of his joy.

The fireworks—if the Committee will permit such a terrestrial cliché—began when J. B. offered to buy Cassie a highball and she declined. J. B. had a few of his usuals, which is no longer unusual, since he is having them unusually often. Cassie clearly had something on her mind that she knew J. B. would find unpleasant. J. B. insisted that she loosen up with him by having one of her usuals. "J. B.," she said, "I don't want to loosen up. I know what happens every time we get 'loose.'"

J. B. was afraid. "Come on, Cassie, let's unwind—I've got a new kind of Chablis I want you to try when we get to my place. It's going to be a great evening!"

"Not for me!" said Cassie.

Cassie was afraid that for her refusal, J. B. would call her a "prude" right on the spot. A prude in Muddyscuttle usage is an over-virtuous woman. There is such colloquial malice in the word that American women would rather do anything than be labeled by such a term. There are whole movements of women in this hemisphere that have dedicated themselves to the extinction of such labels.

J. B. looked into his drink, studied the ice cubes, and then blurted out, "What are you, Cassie, some kind of prude? For God's sake!"

"Yes, it is rather for his sake, I suppose," she said.

"Whose sake?" thundered J. B., banging his glass of ice cubes on the small table.

"God's."

"God's? Don't tell me you're getting mixed up with God. You're not only a prude, but a God-nut. . . . Cassie, for Christ's sake!"

"His, too!" she said in the face of his hard anger.

A long period of silence followed. It seemed for a moment she might abandon her prudery and agree to go home with him. I have not seen two souls more in agony than they appeared to be. I could tell she wanted to please J. B., but even more than that, she seemed possessed of a new allegiance. He could neither understand nor accept it. She wanted to have a little drink with him, but was afraid that even one might weaken her resolve. He stared at the bottom of his glass.

After an agonizing silence, she spoke nervously, but she was firm.

"Look, J. B., let's face it. We have a cheap relationship, always plastered over with too much booze and a lot of cheap scenes in your apartment."

Alphalite beamed.

"It never bothered you before," he said.

"Well, it does now, since . . ."

"Since what?" he almost shouted. He was talking so loudly that several others in the bar turned their heads and stared in the direction of their table.

"Since what?" he asked again, not quite so loudly.

"Well," she hesitated. The words were coming hard for her.

"Since what . . . since what . . . SINCE WHAT?"

"Since I accepted Christ."

Alphalite began buzzing excitedly through the walls again.

J. B. blurted out a coarse laugh and slapped his leg in cruel attack. "You accepted Christ! How could you do that?"

I felt sorry that J. B. was so acid to Cassie. The idea of Cassie "accepting Christ" bothered me some, too. The idea is so humanized somehow. Who are these mortals that they condescend to accept or reject the Logos? The key issue never seems to surface in their small system of arrogance. "Accept Christ" is the way that some Scuttlers in the evangelical world refer to reclamation. I know you will be galled by reading this, for it seems they may have missed the point. Their way of putting it leaves the Almighty under human judgment. Salvation is born in Christ's condescending to accept man, and not man stooping to accept the unworthy love of God. It makes a wreck of excellence.

We dare not dwell long on this kind of human arrogance. The way they speak of it, Christ is life, offered to them on a silver platter, and they ponder whether they will condescend to accept his magnificent sacrifice. What's for them to accept? They should beg his favor. If they miss it, indeed, all that is left to them is Daystar's pit. How fashionable

of them to make their rescue from the pit sound like some sort of bargain for God! What drowning man confers laurels upon the lifeguard because he has been so lucky as to rescue his resplendent victim?

Since so many speak of it this way, we must not be too hard on Cassie for so phrasing it. In the course of this tense conversation, Cassie told J. B. that she had been visited by two visitors from Grace Church who had told her about Christ. These two laypersons had passed through her neighborhood knocking on doors telling people about Christ. In this random fashion, they had happened to call on Cassie. "Suddenly," she said, "I realized how far I was from the path. I confessed my sin, and I plan to go to church on Sunday. I was hoping you might come too, J. B."

"You're talking like my funny aunt," he replied.

"Ida?" asked Cassie.

J. B. nodded.

"But you always told me you loved your aunt as anyone else would have loved their own mother."

"She's been a mother to me, but she's a God-nut just like you, Cassie," he fumed. He seemed suddenly ashamed that he had referred to Aunt Ida with such despicable terms. "Look, Cassie," he said, tempering his volume with calm, "if not tonight, couldn't we get together at my apartment this weekend and talk the whole thing over?"

"Not anymore . . . I'm sorry, J. B. Not this weekend or any weekend. Not tonight or any night! I've come across a new set of standards. I shall need Christ's help to live up to them."

He was offended by the way she spoke of "Christ's help." It is quite out of fashion on Muddyscuttle to just blurt out the words "Jesus" or "Christ," unless one is using them in a coarse context. To use the words in the open as you might use the name of William or Eric is socially taboo.

Soon conversation turned from Cassie's new experience to Grace Church. "What's this place like if it sends out God freaks to menace decent American neighborhoods?" asked J. B.

"What's so decent about my neighborhood?" She answered his question with one of her own.

"Well . . . it's . . ."

"I'll tell you what kind of people live in my neighborhood. They drink too much, make free sex their lifestyle, and are starved to death for any real piers upon which to build their lives."

"You sound like Frankie Williams."

"Maybe our neighborhoods need to be menaced. Maybe the entire nation could use what I have found. Maybe you need it, J. B. What if your Aunt Ida is right?"

"I still can't fathom people talking about God right in the streets, or in their homes, or in lounges like this, for Christ's sake!"

"That's exactly . . ."

"I know, I know, I know—that's exactly whose sake it's for."

"And the people who speak openly of Christ are not weird. They seem to me to be the only ones in touch with their world. One of the men who shared the Christ-life with me works for your company. His name is Beau Ridley."

"Beau Ridley! I know him. He seemed so intelligent, too. He's the guy who says prayer in the company cafeteria before he eats . . . I'll be damned!"

"Could be, J. B."

"Cassie, will you quit interrupting me with these innuendos! . . . Beau Ridley," he said, collecting himself. "The man's a fanatic! Maybe even a lunatic! So he was one of the—how do you say it?—witnesses who came to your door."

"Yes."

"That phony. How can you let a religious nut like that ruin our great relationship?"

"It wasn't a great relationship. It was cheap! I want out, J. B."

J. B. grew red with anger. "You were never in, baby!" he yelled at her.

She picked up her coat and purse and walked out into the snow. Alphalite appeared for a moment in the open doorway, and I could see the snow falling.

Alphalite called back in language beyond them, but expressed the wisdom of new creation. "White is a majestic color, Val."

"Indeed!" I called back.

> *Only blackness ever knows*
> *The shining treasure of the snows.*

Alleluia,
Valiant

The Fire and Image

We are alone tonight. J. B. has had several more of his usuals and isn't thinking very clearly. There is a fire in his fireplace. The room is hot and, yet, there is a chill about it all. He is sweltering from an odd fever set into his system by two loves. One love is the attachment he feels to Cassie, which I thought was only a sexual convenience. Tonight it is becoming clear that she means more to him than I had before supposed.

The second love is the new love he observed in Cassie. He is almost jealous of her new love for Christ. How can one really be jealous of such an exalted and different kind of love? Yet, he is. Besides this jealousy, he is seething in resentment that Christ has apparently doomed him to lonely weekends.

While he was staring at the fire, the dancing flames seemed to hold him mesmerized. "Why . . . why . . . did she do it? I need her so . . ." he muttered, looking again into the fire. "Oh, hell!" he said, throwing his glass against the mantel. It shattered and fell upon the hearth. He barely had spoken the words when the imagery of his words fell upon the flames.

He remembered the fire! It was hell! That fire so long ago had left him an orphan. He remembered how lonely he felt when he knew his parents were still in their incendiary tomb that had been his tight little world. The teddy bear that had been his only surviving toy still glared at him from its slouched position on the corner of the bureau near the window. "Hell!" he said again.

The fire flickered.

Images of things long gone danced in the bright embers.

He beheld himself as a boy wandering on the lawn among the great hoses and red lights. He remembered the fire and his immense gratitude that Aunt Ida had come. How he had clung to her in the most welcome embrace of his life! She had been so different from his own parents. Her love, while only a kind of substitute for the new loneliness that was his, seemed rooted in the firm soil of Kentucky. How he needed the depth of compassion that lived in that good country woman!

Now he wondered if Aunt Ida would even recognize him. He was drunk, lonely, and maudlin over his old rag toy. Nor would International

Investors have recognized this budding young executive, oiled in martinis, crying over his teddy bear, and cowering before the spectres that rose from his fireplace to walk his troubled thoughts.

He got himself a drink. With bleary eyes he walked over to the little bear and picked it up. He smiled and felt the pain of bittersweet memories. He set the bear down, and by odd coincidence, its soft left leg fell upon the Bible. He picked up the book. He stood with the amber flickering of the fireplace upon his young yet aging face. "What would Auntie think? My standing here with a Bible in one hand and a martini in the other?" he asked himself.

He thought of trying again to read it, but only thumbed its pages and set it down again. "Despair for nothing!" he said to himself. "I have it all: a fine job, a sports car, a good salary, and an apartment with the right address." Then Cassie's definition of her neighborhood rang again in the air about him: "I'll tell you what kind of people live in my neighborhood. They drink too much, make free sex their lifestyle, and are starved to death for any real piers upon which to build their lives." J. B. knew that this was not only her neighborhood, but his as well. Even more than his neighborhood, it was himself.

He looked above the rim of his glass. The former glass lay shattered on the hearth. The flame reflecting from the broken pieces seemed somehow to symbolize his life.

Then I urged J. B. to a new plateau. He has somewhat of a strong mind, so I was able to manage this only because he was drunk and offered little resistance. I caused a vision to form on the amber tips of the flames that settled low above the glowing coals.

In the dying fire I managed to float the image of his old aunt as she had been years before. Among the smaller embers J. B. saw the adolescent image of himself. The dream lived. J. B. grasped his aunt. They embraced, and as the boy held her, she grew old and wrinkled, then faded away and was gone.

He was alone. He knew he was.

Then there arose a teddy bear. It seemed friendly to him for an instant. Then it began to enlarge. Its scruffy little face changed as it grew. As last it towered above him in the room. It was fanged. His teddy—once his great security symbol—now menaced him. It beckoned him into the flames. He was afraid to follow. The hypnotic effect of the glowing coals

fixed his trance. With effort at last he managed to close his eyes against the demon bear.

He turned himself from the fire and faced the icy windows. "Oh, Auntie, save me!" he said. The cold air near the frosted window brought him a new view of this world. He was ashamed he had cried out into the room. He turned and looked again and the demon was gone. The only bear in the room still stared at him from the bureau top.

"Well, I'll be damned," he said, but wished he hadn't.

> *The things that thump in semi-light*
> *Can make men fear the pending night*
> *That heaven never sees.*

Alleluia,
Valiant

Of Love and Backslipping

While J. B. has not seen Cassie since the big snow, I have learned something of her from Ridley's angel, Joymore. Cassie has learned that free love is costly in terms of guilt and self-acceptance. Her former weekends will not set free her present ones. Why did she ever live with J. B.?

Like other mortals, Cassie spends her time trying to understand herself. There are as many theories of human behavior as there are psychiatrists. Cassie has read many theories in her search for herself. There are moments of loneliness when she is tempted to call J. B. and opt for a return to her old lifestyle.

Evangelical churchmen on the planet talk of a problem that believers call backslipping. Backslipping is the human tendency to abandon the Logos-life and reenter a former value system. Most new believers return to old lifestyles when they begin to feel that they can handle life on their own without needing faith. Backslipping usually begins in such self-sufficiency. Christ never taught self-reliance. He taught that he himself is the only source of confident living. Self-sufficiency is based upon a defective psychology which teaches that humans can do anything they think they can. Oh, that Cassie might learn quickly that there is a great chasm between her intention and her ability!

I have heard that this strange idea of self-reliance begins in youth. Parents on Muddyscuttle allegedly tell their children about a little locomotive who was asked to pull a long line of cars up a hill. The "choo-choo" is a positive thinker who manages to succeed because he believes so much in himself. He goes along the rails saying, "I think I can, I think I can." Humans often read this tale to their children as an early parable of self-sufficiency. The story is probably a part of Cassie's distant past.

Alphalite told Joymore that Cassie sees herself as omnicapable. Her petty arrogance dismisses most of her need for our beloved Logos. Her tyranny lies in making God her partner in a faith venture. Like most other positive-thinking Christians, she usually has two viewpoints: hers and the one which is not so crucial. She has mistakenly felt that the Logos is on her side and is assisting her in a kind of spiritual imperialism to rise to the top of life. She believes that faith in the Logos gives her the right to control others and be successful, whatever devious path she follows.

She has already read some of the numerous books and magazines on the subject. She has, therefore, heard a score of Christians testify how God exists for her own personal advancement in life. "How to Be Successful" reads one such article. "Jesus Made Me Corporate Head" reads another. "Christ Gave Me the Winner's Cup in the Swimsuit Competition" reads another. From what Alphalite tells me, she is still unable to see that her idealism is naive and motto-ridden. She, like many new believers, reads bumper stickers more than the Bible. There are any number of popular clichés on self-sufficiency. "Turn Your Aches to Steaks" says one; another reads, "Jesus Don't Sponsor No Flops." These are simple slogans of self-sufficiency which, attached to human efforts, displaces the need of Christ.

My fear is that Cassie may be diverted into egocentric Christianity and become unconcerned about J. B.'s need for Christ. That must not happen; her own new faith is the most immediate hope my client has of being reclaimed. Should she backslip at this point, my ardent hope for J. B. would suffer. He is clearly in love with her and so smitten by this romantic madness that he would be most open to anything Cassie said. Oh, that she knew this!

Even though I know my time here is short, I must remind the Committee that I am struggling on through storms of homesickness. I have caught myself distracted at cocktail parties as J. B. has his usuals. I feel a certain planetary revulsion in these moments. I find myself singing the silent songs of infinity. How long a human year can seem when one is separated from the Logos! J. B.'s Cassie does not really want to go to heaven now: She is snared in the sociology of earthly life and, like other Muddyscuttlers, doesn't want to die at all. Earth, not heaven, is the residence she most desires.

All Christians sing of the glory of going to heaven, but no one wants to be carried up on the next load. Leaving the planet is for them a gruesome disinheritance. It is because they love too low. Heaven for them is a great privation where they cannot glut on all their various appetites. Heaven is a dull place without shopping malls, football, television, and ice cream. Heaven is just a better hell, really, than the one with flames and demons; but can heaven be heaven with neither sex nor martinis? Heaven is just below whatever they happen to enjoy. Deep in their hearts they would rather keep all the goodies of their current lives and build such heavens as they can. Even seeing Christ is scarcely prize enough to replace the disinheritance that death will bring them.

They are all afraid of death, and this fear is so natural to them that even the love of Logos does not set them entirely free. With some Christians it is not so much death they fear, but dying. Dying is not just losing Muddyscuttle, but the pain that comes in the process of losing it.

Oh, how I long for the world that neither J. B. nor Cassie can ever imagine while they are prisoners in protoplasm! Always they indulge their flesh and starve their spirits. I know I grumble far too much—I am, as I have said, most homesick. If only I could hear again a great celestial chorus.

At my last rehearsal, the Cogdillians were performing the anthem for Clockstop called "Valiant the Rider in Splendor and Power." It is a magnificent piece whose strains will not settle from my spirit. I remember that the bass accompaniment was an exploding supernova and a comet storm. I do so anticipate giving up these shallow orchestrations that Muddyscuttlers call music. It offends all taste. Has the Committee ever heard of a "jukebox"? The deepest part of Daystar's pit must be long arcades filled with these raucous devices.

J. B. loves these but still swelters in meaninglessness, precisely because he has no real way of perceiving our parallel universe. He suffers from nearsightedness, seeing nothing but the obvious, loving only the transient. He sings only jukebox music and, sadly, never suspects the gallant anthems of our realm.

> *Valiant the rider in splendor and power*
> *Comes upon light and the thunder of force.*
> *Eternity bridles the steed of the hour*
> *And glory unfolds at the source of the Source.*

Alleluia,
Valiant

A Muddyscuttle Fear

I have greatly desired to pass along some spiritual counsel to Alphalite. But I still have not seen him since that last exchange between J. B. and Cassie in the bar. It has not been long in our reckoning of time, but it has been two weeks for them. I do hope Cassie is still "sticking to her guns," as Muddyscuttlers often say of determined resolve.

Several crucial events have befallen J. B. First of all, J. B. took a business trip to a city called Los Angeles. I was hoping it really would be a city of angels, but to my dismay it held the same proportion of angels and guardians that exists elsewhere on the planet.

Most interesting to me was the flight itself. I have never enjoyed time on an airship. How cumbersome and slow the odd things go, and yet they call it flight. How pedestrian is human science! We were lumbering along at such a snail's pace, I wonder that we did not fall upon the planet. It would not have been a long fall, but you know how prone these humans are to injury and death. None would have survived.

Two things happened that caused J. B. to think later of both Christ and Cassie's changed values. The first occurred when the plane made an intermediate stop in a city called Denver. J. B. was approached in the air terminal by a strange group of young people wearing colored robes and chanting strange words I could not recognize. Neither did J. B. They approached him near a newsstand where he had planned to buy a magazine that he refers to as a "girlie book." I will not distract myself to explain "girlie" to the Committee.

He never bought the magazine because these strange young people were trying to sell him a holy book of their own. I reminded J. B. that he had not even read the Holy Bible that his Aunt Ida had given him. I warned him to be careful about buying books of which his Aunt Ida would not approve. The impact of my suggestion was strengthened by J. B.'s reflecting about Cassie and his Aunt Ida and their elusive similarity. He was smitten in conscience and bought neither the holy book nor the girlie magazine.

Later in his hotel room in Los Angeles, J. B. made a discovery as he was standing before the mirror shaving. He noticed a large swelling just under his jaw. He stroked it, felt it, and tried to make it retreat into his neck, but he could not. He seemed alarmed by its defiant appearance.

The next morning it was still there. He had a certain uneasiness each time he beheld it in the mirror. It caused him some pain, and he shaved that section of his neck more gently than the rest of his face. However, his concern did not slow his drinking. He has been hitting the bottle harder than ever these days. He seems to have lost interest in the fairer sex. His relationship with Cassie is "on the rocks." By odd coincidence, that is the way he drinks his Scotch—though I feel sure the metaphors are not connected.

He does confuse me with his feelings. He told one of the accountants in his carpool that he thought he might be "carrying a torch" for Cassie. One hopes he will "carry his torch" while she "sticks to her guns." (Aren't these clichés dreadful?) I shall need both his love of her and her commitment to Christ to draw him on toward reclamation.

We returned from Los Angeles on a non-stop flight. Human aviation would beggar a handicapped angel. They have two good wings on these contraptions, yet they dawdle along at the speed of sound. I could certainly have flown faster outside the plane.

It was most disconcerting to learn that J. B. could get his usuals even on the airplane. Of course, he did. He never passes them up. He is drinking out of a general lack of interest in life. He may have a touch of Muddyscuttle depression called the "blahs," which only makes his drinking worse.

I am sure now that he is in love. Can you understand this condition of violent infatuation that these humans experience? I wish J. B. would see Cassie long enough for me to see Alphalite. I would like to find out how she has been behaving. She could possibly be "carrying a torch" as well as "sticking to her guns."

At work yesterday J. B. agreed to have lunch with Beau Ridley, Joymore's charge.

This could be a new breakthrough for the Logos. I am still doing my Alleluias with joy even when J. B. mopes about his apartment with the blahs. I dare not cease my Alleluias, lest I lose my joy. Think of me.

When any realm learns how to love
The universe rejoices.

Alleluia,
Valiant

A Special Word to the Committee

My days grow short, my conflicts violent. Here is the essence of my inner wrangling. Humans know only a lateral geography—east, west, and whatever the other two directions are. They know nothing about the upper and lower dimensions. This is most unfortunate because east is about like west, but upper is immensely better than lower, as I am now discovering. Christ is the example of obedience for both humans and angels. He left Upperton for Muddyscuttle because he loved the Lord High Command, who loves every living being in the universe.

I have often marveled at this creation when I can see no reason for its being. I have heard of the planet Hopeton that is similar to Muddyscuttle. It lies yet unspoiled in the starlets of Firehalls Down. It is a lovely stopover where men are as pure as angels, holding the exact same values. What a world it must be! Still, loving unlovely worlds is the best evidence that the High Command exists. I marvel how the Logos once wept over the lost humans of this planet. At the end of his humanization he grieved their estate even though their behavior was reprehensible. But when he opened his mouth, even dying as he was, he only begged God to forgive the cruel planet.

All Upperton fell and wept.

Now I am learning how much this fallen planet means to God. Take J. B., for instance. I too care for him. I maintain a secret hope for J. B.'s Aunt Ida. According to a friend of mine in Human Petitions, she is regular in her prayers and many of her petitions focus on her dear nephew. She is concerned for "his soul," as she phrases it. So there are at least two of us down here who care. Perhaps Cassie is praying for J. B. too, but I cannot be sure.

The lump on J. B.'s neck may have little relevance, but it is getting larger, and he is frightened. My clients on earlier tours also became concerned about the various lumps and bumps that appeared on them from time to time. I do remember that some of the lumps were called "mumps." (You would think they would have called them lumps.) While they caused my charges a great deal of discomfort, I couldn't help thinking about how humorous they were, these "mumps." Oh, the great day when both J. B. and I will be free of mumps and bumps and time!

Mumps seem not to be so terminal a state as being in love. It has such a profound effect on my client. He is lost these days, rubbing his poor neck and grieving Cassie's absence. He can barely stand to eat. Whether you on the Committee can accept it or not, J. B. is in love. And shallow as it may seem in heaven, it is a deep matter in Cleveland.

Small men and tiny worlds should know
Great love will make a planet grow.

Alleluia,
Valiant

January

Here is the astounding news! J. B. went to a physician, who told him he must enter a hospital as soon as possible. The doctor said the unusual swelling could be lymphatic carcinoma. This is a serious human condition and far more dreaded than mumps. J. B. is to have a biopsy immediately.

He was so alarmed that he quickly called Aunt Ida and asked her to pray. Aunt Ida plans to come to Cleveland straightway. The biopsy may be immediately followed by more serious surgery.

J. B. is so frightened he is trying to read the Bible again. He threw away most of his girlie books, keeping only the best, which are really the worst. He has been trying to live in a way he feels will please his Aunt Ida. This is a secondary reason for being good, at least when compared with the higher motives of the saints. But while he is being good for all the wrong reasons, he is managing an unbelievable amount of reform. He is to go into the hospital next Monday.

Here is the spectacular news! He is going to church with Beau Ridley on Sunday. I think there are two reasons. First, he knows that Cassie attends Grace Church, and he is anxious to catch a glimpse of her. Second, he is frightened by the prospect of surgery. He hopes to make a last-minute impression on God. "I would like to get God on my side," he said, accepting Beau's invitation.

He and Beau had an interesting conversation over dinner. I must try to tell you exactly what transpired. They ordered a rather expensive human food called lobster tails. I wish I could draw you a picture of these delicacies as they lay on the plate. When I saw these tails, I wondered what their heads must have looked like. Anyway, after the food was served, Beau asked if he could say grace.

"Grace? Right here in the restaurant?" asked J. B.

"Yes, if that's all right?" asked Beau.

"Why yes, I . . . I guess so."

Beau did pray rather loudly, and J. B. looked around at other guests and smiled nervously. Mercifully for J. B., Beau's prayer was short.

"I used to pray when I was a boy," said J. B. sheepishly.

"Oh, really? Do you now?" Beau responded.

"Not so much. In fact, I leave that to my Aunt Ida. She's more regular than a preacher."

"What did you pray when you were a boy?"

"Oh, you know. 'Now I lay me down to sleep, I pray the Lord my soul to keep. If I should die . . .'" At this point, J. B. stopped and felt his neck lump. He seemed choked for a moment and then continued, "'. . . before I wake, I pray the Lord my soul to take.'"

Taking a bite of his lobster tail, Beau asked, "And if you did, would he?"

"If I did would he do *what*?" J. B. responded, making it clear Beau's question was confusing.

"If you should die before you wake—would he take your soul?" asked Beau.

"I . . . I . . . I guess so. I mean, my Aunt Ida is a special friend of his and . . . I . . ."

"I'm sure she is, but Christ will not accept you on the basis of family faith. Your Aunt Ida's faith cannot avail for you. J. B., you need a relationship of your own with Christ, just like your friend Cassie has."

By this time J. B. was ill at ease. He clawed at his collar, then seized on Cassie's name, "Have you seen Cassie lately?"

"Yes. She has become a regular at church. I frequently see her in worship. Cassie seems to have made a sincere commitment to Christ, but she seems a little lonely. My wife seems to think she's in love."

"With whom? How can your wife tell?" J. B. seemed to be on the edge of cardiac arrest.

"She may be entirely wrong," said Beau. "Women seem to understand these things. I'm quite pleased with Cassie's determination to serve Christ. She really seems to be sticking to her guns. You know, I think my wife may be right. She does seem a little misty-eyed and faraway. I think she may be carrying a torch for someone."

I was delighted with Ridley's insight. So, she is "carrying a torch" and "sticking to her guns" after all. It was welcome news.

The conversation resulted in J. B.'s promising to attend Grace Church on Sunday morning. That afternoon he'll be going to the hospital shortly after Aunt Ida arrives in Cleveland, so his Sunday will be busy.

There is one more aspect of glory. Frankie Williams is coming to Municipal Arena with his Greater Cleveland Conquest. Beau mentioned it to J. B. He said he would be counseling inquirers on the floor each evening.

Maybe all these circumstances will leave my client open to a new consideration of the Logos. J. B. seems to be more spiritually sensitive in every area. I don't mean to bore the Committee with trivia, but J. B. actually tipped his hat to a nun. Perhaps it is not a great sign in itself, except that in his heart J. B. was thinking, "I must see what these creatures believe that gives them the ability to live without sex." Celibacy to J. B. is an insane idea. Still, he sees it as a great achievement for those who put up with the affliction.

I am hopeful that with the lump, Aunt Ida, Frankie Williams, Beau Ridley, Grace Church, and Cassie above all, J. B. will soon discover the Logos. Ah, if it happens! Greatness will come! J. B. will see a world where he can be of service. He will hear the cry of orphans for the first time. He will see the dispossessed and homeless. He will read beyond his questionable magazines the literature of a suffering world. He will be born anew to the possibilities of a life that is courageous enough to look upon all the hurt that exists just beyond the blind indulgence of his cravings.

Come, Logos!

> *A star exploded and*
> *The fiery band*
> *Held at its heart*
> *The Great Command: Go! LOVE!*

Alleluia,
Valiant

Star Thoughts

Things seem to be coming my way at last. I must "strike while the iron is hot," as they say in Cleveland. My fear is that I may be pinning too many of my hopes on the coming Frankie Williams Conquest.

The danger of Conquest services is that they are often emotional in their appeal. Conversion at its basic level is the sovereignty of the Logos. Only last week I learned that several were turned back at the gates of Upperton. They had terminated in a car crash on the way home from some evangelistic worship service. They had arrived at the gates singing sweetly a song they had heard at the Conquest service. It was with some terror that they were turned back, for they had no real knowledge of Christ.

I am always sad for those who have a form of religion but fail to understand real faith. No one is admitted to Upperton except those filled with the substance of the Logos. I cannot allow my client to rely on shallow understanding. The world swelters under a thousand griefs: death, war, hate. He must be reclaimed or he will never care about the things Upperton cares about.

During the humanization of Christ, he observed much shallowness of spirit. He warned all Muddyscuttlers, "Not everyone who cries 'Logos' shall enter Upperton, but only he who does the will of the Lord High Command." It is the will of the Lord High Command for men to fill their hollow existence with service to a broken world.

My client must constantly face this issue of inwardness. Upperton is off-limits to Scuttlers whose only attribute is outwardness. I remember a surprised atheist who came to the gates unable to believe he was still alive when he knew he wasn't. He was trying to get into heaven without that inwardness that is the one inviolable standard of Upperton. He was honest, having come straight from the philosophy department of a large university. He kept mumbling that he had many degrees and had never seriously believed in either heaven or God. He assured us that he finally knew that both were as real as his doctor of philosophy degree. But he was so late in coming to us that, of course, we could do nothing to help.

I fear that J. B. may be frightened into shallow commitment by this lump. He may make some spurious decision to regain Cassie's lost esteem. I must hurry him to better understanding. He must receive Christ out of his own sense of spiritual desperation or he, too, will be turned from the gates.

Most Scuttlers have fuzzy notions about what it takes to be admitted. I once knew a man who arrived at the gates of heaven offering the God-and-Nation badge he once earned in Young Campers. He insisted it wasn't fair to turn him out of heaven when he had helped so many little old ladies across the street. I would have helped if I could, but the imperative inwardness was missing, so I was powerless.

J. B. must come to understand that the nature of conversion lies in Christ's demand that true penance be offered in place of human arrogance, or inwardness has no validity.

Christians have a way of codifying and reducing the mysteries of their spirituality to clichés. (This grievous tendency is behind the "Honk-If-You-Love-Jesus" syndrome.) One American evangelist from the Bible Belt codified the mystery of salvation in a most curious metaphor. He called it the "Thessalonian Turnpike to Salvation." There were three lanes on the Thessalonian Turnpike, he said: Lane One, all must turn from sin to be saved; Lane Two, all should follow Jesus to be saved; Lane Three, we must turn to the living God to find salvation. His approach was little different from one of J. B.'s sales seminars. Here's how one uses the Thessalonian Turnpike: First, one rings the doorbell (while the angels presumably come to attention) and says, "Excuse me, sir, but if Jesus were to come this minute, would you be holding a harp or a pitchfork?" If the answer is "harp," fine, but if "pitchfork," then you should begin the presentation of the "Thessalonian Turnpike to Salvation."

My fear is that J. B. could be led down the path of Christianity where the machinery is great and the mystery is small. Although I will rejoice at any experience which brings him to Christ, he must know that salvation is in the Logos alone and not the rote schemes that evangelicals use to pry the gates of heaven open. Muddyscuttlers ever obscure the Great Chair with petty formulas.

Once more my hope rides on circumstance. I must trust in the combined influences of Aunt Ida, the neck lump, Frankie Williams, Grace Church, Beau Ridley, and of course, Cassie.

> *Praise all human need and place*
> *Where the wounded hand of joy*
> *Beckons littleness to Grace!*

Alleluia,
Valiant

The Rural Saint

I am in church trying to focus on the sermon. This pastor *can* communicate. His sermon is on life after death. Nothing could be better for J. B. His neck lump being what it is, he is most concerned about his future and is trying to get all the information on heaven he can. So J. B. is listening hard.

This sermon on heaven is obviously being preached by a man who has never been there. Yet those here this morning are listening intently as though he has just come back from the place. Fortunately, they are unable to see the pastor's guardian, who is standing right beside him grimacing at the parson's naiveté. How shall humans ever learn what angels find so commonplace?

Perhaps the Committee can tell by my last entries that, while my enthusiasm is better, I am still suffering from the dingy illumination of Muddyscuttle. At least this sermon makes me see again the delightful world that is only a few months away now. I anticipate the glorious day I shall return to Upperton. I shall blink for days in the incandescence.

I am glad J. B. is at least hearing of the other world this morning. How he needs to learn of it! He will never be allowed in heaven just because he tips his hat to female clerics. I must say, it is deflating to leave my own celestial preoccupation and deal with nuns and bumper stickers. But I am trying to keep our friendship usable across the reaches of our very different worlds. And sermons like this one do bring our worlds closer. J. B. doesn't know it, but only as he accepts my world will his really have any meaning.

I have continued to meditate upon the words of the pastor. Perhaps that is the mark of a great sermon. It was clear even as he spoke that he had never been to Upperton, and yet there was a fundamental worth to all he said. It was he himself that impressed me. What the man *was* preceded all he said; isn't it always that way?

He was in league with the angels. He was standing firmly on the planet but free of materiality. He spoke about the reality of the Logos and cried in an honest passion I have not seen to date on this orb. Mystery clung about him, and yet, he was stripped to a nudity of soul and power of essence. He seemed to give full human vision to those things which do not appear. His manhood was there, but was only the slightest encumbrance to his inwardness. His words, gilded with joy, flew at J. B.'s encrusted resistance.

J. B. had attended the service to see Cassie. She sat a half-congregation away from him, but once the sermon began, he never saw her again. He did see his sodden interior and his thin veneer of respectability. He was close to reclamation as the sermon ended—I am sure of it.

After the service Cassie greeted him with reservation, but welcomed him to the services of *her* church. (Evangelicals tend to be possessive of churches. They know the church belongs to the Logos, but you rarely hear them say so.) J. B. *is* in love. He was dying for her to say something, anything, to him. She maintained her reserve. He asked if he might call her sometime, but she said that there was too much between them. She told him she needed to put some distance between her past and herself. "I would prefer that you not call," she said kindly but firmly.

She turned to walk away when he said, "Very well, Cassie. If you would remember to say a little prayer for me, I'd appreciate it. I am going into the hospital today. My doctor is concerned that I may have a malignancy. I'm distressed . . . frightened, I guess."

Cassie turned back and tried to speak. She choked. She tried a second time, but was still overcome with emotion. Finally, saying nothing, she turned and walked away. Her steps were weighted with an agony of soul that made it clear even to J. B. that she was in love. In spite of the agony of this abruptness, he was ecstatic to see her so visibly affected.

Alphalite told me in a brief exchange that Cassie has been picking at her food and is very much in love. He says she is determined not to tell J. B. because of her love for the Logos. She still feels a lot of guilt over her past relationship with my client. She will not leave her past where she lived it. She presumes against our Logos by not letting him forgive the kind of life that she and J. B. once shared.

Cassie's friends at Grace Church have counseled her to forgive herself all that she has already been forgiven by the Logos. She should live in the freedom of reclamation. Still, she suffers. To be guilty of guilt is a great affront to God. Guilt is man's great reprimand. Muddyscuttlers are so reluctant to let our Logos provide atonement; there is ever the feeling that they must pay for their own sins. As if they could! Why can't they accept the overcoming power of crucifixion they forced upon the Beloved? What is this foolish notion that they can pay for their sins just by feeling bad about them after they have been fully forgiven in heaven? How dare they think their little acts of self-incrimination are even visible beside the grandeur of his sacrifice? Yet that's what homemade atonement is: The foolish attempt to purchase forgiveness with guilt.

J. B. ate a lonely lunch after the services. He drove to the airport to pick up Aunt Ida, who arrived on one of those dawdling airships I mentioned earlier. She got off the plane with a small valise and a large Bible. J. B. was most happy to see her! I spent a few moments getting re-acquainted with Nova, Ida's angel. He's a regular sort, solidly attendant. Nova says that while Ida has certain idiosyncrasies I might find tedious, she practices utter submission to Christ.

After the initial hug and kisses, J. B. and Ida passed some idle chatter. He said he had been living just "like she had taught him." He was uncomfortable with his own words. She promised to make him kolaches and liver dumplings just as soon as he was out of the hospital. (Aunt Ida was once married to a Slavic man who ate unusual food.) This promise did not seem an incentive to health to me, but it did to him. I suppose it was not too unusual for someone who eats lobster tails.

After visiting for an hour or so about old acquaintances and their welfare, Ida drove J. B. to the hospital. He checked in and went to his room. As soon as he was dressed in curious bedclothes, Aunt Ida came in and visited until his supper was served. At one point the dialogue became interesting. Nova and I made some rough notes on what they were saying, and here is how it went:

Aunt Ida asked him with great concern, "Jay-Jay, are you worried about your surgery?"

J. B. answered with more than a little anxiety, "What will I do, Auntie, if it is cancer?"

"Do you remember what I taught you when Uncle Harvey was alive?"

"You taught me so many things, Auntie, I can't think of which one you mean right now."

Aunt Ida became forceful. She leaned on the hospital bed, moved in close and said, "Jay-Jay, I mean what I taught you about Jesus bein' the answer to your every problem. Are you still talkin' to Jesus, Jay-Jay?"

J. B. was clearly nervous. "Some, Auntie."

"Some! SOME! What are you saying?" Ida's voice rose higher. "I find that when people only say they are talkin' *some* to Jesus, they really aren't saying anything."

J. B. decided he would be honest. "Oh, Auntie, I can't lie to you. I don't talk to God. I didn't even think there was a God until recently. Now, I just don't know. Maybe there is and maybe there isn't."

"Jay-Jay! What do you mean, you don't know if there is a God?" She became animated and wagged her index finger just under his nose. "Why, if Uncle Harvey—God rest his soul—could hear you talkin' this way, he'd turn you cross his overalls and give you what-for. He'd beat these funny notions out of your head for sure."

"I don't know if you can beat atheism out of people or pound God into them," J. B. said.

"Maybe not, but it just isn't right for you to be here, created by the good Lord, and say the good Lord didn't make you. 'Member them little brown coveralls I made you in the third grade?"

"Uh-huh."

"Well, the coveralls had a maker, didn't they? And no matter how much you or anybody else would say they didn't, they did." Ida's homespun logic seemed to J. B. like something he once dredged from a philosophy course—only more rustic.

"I know that, Auntie."

"Well, you're a lot more certain about the coveralls than you are about yourself, Jay-Jay. You think you just sorta sauntered into being without any God at all?"

"I dunno. Maybe."

"Maybe! Is that what your professors taught you down at that fancy school? When I think of all the money Uncle Harvey and I spent educating you, too. Did they teach you that there is no God? Did they teach you that he didn't make you whole and perfect?"

At this point she seemed to be through making her point. Then she gathered herself and began again without giving J. B. a chance to reply.

"Well, let me tell you, Jay-Jay, God made everything, and he made it whole and perfect. He never made anything that wasn't perfect and fine . . . except, maybe atheistic college professors."

"And carcinoma, maybe. Did God make that, too, Auntie?"

"Aha! So that's it, isn't it, Jay-Jay! You're not so much doubting God as you're just plain mad at him! Well, why didn't you say that in the first place? Everybody gets mad at God every once in a while—even your Uncle Harvey!"

"Well, what's he ever done for me?" J. B. asked, waiting for Aunt Ida's wisdom to deposit some security on the threshold of his mind.

"What's he ever done for you? I'll tell you what! He gave you an aunt and an uncle to care for you after your folks were killed in the fire. And he gave you a good mind and a college education. He gave you a good job. He gives you fifteen breaths a minute and a pulse of sixty-eight. He gave you . . ."

"Carcinoma!"

"No! A thousand times NO! He doesn't do things like that, Jay-Jay! But after everything else he's done for you, how can you turn thumbs down on God? One little neck lump and you're all through with him, is that it?"

"Lately, Auntie, you'll have to admit, God's been walking by me and kicking me every chance he gets. I've got a better-than-average chance of cancer, and I've lost Cassie—"

"Cassie? Who's she?"

"Oh, nobody. Just a girl I lived with—I mean dated—for a while, that's all."

"How'd you lose her?" asked Ida, probing uncomfortably as I cheered and winked at Nova.

"Well, she got religion and won't have anything to do with me anymore."

"Why not? What've you been up to that turns off decent folks?" Ida still probed.

"Er, nothing, Auntie. I'm decent. It's just that . . ."

"Now, Jay-Jay, you gonna hold out on Auntie? What have you been doin' that isn't proper? You haven't been philandering 'round here in Cleveland, have you?"

"I don't want to talk about it anymore, Auntie. I have to be up early in the morning for the biopsy."

J. B. was perspiring by this time as Aunt Ida was clearly closing in. As she drew the strings of her pursuit, he became anxious. She opened her big black Bible and read him the most ominous words. "The fool hath said in his heart there is no God." Then she closed the book and took his hand and prayed with sincerity and great volume. She sounded like a prophetess in a thunderstorm.

"Now, God, Jay-Jay doesn't know any better than to say you don't exist. So you gotta help him, 'cause he's scared to death. God, if you wanna heal that little old lump on the side of his neck, you just take it away. I'm gonna have to ask you for this and trust you for it, 'cause poor Jay-Jay's in no shape to ask you for anything . . ."

Her tone became earnest, and tears began to flow from her tightly closed eyes. She continued, "Oh, God, my poor Jay-Jay's been so lost in his sin and now Cassie's turned her back on him and his low ways. I pray you'll help him be more what he needs to be, not jus' so Cassie can respect him, but so he can respect himself. Mostly, God, give some direct attention to that little lump o' cancer under his jaw. I'm just trusting him to you and Jesus. Amen."

When Aunt Ida finished, she kissed him on the forehead. Then she gathered up her Bible and her handbag and left the hospital room. She had a less scholarly but deeper impact upon him than the pastor at Grace Church. He was glad to be alone and yet he wasn't. Nova and I could hardly take notes on their conversation for cheering Aunt Ida. She was magnificent! I hope we can get her into Upperton without revision.

Now the hospital is quiet. J. B. is not quite asleep. He's wishing that he had stayed after worship this morning to talk to the pastor. He is neurotic on most issues of the spirit. One moment he is an atheist and the next a desperate seeker. Still, in his seeking moments, he will not yield to Christ. He does seem to feel the burden of his previous life with Cassie; at such moments he feels he has sinned against God. The next moment there is no God. Human nature is fickle beyond description.

I am on the side of Nova's charge. How can any Muddyscuttler stand in the middle of our universe and judge the Great Chair to be nothing at all? Human arrogance reaches its apex in atheism. I found myself wishing that Aunt Ida could become a mandatory lecturer to every university philosophy department. Her wisdom is uncongested. How well she understands the intellectual tendencies of men! They force God to be nothing and by this devious process rise to the spot God occupied before they deposed him. They are to be pitied.

Aunt Ida has a formulated faith, to be sure. Her view of sin is as small as J. B.'s, for different reasons. J. B. has been blinded to the great injustices of this world by his hedonistic ego. Ida's view of evil has been rehearsed in an atmosphere where drinking and sex are the little sins so often denounced while the universe aches with genocide and poverty.

But she is alive to the hurt that afflicts her world and she does care.

She has demonstrated a quality of compassion that can come only from Christ and the whole substance of inwardness which he imparts.

Tomorrow my client shall know whether his life is to be shortened by disease. It is a heavy night for me. I love him and wish he didn't have to suffer. But from moments like these, our Beloved often gains a foothold in the human heart.

> *Come watch our Beloved leave footprints in air,*
> *Evermore reigning where flesh may not dare.*

Alleluia,
Valiant

101

A Silent Winter's Night

It is a long winter's night. J. B. is waiting in dreamless sleep for tomorrow's surgery. He is "mixed up." I should think there is little "up" about being "mixed." I should rather have the cliché be "mixed down," since there is nothing elevated or lofty in the kind of indecision that J. B. now deals with.

J. B. may be deliberately choosing indecision because it is a safer way. Procrastination always eliminates the immediate risk. "The safest of all courses is to doubt," one old mortal said. In the battle for truth, doubt sometimes peeps cautiously over the ramparts to watch in safety while those who have courage state their convictions.

I cannot force J. B. out of his mixed condition. Uncertainty about values results in confusion. My client is always asking about the value of Christ-life while he clings to the value of life as it is. He thinks of conversion as the restrictions of a God who enjoys breathing down the collar of all who want to have a good time. J. B. accepts the axioms of his peers: "God is a killjoy." Part of J. B. wishes to be under a higher dominion. On the other hand, his ego rebels fiercely in favor of his spurious independence from all outside spiritual intervention. The reclaimed often talk glowingly about the "lordship of Christ" while they live in the egoistic glory of their own lordship. Here is their neurosis. Shall they have a Lord or be a lord? It keeps many from salvation, and it keeps most of the saved from deeper joy. Few resolve it.

Mortals have a burden that we guardians never deal with—flesh! I know I have earlier in this report lamented its absence at moments when I would like to give my client a reassuring touch. But for all the good qualities of flesh, I have never been able to understand the control this infernal substance has over spirit. What is it? Protoplasm? Bones? Follicles? Sinews? Whatever it is collectively, it makes demands. It drives Scuttlers until they become gluttonous in their appetites and overfill their every desire. And ultimately flesh destroys life, for it gets worn and old and diseased.

J. B. is sick—his flesh betrays his well-being. He suffers the curse of the neck lump! There is a real chance he could die from their cancerous betrayal of his own flesh. He cannot imagine getting on without this

180 pounds of flesh and blood that he believes himself to be. So he lacerates himself with the possibility of disease. Oh, that he could see the liberation of spirit! It would end his captivity!

> *There comes but one great liberty*
> *When morning wakes the world to see*
> *That living after life is free.*

Alleluia,
Valiant

The Middle of the Year

During the night, J. B.'s neck lump deflated and disappeared. The surgeon made a preliminary incision but found nothing. J. B. had extensive testing here at Memorial Hospital, but nothing has confirmed his early fears. It appears J. B. has been "healed," as churchmen say.

He is ecstatic! He is giving credit to Aunt Ida and God—in that order, I'm afraid. Aunt Ida has now asked the Lord to give him spiritual health as well. I owe the order and correctness of these notes to Nova.

When J. B. emerged from surgery groggy with anesthetic, he said with murky cheer, "Hi, Aunt Ida."

"Hello, Jay-Jay," replied his aunt. "Did you see the Lord in any of those pretty dreams?"

"No, I didn't see anybody," he said. Then coming to himself, he quickly asked, "Is my surgery over?"

"It's all over. And best of all, there isn't anything under that big bandage on your neck."

"What's that?" he responded as though he had not heard her properly.

"It's all over. There isn't any neck lump. There wasn't when you went into surgery. The doctor said he'd never had a case like this. The tumor just seemed to go away in the night."

"What are you saying, Auntie? They didn't take the tumor off my neck?" His question represented his incredulity.

"They didn't need to, Jay-Jay. There wasn't any tumor there."

"That's amazing!"

"The word is miraculous! Your doctor said he thought it was amazing, too. But I asked him what was so amazing about the Lord healing my little Jay-Jay."

"Auntie, you're a marvel!" he said as if he had just faced the Virgin of Lourdes.

"Jesus is the marvel!" said Aunt Ida, giving the credit where it was due. "I'm just glad to be his child and able to see him work his marvelous power in every life—especially yours, Jay-Jay. I'm gonna pray right now and thank Jesus for beatin' these fancy doctors to that neck lump." So saying, she clamped her eyelids together and began. "Now Jesus, you took care of Jay-Jay and healed him completely. I'm just gonna pray now that you'll help him quit saying you don't exist. He doesn't really mean anything by it, Lord. You know he's always been a questioning child and he thinks he's being honest with himself. At least now he knows that you can deal with cancer, and he needs to see you heal his doubts and confusion, too. Now, Lord, about his low life: You've seen ever'thing he's done—and I'm sure he's had the angels blushing 'round the throne. Lord, I pray you'll help him give up all his sin and think like Uncle Harvey and I raised him to think. And Lord, help Cassie—whoever she is—not to be too high-brow and goody-goody to help Jay-Jay till he comes around. Thank you for every little blessing from your mighty hand. In Jesus' name, Amen."

Much has transpired in the past twenty-four hours. Aunt Ida left yes-terday, but I wish she was still here. There is a kind of power in her rural faith one does not often see around Cleveland.

There is one other incident you should know about. Cassie brought Jay-Jay—rather, J. B.—a box of nougats. It was good to see Alphalite again.

Cassie was delighted to learn of the "miracle." She said, "God, indeed, was merciful." J. B. was excited that she had come to see him—was sur-prised and delighted. She could not stay long. J. B. asked if he could phone her when he left the hospital. She said it would be okay, but she was becoming more involved in church activities and was not often home in the evenings. She said that she was going with the gang to a "Chris-tian Life Seminar" and would be involved for several weeks. When the seminar was over, she agreed that he might call. J. B. asked her for a "good-bye kiss." She declined. She said they both had their lives to live, and little good could come of opening old wounds.

As she spoke of wounds, she glanced at the bandage on J. B.'s neck, then quickly looked away as though it hurt her personally. She then walked briskly out of the room. She is determined not to be in love with him, though her determination seems to be weakening.

Beau Ridley called. Because of the "miracle," he was able to secure two promises. First, J. B. promised to go to Grace Church again on Sun-day. Second, he agreed to attend the Williams Conquest of greater Cleve-land when it begins next month.

In spite of the miracle, J. B. was glum the rest of the evening. I find myself participating ever so slightly in his mood. I understand Cassie's effort to break with her old way of life, but I almost wish she wouldn't be such a "prude."

On the day of a great miracle, I am less hopeful than I should have supposed. J. B.'s healing, which seemed so glorious in the morning, was an uninteresting event by evening. I cannot understand how the glory of his miracle has so soon faded and does not mark his experience more deeply. Immediately after his recovery J. B. fastened a great deal of theological importance to the whole thing. And for his sake, it may be well. Still, contemporary miracles are less basic to the nature of faith than generally supposed. On their own, such great signs do little real good in helping people come to faith or in confirming them in it. Believers need, rather, that process of inwardness which feeds daily on spiritual substance. Only then will they adore Christ more than his miracles.

Oh, that he might know the Scriptures. Scuttlers suppose that if they could only see something "un" or "super" natural, they would immediately come to faith. Now J. B. has arrived at point-blank truth. God has affirmed himself in personal power at the point of J. B.'s need. He has seen the magnificent evidence of the supernatural. Yet he doubts. The miracle meant more to Aunt Ida than to J. B. She didn't need the miracle to believe in God; she believed in God as much before it happened. J. B. still disbelieves in spite of it.

Faith neither begins nor grows by miracles. The Logos chose the route of humanization in the glorious process of Muddyscuttle's reclamation. But this miraculous experience has never been witnessed by human beings as a whole. "Eye knowledge" is important to mortals. They have a proverb here that says "Seeing is believing." What a curious dependency! The corollary proverb is damning: "Not seeing is doubting."

Isn't it odd that having seen the supernatural, J. B. so soon regards it as natural? Why won't he learn that believing comes first and seeing later? If he would believe, he would see all that now mystifies and perplexes him. He would join those liberated Scuttlers for whom miracles are evidence to the heart and not the eye.

My client would be reclaimed already if he could accept his own spirituality. His thinking is materialistic. If he were pulverized to fine ash and scattered on the planet, nothing would change. He would still be J. B., as real as I am, without the curse of his own flesh obscuring his true existence. This is a cosmic riddle! It is a materialistic joke! By the time Muddyscuttlers discover genuine existence, it is too late to see the fleeting nature of the materiality they once thought was true reality.

How slow is flesh! Hordes of humans followed Moses through Muddyscuttle wastelands. Time and again God performed magnificent miracles for them. He split seas, gave water from stone, and fed them bread from the desert floor! Did they believe, having seen? Not for long. They died doubting in aching blindness.

The great miracle of Jesus' humanization should produce faith. He divided loaves, walked on water, and drew the dead from coffins and tombs. His reward for all this was not belief, but humiliation and execution. At his death we in Upperton did not cry over the mutilation of his flesh—we knew that for what it was. It was the insult to love that left his Father reaching in agony from the Crystal Chair.

Some Scuttlers used to debate the question: Do miracles create faith, or does faith create miracles? Their question is absurd. Miracles transcend science and reason in demonstrating the supernatural realm. The one great miracle is reclamation. Most are reclaimed before they gain any perception of our realm. They meet Christ before they ever learn the significance of miracles. I must not despair. J. B. will be better motivated toward reclamation by his own sense of need than by Aunt Ida's miracle (and that is still how he refers to the neck-lump miracle).

When I am discouraged, I think of this. During his humanization, our Lord said, "If I be lifted up, I will draw all men to myself." It is not by little miracles, great arguments, nor threatening circumstances that men come to life everlasting. Life is Christ alone, eternal in power, pervading the cosmos, yet living in men and women. The great miracle is this reduction: the great Christ spiritually camping in small spirits.

Yet the Logos is the Lodestone. He will draw. I feel that J. B. may already be caught in the magnetism of Christ's life. Let us wait and see if he may not soon experience the only great miracle there is—the transformation of pitiful mortality into eternal life.

In the meantime I must clear the debris from the rails. Assail the barriers. Desire. Wait.

Miracles are frequent
And all the blind can see
A simple splendor coming
In dull complexity.

Alleluia,
Valiant

The Month of the Logos

I am coming to understand that faith is a matter of hearing.

Words have immense power over mortals since they form the fabric of all reason. Cleveland is under siege by a new and powerful word that Frankie Williams calls the Word of God. This word is now the subject of the press, and all souls who dwell in these environs seem stirred to stop and listen to it.

The Frankie Williams Conquest is in full swing, and J. B. has gone for the past three nights. Beau Ridley has been taking him to the Conquest, and Joymore and myself have derived great pleasure from these experiences. You may think me plane-bound, but these arena services seem to smack of Upperton. Each night thirty thousand Scuttlers sing and pray for the reclamation of Cleveland. Best of all, there are thirty thousand guardians present, too. It is the best angelic singing I have heard since I left Cogdill. They are a superb evidence of what guardians can really do in the rarified spiritual atmosphere of a fallen world. I know I have often railed upon the quality of religious music, but I have made an interesting discovery: One reason why mortal hymns are so bad is that mortals sing them. The same melodies, harmonies, and words are really quite beautiful when properly sung by our own kind.

The Conquest Songster is a fine human singer as he leads his stadium congregation. His guardian, Constellation, has been leading us guardians in the better music. If these Scuttlers could hear us, they might have an immediate experience of grace. Some of their hymns have dreadful lyrics that speak of human depravity and destitution. They really do not apply to us angels, but we sing them anyway. Here is a good example of their not-so-angelic lyrics:

> *Just as I am and waiting not*
> *To cleanse my soul of one dark blot,*
> *To thee whose blood can cleanse each spot,*
> *O Lamb of God, I come!*

But to mortals with what Aunt Ida calls "low ways," such lyrics are not so outlandish as they seem. Such ideas definitely need consideration.

Frankie Williams is a good evangelist. His words sear the human conscience. More than five hundred Scuttlers were reclaimed as the choir sang about human sin and spots and blots. How wholesome for them to consider their estate before our Beloved! Few such moments of truth and light occur upon this dismal orb.

Cleveland is aglow with a strange light. The High Command must have been overjoyed to see five hundred reclaimed at a single service. I doubt whether Upperton can imagine anything like this stadium full of men and angels joined in song. It was so ecstatic that we sang our way out of the arena and into the parking lots in a baptism of light.

Fervent angelic singing rose from those guardians whose clients were reclaimed. I wanted so to join them, but J. B. would not go forward. He listened to Frankie Williams intently but refused to budge throughout the invitation.

At one point J. B. appeared almost repentant and seemed as moved as he was the night Aunt Ida left him alone in the hospital room. He had resolved not to go forward and so clung to the stadium seat before him. He gripped the iron rail until his knuckles whitened. If he had released it for only a moment, he might have come to faith.

He is struggling against the Logos, but he is losing. He is being propelled to faith by a motivation stronger than I alone could compel. He is caught in the magnetism of the Spirit.

Now, about his romance.

Today he finally called Cassie. She seemed pleasant, but declined his offer of a lift to the Conquest tonight. Because she declined, he has decided to stay home. I am disappointed in this decision. J. B. is so close, and I desperately hope that Clockstop will be stayed until he is safely reclaimed.

One important incident you must know about. Yesterday J. B. and I had lunch with Beau Ridley and Joymore. Beau talked to J. B. of the Christ-life. He used a tool that the Committee will deplore—the Thessalonian Turnpike. I hope you will not think ill of Beau, for he does it with his whole heart. While I don't like the concept in general, it had a powerful effect.

Beau's earnest entreaty came cloaked with clichés. While he lacked John MacDonald's self-righteousness, his witness sounded similar.

"J. B., tell me this. Have you come to the place in your spiritual life that you know for sure if you were to die right now, you would be holding a harp instead of a pitchfork?"

"Well, I suspect it would be the latter," answered J. B. "All I know is that since I have been attending the Frankie Williams Conquest, I have been confused."

"That is just my point, J. B. Why do you think God had you and me become friends?"

"Was it God who did that? I didn't know that! I thought it just sort of happened because we both work for the same company and eat in the same lounge."

"No, J. B.! I've never found things to be that happenstance. God has a definite plan for even those events that seem small and insignificant." Beau seemed to speak with the tone of a bishop. "Everything that happens to us, God engineers in such a way as to get us out from under our circumstances and put us under the blood."

"Under the blood? What an unpleasant idea," objected J. B. "Besides, how can God, who is busy doing all the things he has to get done, manage to care about International Investors, much less the man in cubicle thirty-two?"

"The gospel is the great plan of a Holy God. He wants everyone to get to know Jesus Christ. J. B., have you ever considered receiving Jesus as your personal Savior and getting saved by the blood?" Beau spoke in "churchese," but J. B. responded in good faith.

"Oh, Beau, I don't know that much about God. At Grace Church and at the Conquest I think about the idea, but it looks impossible for me. Faith is easier for people like you than it is for those like me."

"Nonsense, J. B.!" protested Beau. "All things are possible through prayer. God can do anything but fail. You should really go after Jesus, 'cause where you go hereafter depends on what you go after here." Again the clichés flew.

J. B. became painfully honest. "I don't think I could be a good Christian even if I tried. I could never be as dedicated as you are, Beau. I've seen the changes in Cassie. I don't think I have the stuff it takes. Even if I could really make up my mind about God, I just don't think I could hold out, no matter how hard I tried."

"You don't have to hold out, and you don't have to try. Just quit trying and start trusting," Beau said. "Now, let me show you here from the Book of Thessalonians how you can be a part of that great Turnpike of Truth.

I can show you in ten minutes how you can get out from under life's circumstances and get under the blood. You see, life is a matter of the Three Rs."

"Reading, 'riting, and 'rithmetic?" asked J. B. naively.

"Nope," grinned Beau, smiling that J. B. was so ignorant of the Thessalonian Turnpike. "Recognizing, Repenting, and Receiving. First you recognize your lost condition. Then you repent of your sin, and then you can receive the gospel and be saved by the blood."

"I'd like to believe in the Book of Thessalonicans—" said J. B., seriously mispronouncing the word.

"Thessalonians! Thes-sa-lo-nians!" Beau corrected.

"Yes, but right now I've got more important things to consider."

"J. B., there are no more important things than to believe the Three Rs and save your soul from an eternal devil's hell."

That is how it went. Beau's concern expressed itself in clichés. He is deeply earnest about it all, however. J. B. appears anxious to be "under the blood." He seems earnest, too.

I must close. J. B. has just accepted an invitation to tonight's Conquest after all. What a rapturous turn of events!

> *Just as they are, they have come from the night,*
> *Invading infinity, dwelling in light.*
> *From the kingdom of graves and realms of the dead*
> *They have turned to the Dayspring of Life.*

Alleluia,
Valiant

On the Way to the Conquest

Well, here we are in the automobile on the way to the Conquest. I know I am trying too hard, for I am too concerned with J. B.'s anxieties. Still, I believe that he is very near the most important decision of his life.

I gasp at human possibilities. J. B. has the possibility of grandeur we angels never can experience: reclamation. Can you imagine? Beginning existence as ordinary flesh and ending it in obvious love. Scuttlers taste forgiving grace, while we angels only know what it is like to be loved in foundational purity. Ah, to be lifted from dank materiality by the loving hand of the Lord High Command! I hope soon to enter into the full joy of my client.

When J. B. attended Grace Church, he was less impressed with their praise. Now I wonder whether it was because the number who gather in Grace Church is smaller than the Conquest crowd. Scuttlers themselves are prone to evaluate the success of religious meetings merely by the number in attendance. It is a shallow habit. J. B. must drop this assumption. His fascination with the mass assembly lies in his need for personal identity. There is truth in the human cliché: "A man is known by the company he keeps." J. B. feels bigger in big gospel meetings. Being a part of 30,000 sinners at once makes being a sinner seem less sinful. They have been publishing Conquest attendance in the daily papers. It excites J. B. to be part of such a large venture.

The success syndrome of Christian enterprises that fascinates J. B. bothers me. He watches Frankie Williams with all the adulation he would give a resurrected saint. In his misplaced esteem he again confuses "bigness" with "greatness," and "popularity" with "spirituality."

It disturbs me that J. B. has so little adulation for Grace Church. By contrast with the Conquest, Grace Church appears small and unimpressive. This is unfortunate, for much of the human dedication at Grace Church is beautiful. It has all that the Conquest offers plus a spiritual rapport that is warm and affirming. I cannot expect you to understand baseball. It amuses me only because it keeps guardians flying over a large grassy area to stay near their clients. They must feel as I do when J. B. and I are on the tennis court—a frenzied act of guardianship I must not try to describe.

I distract myself . . . where was I? Oh, yes . . . well. . . . Baseball teams are divided into leagues. Those that hold less interest are referred to as the minors. Well, J. B. is giving the Conquest major league esteem, and Grace Church, minor. I regret that I am earthbound in my illustration. I hope mortal esteem for Williams does not blunt the esteem they ought to feel for Christ. Misplaced admiration thrives on Muddyscuttle. Still, Frankie Williams seems worthy of the confidence placed in him. He is a man snared in the web of his calling. He does not covet prestige. He has strength without arrogance in spite of his major league status. Whatever I might say of Williams, he does play a critical role in J. B.'s hoped-for reclamation. I trust that when Frankie Williams leaves this city, Grace Church will continue all that the Conquest began in Considine.

But neither Frankie Williams nor Grace Church shall determine this matter. I have become all the more aware that it is Christ who draws men to himself. The universal love of God designs the best circumstances to guide every person to life. I see what J. B. cannot see—that he is not alone in his struggle. He thinks that everything depends on himself. He thrashes like a new swimmer making a desperate crossing. Christ endured the agony of death for my client. It is Christ, I tell you, who has erected a thousand barriers of love to keep J. B. from traveling his hapless way to nothingness. I thrill at the thoroughness of divine love. To end in Daystar's pit, J. B. must struggle over a hundred barricades of grace. Think of the obstacles God has already laid in J. B.'s path to self-destruction: Aunt Ida, MacDonald, Beau Ridley, Grace Church, Cassie, Frankie Williams, and even the biopsy. But Cassie is the key.

Cassie is preparing to attend a spiritual renewal weekend when the Conquest is over. She and many other singles will travel on chartered buses to a mountain retreat for extensive Bible study and prayer. As for Cassie and J. B., their relationship cannot maintain this distance much longer. They are clearly in love. Cassie consumes his thinking. Alphalite says Cassie has intense reciprocal feelings.

The last reckoning is desperate and close for my client. J. B. must come to know the Logos, and soon. Still, the ever-reaching love of God is constantly thwarted by J. B.'s pursuit of mere romance. Humans rarely seek higher affection if a lower one is accessible.

Human love is, indeed, powerful, if only to humans. Nonetheless, I may have given such love a lower rating than it deserves. It is unfortunate that I lived so closely with the gluttonous sexual side of romance during my first assignment on this planet. In the case of J. B. and Cassie, their sweating, grunting, selfish indulgence may at last have risen from its muddy roots to become the very image of God's love.

What of J. B's love for Williams? Call it esteem, if you will. Still, J. B.'s reverence for the evangelist may be more natural than I should like to admit. Humans tend to admire those who assist the Logos in reclamation. I was aghast that Ridley approached my client with the Thessalonian Turnpike. Yet it accents the substance of the last human command of the Logos, "Into all the world—preach the gospel to every creature." Those were his last words. So what if Beau Ridley is not very far advanced in the way he goes about it? He is being true to Christ's command even as he uses his zealous, mechanistic, and mundane cybernetics. And when Frankie Williams is no longer in Cleveland, I will then be glad that Beau is working with J. B. in any way.

Comes now the great and holy state,
And promise beckons us to wait.

Alleluia,
Valiant

The Triumph

Hallelujah! Reluctance has been slain! J. B. has been set free from the bonds of Daystar! It happened at the Conquest on the last night that Frankie Williams was in town. It is difficult to tell of the soul-struggle J. B. encountered.

As he made his public commitment, all my fears of spurious identity were allayed. Neither the size of the crowd nor Frankie Williams was much in his mind at the time of his reclamation. Glorious truth! Wherever true reclamation occurs, it is always a highly individual matter. Although he stood before the Conquest crowd, it seemed to J. B. that he and the Logos were the only two in Cleveland.

His joy can hardly be described! He is filled with peace and a feeling of enlightenment. His whole being seems to have a quality of richness—a new wealth that derives from his spiritual inheritance. There are many aspects to this.

First, he has acquired the wonderful inwardness that is the inviolate principle of Upperton. This inwardness is not *sui generis*. He has created neither its being nor its value. It is the substance of an invasion that has flooded his life, through the narrowest opening of his will. He desired this inwardness only in little amounts, but it came in torrents. The flood has dumbfounded him with light. He willed it all, and yet there is so much more than he willed.

Joy is so innate to us that I can barely understand its impact, first discovered. These who have been born empty often come to fullness in a deluge of mood. Their joy makes visible the existence of our realm. It is not the only evidence of Christ that the planet sees, but it is most dynamic.

To be sure, new joy has an element of exhibitionism in it. J. B. sings constantly these days. His vocal quality is as poor as his spirit is rich. Thankfully, his musical expression is covert. He reserves it for himself and the angels. He sings in the shower—a common human tendency I do not claim to understand. But singing anywhere is new to my client since his joy came upon him. It is not sterile joy. He now has an interest in Bible reading that is spontaneous and no longer motivated by his threatening memory of Aunt Ida. Further, he no longer resents Scripture for its long "begat" passages. Wondrously, he reads and has not been stopped once by the "begat" passages.

He is making a marked effort toward personal reform. He now questions himself about every form of indulgence that he once freely allowed. He is viewing gluttony and drunkenness, lust and jealousy from a new perspective. The accursed "girlie books" are all gone now, even those he considered the best. He has canceled a planned trip for rest and relaxation which was to include the loosest sort of activities. He no longer uses the name of the Lord High Command in Muddyscuttle phrases. But most impressive of all is a formidable new mental discipline with which he garrisons his thoughts.

It is spring, and even I am taken with the beauty of earth. The greens and blues of planets such as this have a charm all their own. There are still evidences of the fall of man all about—bits of rusted steel, candy wrappers, and crushed beverage cans. Yet a strong joy gathers new life from buds about to break into flowers. This feeling blankets the fields and hills. I wonder how this wondrous planet would have looked without Daystar's contamination. How foolish Adam and Eve were to blight their world for the slithering propositions of evil.

The world seems suddenly so new that I can scarcely believe I have been on the planet for years. I wish J. B. would go into the country alone to celebrate his new joy and leave me dumbfounded on the warm earth. Earth is not the pigsty I had first thought. Now, in the explosion of spring, I understand how our beloved Logos felt. I know at last why God so loved this world that he permitted the humanization.

I must not give you the impression that J. B. is altogether changed. He is not ready for canonization. He is still struggling with his lower nature. He noticed Cassie yesterday during a less captivating moment of the sermon. Even in church his mind descended rapidly below his higher nature. He was almost engulfed in the same lust he experienced when they were living together. It was seething, if unexpressed. Yet he maintained a reverent look as a masquerade.

As I looked around, all the other Scuttlers in pew twenty-eight looked the same way, and I was hit by a cold chill. What ghastly indulgences lurked behind all those pious faces! Had I pores, I should have sweated.

Soon the pastor spoke a sharper thought, and J. B. left his fantasies and returned to his old sweet self, as they say down here. I was alarmed—his self was not so sweet after all. His hypocrisy was instant and stifling.

117

He could entertain rank gluttony while appearing to feast on the adoration of the Logos.

His lust was intense and real. I did not imagine it. He experienced it! And all right in church! It has left me with a strange foreboding, and I cannot stay my fear. Are my hopes to be dashed by his permissive mind?

Further, while friends rejoice over his reclamation, I fear that Grace Church may dilute his zeal. He is being rushed all at once to join too many church organizations. He has been asked to join two choirs, two Sunday school classes, the bowling league, the men's club, the discussion team, and the Saturday Night Meet-a-Friend club. Should he try to join all these church groups, he will become busier than he is spiritual. He will be all legs and no heart in a short time. He has so far resisted the recruiters, but I don't know how long he can hold out.

I fear that this new fervor may be diverted to secondary allegiances. I shudder to think he might join so many good causes and yet miss the best.

> *Joy is here*
> *For life has come*
> *And death is speechless,*
> *Ordered dumb.*

Alleluia,
Valiant

In the Bus Terminal

A week has passed since J. B.'s reclamation, and I now find myself in a bus depot. As always I have my journal with me, including copies of this document for the Committee. I carry this file with me because of the certainty of my client's termination. But I must hurriedly conclude these papers, for the time is at hand. It is time to board the bus that J. B. must ride into foreverness.

May I tell you of my client's latest joy? He and Cassie have been exploring a tentative relationship. They are here with forty or more others waiting to board a motor bus for a trip they suppose will take them to a renewal center.

J. B. is unsuspecting. For him this is an opportunity for participating in a time of Bible study. Being with Cassie has doubled his joy. He is full of promises yet unspoken to both the Logos and to Cassie. J. B. and Cassie are sitting and talking quietly about the new meaning which is so abundant in their current relationship. Their new rapport has blotted out their past affair. It seems so sad! Now that they openly celebrate their relationship, it is over.

Now I can accept the great wisdom of the Committee. A divinity student would have been all wrong for me. At last I agree with my assignment. During J. B.'s struggle to become, I have arrived at a new plateau of angelic understanding. We have both been changed by the strange process of refining love.

I do love him. I know the High Command loves him, and we are in complete agreement. He is mine for only a few more hours. Shortly we shall both be back before the Chair. I anticipate the moment.

The chartered motor bus has pulled in and the passengers are called for. J. B. and Cassie are standing hand in hand. They are the joy of the Logos and could teach their world the glory of a good confession. Unfortunately, they are out of time. They would be grieved if they suspected they will never see Cleveland together again. It is not horror, but a delightful surprise that awaits them.

Excuse me that I've left this report so truncated. But I must go and

watch these lovers safely across the chasm of mortality. They have run out of time. But no matter, they can get on without it now.

> *Summon the herald trumpets*
> *Beneath the vast glass dome!*
> *Love redefining death and love*
> *Escorts her pilgrims home.*

Alleluia,
Valiant

The Philippian
Fragment

Preface   127
The First Letter   129
The Second Letter   145
The Third Letter   165
The Fourth Letter   177
The Fifth Letter   187
The Sixth Letter   195
The Last Known Letter   204
Afterword: Who is Helmut Niedegger?   207

Preface

This manuscript has traveled an indirect route from its discovery to its publication. I am indebted to so many for these pages:

To the brothers of St. Thaddeus whose vow of silence spoke thunderously of my obligation.

To the members of my own congregation who encouraged me by allowing this material to be published in our newsletter until a wider audience could be gained.

To Helmut Niedegger—above all, to him—the elusive German scholar whose inspiration I have properly credited in the afterword of this book.

Calvin Miller

The First Letter of Eusebius of Philippi to His Beloved Friend Clement

The Assuming of a New Pastorate

1 Eusebius, newly appointed bishop of Philippi, to Clement, pastor of Coos. [2] Peace and joy and the kindness of Christ possess you.

[3] I have newly arrived at my parish, and am delighted at the reception I have received. There is no joy quite so effervescent as a new pulpit responsibility. Everyone loves my sermons, and most are generous in telling me so. [4] I am preaching my gold-scroll series on the Beatitudes of our dear Lord, and the response has been more than adequate.

[5] The church and I are like newlyweds. [6] We love each other with a kind of ecstasy that can only grow in its fervor. At one point in a sermon they all broke into applause. [7] One dear sister tells me every week that my sermons are getting better and better.

[8] Last week I finally met Brother Glandus of the congregation in Dorsinius. It is not a large assembly, and he has been pastor there for several years. [9] Some are apparently a little weary with his preaching, and I only wish that he could have a little of the rapport I feel with my flock here in Philippi.

[10] Pastor Glandus is in jeopardy. His congregation often protests that he is putting them to sleep. His tonus is mono and his tempus is longus.

[11] He is a fine pastor. His deportment is open and his attitude is good. He loves all men and especially those who are of the household of faith. But his preaching is a persecution of the saints.

[12] The days are hard on Glandus. I sense in him the frustration of the disinterest he creates merely by standing up. [13] He went on a short vacation and the church was packed in his absence. Guest speakers are nearly a festival event for his congregation.

[14] There is some truth to the adage that interest is the key to love. Certainly the church is more than a forty-minute sermon. The church is the body of Christ. [15] But boredom is the enemy of fellowship.

[16] It has never been a function of the office of the Holy Spirit to make

the sermon interesting, only true. Integrity is the authentication of a sermon and not interest.

¹⁷ Glandus is telling the truth, but he takes longer than necessary to tell it. ¹⁸ As certain of our laymen have said, "The mind will absorb nothing beyond the fringes of boredom."

¹⁹ Glandus must tell the truth more quickly. If he needs a model, let him remember that our Lord's Sermon on the Mount took only about eighteen minutes to preach.

²⁰ He was able to keep a crowd of thousands at rapt attention. Why did our Lord not take longer? Was it that he ran out of material or decided to save his exposition of the Shema for a bigger crowd or a later occasion? No, he simply knew that interest comes garbed in brevity.

²¹ I have resolved that my current wave of acceptance must continue. I will make the truth as interesting as possible, and I will tell the truth minimally.

²² Here's the great commission of the pulpit:

²³ Take the fewest words possible to tell the greatest truth of all: God was in Christ, is yet, and ever shall be.

²⁴ I am sure I am all the more sensitive to the ills of Glandus since my own new ministry is a whirl of great preaching and long compliments.

²⁵ I am sure your preaching brings on the praise it deserves. ²⁶ I hope that one day we can be together and share outlines and manuscripts. ²⁷ In the meantime let us both pray that Glandus may survive the fire that gathers about his ministry but is absent from his pulpit.

Why Eusebius Left Bythinia for His New Parish in Philippi

2 Clement, how much I love Philippi. ² Glory be added to glory that I am once again the center of congregational esteem. ³ Phoebe of Phrygia brought us a squab-and-honey casserole for dinner on Thursday. Hiram of Hellespont gave us an expensive scroll of the Septuagint. Publius the Paralytic did his part by bringing us seventeen sheets of high-grade Egyptian papyrus for the epistles I must write.

⁴ There is no church like a new church. So far, in a single month of serving this congregation, I have been given a new toga, a new tunic, and a pair of Nubian lizard sandals. ⁵ There was a grand reception where everyone brought snacks to the atrium for Koinonia and Kippers. Yes, I am loved here in the city of Philippi.

⁶ How well I remember my last year in Bythinia! It was not so pleas-

ant, I can assure you. I only served the church as pastor for eighteen months, but it was a stormy year and a half. [7] There was a brother named Severus who wanted his son, Constantius, to be ordained as a deacon, and the church refused to comply. [8] Constantius had little about his life that seemed to merit his name. [9] He not only kept late hours with wineskins, but it was generally agreed upon that his chariot was often parked in front of the puellae bonorum temporum or the "good-time girls," as Romans are wont to say. [10] He was churlish and roguish and loose with the opposite sex, but this virtue was his: He never missed church. Still, his father, Severus, wanted to see him a deacon.

[11] Constantius had an elevated view of the office. He wanted very much to be a deacon. He spoke of it as being "crowned as a deacon" when it is proper to refer to it as being "ordained as a deacon." [12] There were some other things that seemed muddled in his understanding. He felt that deacons should be given clerical deductions in the markets of Bythinia. He also desired to avoid the Roman military conscription and receive certain compensations like tax credits of one kind or another. [13] He did not understand servanthood. I asked him if he was prepared to visit the leper colony to minister once he was ordained, but he declined unless the church could pay him mileage on his chariot and per diem expenses. [14] The idea of the leprosarium had some appeal to him since it was on the way to the houses of the good-time girls.

[15] I had to agree with the action of the church. Constantius was definitely not the sort of man who should be "crowned" or . . . er . . . rather . . . "ordained" as a deacon. [16] When his father, Severus, discovered my stand, he became very angry. Severus immediately felt the Lord might be calling me to a smaller parish in rural Arabia. Being a wealthy man, Severus's donations paid much of my wage. [17] His money was a canker in the assembly. Not only did it furnish Constantius with racy new chariots, but it also gave him the deciding vote in every action of the church.

[18] Remember how Simon the Apostle reprimanded Simon the Magician who tried to buy the power of the Holy Spirit? "Thy money perish with thee!" he cried. It was, indeed, a powerful phrase, and one I had much admired.

[19] Well, Severus came to me and offered me an arrangement. He promised me that if we ordained Constantius, he would see to it that my salary would climb several shekels in a single annum. [20] He promised

me that I would never want for the common necessities. It was clearly an ecclesiastical bribe, so I also cried, "Thy money perish with thee!"

²¹ Things went downhill after that. Severus withheld his tithe. There was usually not enough money to pay my wage. Constantius finally quit church and married one of the good-time girls. ²² Most of the church withdrew from me fearing to risk the displeasure of Severus.

²³ The other deacons refused to go to the leper colony. I took over that ministry. ²⁴ As my reputation eroded in Bythinia, I grew more fond of the lepers, particularly Lenia. She taught me that need alone causes us to hunger for Christ. "Health and wealth wean us of our need for Christ," said Lenia. "It is only to the poor in spirit that the Spirit comes," she said. "It is not so bad to lose a wealthy member. It may be the very insufficiency that turns you to Christ. ²⁵ It is amazing how much I have learned of the love of God in a decade of leprosy. The pain of life best buys for us that intimacy with Christ that money is powerless to purchase." ²⁶ The membership of Bythinia finally asked me to go. ²⁷ Having no church of my own, I went to serve among the lepers until the church here in Philippi invited me to be their pastor.

²⁸ Ah, Clement, they love me. They care for all my needs. ²⁹ But yesterday I was confronted by Coriolanus who has been a member of the church here in Philippi for thirty years. He has a daughter he would like to be a deaconess. ³⁰ He promised me a consistent wage if I would see that his daughter becomes one. I told him that I would see what I could do. ³¹ He would like for her to be "crowned" as a deaconess by the Ides of Janus. I reminded him that the word was "ordained."

³² Even in this sea of acceptance I am suddenly afraid. Coriolanus is a big giver, and in some ways reminds me of Severus. Maybe I shouldn't worry. After all, I seem to be so well loved. ³³ I remember the haunting words of Lenia the Leper of Bythinia, "Only in the poverty of our need may we discover the riches of Christ." May I choose such poverty as will make me truly rich.

The Unkind Outcome of the Former Pastor in Philippi

3 I am pastor! Oh, the exhilaration of the very words *Reverend Eusebius!* One of these Philippians called me Doctor Eusebius the other day. It sounded so good—Dr. Eusebius! ² I was jubilant thinking how it would look in Doric letters on the church sign. What joy there is in being pastor!

³ But some of the joy I would otherwise feel is blunted by the remembrance of my predecessor, Quartus. I watched one of the members with a bucket of white paint taking his name off the church sign last week. ⁴ "Is it as hard to erase the memory as the name?" I asked our church sign painter.

⁵ "Oh, no," he said. "Third time I have painted out a pastor's name in this decade."

⁶ "Did you like Quartus? Was he a good pastor?" I asked.

⁷ "Yes, but he crossed Coriolanus. I heard his daughter wanted to be a deaconess and Quartus refused."

⁸ I said nothing but swallowed hard. The sign painter continued.

⁹ "Quartus wasn't really his name, you know. His name was Cato, but it gets easier to call your pastor by a number rather than by his name. Tertius came before him."

¹⁰ "What was his real name?" I asked.

¹¹ "Can't recall . . . He only lasted seven months."

¹² "Thrown to the lions?" I asked, almost preferring that Tertius had been devoured by lions than by Coriolanus.

¹³ "Nope, that would have been easier! No, we all heard that Coriolanus didn't like a certain sermon Tertius preached against rich Christians who tried to buy preeminence. He reminded the rich that while they might buy position in this church, it was not for sale in heaven. He picked an unfortunate text for his sermon."

¹⁴ "What?" I asked.

¹⁵ "Thy money perish with thee."

¹⁶ I swallowed hard. "Maybe I should have gone to Arabia," I thought to myself.

¹⁷ "Seven months, huh?" I asked when I had regained my composure. "What happened to the pastor before him?"

¹⁸ "Secundus?"

¹⁹ "Yes, Secundus."

²⁰ "Well, let's see. That was the split led by Demetrius because Coriolanus wanted to be the moderator and . . ."

²¹ "Secundus preferred otherwise."

²² The sign painter looked at me. "How did you know?" he asked. "Do you have the gift of prophecy?"

²³ "No," I replied, "but I can sometimes see trends."

24 "Trends?"

25 "Never mind, just tell me about Quartus, my immediate predecessor. How did he escape Coriolanus's struggle to have his daughter elected a deaconess?"

26 "Well, he looked very tired just before the business meeting when he would have been ousted as pastor. 27 He was solid on the point—he would not permit Coriolanus's daughter to be 'crowned.' He wanted out! He was tired of the church and Coriolanus's congregational briberies. So he went through a big crowd on Lupercal singing hymns to the praise of Christ."

28 "That was foolhardy! Was he arrested?"

29 "Immediately, and thrown to the lions the very evening the church met to consider his dismissal. Things being what they were, some considered it a nice way to go to be with our Lord. 30 Many of Coriolanus's camp said it was a coward's way out, but Quartus was not much of a fighter, I'm afraid."

31 By this time he had painted out the name of my predecessor. As he walked away, I asked him where he was going.

32 "To the marketplace to get another ewer of whitewash. You can't afford to get low on white paint in this church. I've got to keep the sign in good shape—all the names current."

33 I was disenchanted as I saw him walk away. "I have been most popular here in my first few weeks. Surely I have nothing to fear," I thought. "The fates of Secundus and Tertius and Quartus will never be mine," I reasoned as the sign painter left. 34 When he was all but out of sight, he turned back and called out, "Eusebius, will it be all right if I call you Quintus?"

A New Friend with the Gift of Healing

4 Shortly after my arrival in the city I made another new friend, Helen of Hierapolis. She is a dynamic lover of people and is so bound up in her love for Christ that she walks in an aura of esteem. 2 I am not usually so taken with traveling healers. 3 You will remember my disaffection for Hiram the Healer of Hellespont who claimed instant health for all who would in faith touch his sequined toga. 4 He lost much of his following in West Asia because he couldn't get relief from a toothache.

5 But Helen is different. She came to Philippi with a conviction that

God loves the suffering and she determined to participate with God in this love. [6] I met her near the synagogue when she was talking to a group of blind beggars. I was surprised when she didn't even try to heal them, but bought each of them a new cane and reminded them that the curbs on Caesar's Boulevard were particularly high. [7] She reminded them that they should be especially careful because it is so hard to hear a chariot coming down an unpaved road. [8] "Someday," she told them as we walked away, "light will be universal, and every eye will behold eternal love."

[9] They didn't feel as though she had cheated them. [10] She is not much of a show woman, I'm afraid. She just mixes with humanity in order to take divinity as far as it will go. [11] I am the richer to know her.

[12] Sister Helen opened a great crusade in Philippi on Thursday and is the sensation of the leper colony. [13] She rarely does anything one could call a miracle. [14] Last week she laid hands on a little crippled boy and was not able to heal him, but she gave him a new pair of crutches and promised to take him for a walk in the park here in Philippi.

[15] Yesterday with my own eyes I saw her pass an amputee selling styluses. She touched his legs and cried, "Grow back! Grow back! In the name of Jesus of Nazareth, grow back!"

[16] Well, Clement, I so wanted to see the legs grow back, but they did not. Poor Helen. What's a faith healer to do with an amputee that refuses to grow legs on command?

[17] She sat down with the little man, crossed her legs on the cold pavement, and began selling styluses herself. [18] Soon she was talking to him, and before very long they were both laughing together. For an hour they laughed together, and by nightfall they were having an uproariously good time.

[19] When it was time to go, Helen's legs were so stiff from disuse, they refused to move. [20] Her legless, stylus-selling friend cried in jest, "Grow strong! Grow strong! Grow strong!" Helen only smiled and staggered upward on her unsteady legs.

[21] She looked down at her lowly friend and said, "I offer you healing, you will see. It is only one world away. Someday," she stopped and smiled, "you will enter a new life and you will hear our Savior say to your legless stumps, 'Grow long! Grow long!' Then you will know the glory that Sister Helen only dreamed for you."

[22] He smiled and said, "Do you heal everyone this way?"

[23] "It is better to heal with promises than to promise healing."

²⁴ "You are right, Sister Helen. But more than right, you are an evidence that our Father yet heals the spirit of amputees—even when they will not grow legs. And, once the spirit is healed, the legs can be done without."

²⁵ Helen turned and walked on down the street. She was near the amphitheater where she holds her great crusade when she saw a young girl without any arms.

²⁶ "Grow long! Grow long! In the glorious name of Jesus Christ, grow long!" she cried.

²⁷ The girl looked puzzled and looked at her shoulders where her arms refused to be. They did not seem to her to be growing.

²⁸ "I was afraid of that," said Helen. "Oh, well, I can miss my meeting one night, I guess. Young lady, how long has it been since anyone combed your hair?" ²⁹ And she sat down beside her new friend and took out her comb. For the first time in my life I wanted to be a faith healer, Clement.

³⁰ After the crusade was over last night, Helen came to our home for squab and honeycomb. Wouldn't you know it, she brought a couple of hungry lepers.

On Positive Thinking in Disastrous Times

5 My joy abounds. The congregation works hard to affirm me. Helen the Healer of Hierapolis is my friend in whom I clearly see Christ. At the moment there is little persecution in Philippi. ² One week ago as I passed through the agora on a quick shopping trip, a voice interrupted my thoughts. The voice had a bugle-like quality and had gathered a rather impressive crowd of men about it. ³ I could tell by the wrinkle-free togas, they were all merchants with an eye to the future. ⁴ The name of the speaker was being whispered all about me with great respect— Marcus Sparkus, an up-and-coming Christian motivator.

⁵ Has he ever been to Coos? He has come to Philippi to lead a cogitation rally. ⁶ I may enroll to see if I can add to the Holy Spirit a better mental outlook in the living of my life.

⁷ Marcus Sparkus has written thirty-two scrolls now, with such titles as *The Impossible Possibility, This Way to Success, The Zeal Deal,* and the ever popular *You Are Numerus Unus.* ⁸ In the first session he tells his eager listeners that God is on their side. In the second he lists how God

has given all things and people for our use to make us richer, happier Christians. [9] In seminar three he instructs his audience to pray for our enemies in such a way that we can triumph over guilt, live a devoted life, and become wealthy. [10] I decided to take the course feeling that it might help my already successful ministry. [11] But just as I was working out my chart for the future and recording my "Life Action Goals," there was a knock at the door. I learned that the authorities had arrested Sparkus and hauled him off to be thrown to the lions.

[12] It left the class unsettled. Now we are not sure about how to make our "Life Action Goals" harmonize with the unexpected difficulties of life. [13] I do wish Sparkus had been able to finish the seminar and perhaps shed a little light on this conflict. [14] I did find this curious passage in his *Successful Living* scroll, numerus duodecem: [15] "We are reminded of the little ant who saw a big, strong grasshopper carrying a leaf. The ant was afraid to try to carry such a large load until the wise old grasshopper said, 'Son, you can do it if you think you can.' The little ant realized that it was not his muscles that were defeating him, but his mind. He began to say to himself, 'I think I can . . . I think I can . . . I think I can.' Thus thinking he could, he picked up the leaf and trudged off after the grasshopper. Like that ant, Christians are often defeated in their minds, and they never learn to think in terms of possibilities."

[16] Who knows what the epilogues shall be to all these things. [17] We are not permitted to question, I suppose, if optimistic ants ever dislocate their backs on large leaves or check into their physicians with double hernias. [18] And what of Sparkus and the big cats in the arena? Can he triumph over them with positive thinking? [19] One thinks, too, of his scroll titled *Banqueting on the Difficulties of Life* and wonders what will be the main course at the arena the night of his ordeal. [20] Can he get out of this one even if he thinks he can? And what of his great work, *Put a New Man in Your Toga*? It looks as if they will at least put another man in his, if anything is left of it.

[21] I understand he has a group of scribes rapidly copying his new book for publication, which will probably be published posthumously, *Thinking It Through to a Lovelier You.*

[22] Thursday night is Christian Writer's Night at the arena. I think I will go and see how he finishes it all up. [23] It will be interesting to know whether in the midst of all the tawny, snarling beasts he lifts his hands

and says to the ticket-holders as he did at each of the seminars, "You can win if you think you can," or if he merely cries, "Let me out of here!"

²⁴ I have two more chapters to read in his *Walking into Prestige in Your Own Sandals.* But I keep thinking of Jeremiah who said, "It is not in man that walketh to direct his steps."

²⁵ I am torn between the desire to think positively or to confront life as it is. ²⁶ If I am prone to remember that Christ said faith could move mountains, he also said that in the world you shall have tribulations. ²⁷ I like moving mountains and seeing miracles occur all around me; it's tribulation that makes me nervous. ²⁸ I wonder if Marcus will escape the lions. "I think he can . . . I think he can . . . I think he can."

On Gluttony and Indulgence

6 My first year here in Philippi was earlier eclipsed by a wave of persecution. ² But for the moment the church is free; and in the freedom to practice faith, worship sometimes seems less important than it might in more desperate times. ³ In truth we are enjoying the economic prosperity, although I cannot believe that our good Lord who always cast an eye to the poor would agree with all the various forms of indulgence that one sees around our parish.

⁴ Persecution has now subsided and there is so little stress that I feel the peaceable kingdom may be about to set upon us.

⁵ What, dear Clement, is a Christian to do when we have so much that we feel so little need of Christ? Who can say? ⁶ Jesus once blessed the poor in spirit. I remember Lenia the Leper of Bythinia. Perhaps Jesus blessed the poor in spirit because in our poverty we acknowledge need and turn toward him who is the source of plenty.

⁷ Now we have plenty and see our abundance rising from our own ability to provide for ourselves. ⁸ The things that God gives us do not cause us to love him. ⁹ Ever more we treasure the gifts and not the giver.

¹⁰ We are made neurotic by having too much. Indulgence stands opposite self-denial and incriminates us with our very love of it.

¹¹ Saturnalia is gone and most of the believers here in Philippi have become confessors of the number one sin of the season—gluttony. ¹² For a fortnight Christians were saying grace over horrendous portions of goodies that filled out the pleats in their togas. ¹³ Now many of them are waddling off as guilty and unreformed chubbies, unrepentant in their indulgence.

¹⁴ We sin so often against temperance, and how comical our atonement must look to our God. My dear Clement, what forms our penance takes!

¹⁵ Have you ever heard of the Ovum Fast? If you eat only eggs for a week while you drink the juice of bitterfruits, you may atone for all indulgence. One hefty believer in Antioch lost a couple of kilos by this method.

¹⁶ Then there is the Aqua Concept where heavies lose weight by drinking all the water they can stand for a fortnight. Anna Magna drank forty-three firkins a week while she ran three furlongs down the Athenian Way every morning. ¹⁷ Her weight loss was impressive. And now she lectures intemperate believers on the need for lighter witnesses.

¹⁸ Time would not permit to tell all the diets that abound after Saturnalia is over. ¹⁹ Must life ever be seasons of gluttony and starvation? Is there no moderate way to health?

²⁰ All of this is bewildering when you consider that indulgence is a sin which most of us Christians observe too frequently. ²¹ How long will it be before all of us learn that overfilling our bodies is a kind of abuse? ²² Our Father in heaven created our bodies as the temples in which he could live and be a witness to himself.

²³ How good was our Lord's example! When he fed the five thousand he multiplied fish and bread and not sweetmeats or honeycakes. ²⁴ Perhaps it was his way of saying, "Thou shalt not glut, and he that does shall never squeeze through the narrow portals of life."

²⁵ Forgive me, Clement, if I seem obstinate on the subject, but after all, a witness is liable for all areas of his example. ²⁶ I remember a portly disciple preaching against strong wine in Berea. His message was abrogated by his own unwillingness to practice a form of denial we all must deal with. ²⁷ A thin winebibber is no less credible than a thick teetotaler.

²⁸ I, too, am overfed, but I cannot bring myself to drink a firkin of water or trot along the Athenian Way.

²⁹ Prosperity and acceptance make us neurotic about such things as these. ³⁰ Probably self-control, not the spastic attempt of the overindulgent to fast away their ill-begotten intemperance, is the mark of a Christian.

Christian Symbols and the Danger of Syncretism

7 There is perhaps one other evil of prosperity for us who believe. It is the emergence of movements which surround the church with

alternate channels for serving our dear Christ. ² It seems that various speakers have become popular throughout Christianity, and there are many itinerant spokesmen espousing any number of causes.

³ The faith now fractures and splits into all sorts of special interest groups. ⁴ Now there is a host of popular speakers who come through Philippi renting halls for rallies that center on one kind of partisan Christianity or another.

⁵ I am plagued. In less than a month we have had a score of Christian artists, evangelists, and lecturers come through our city.

⁶ Titus the Consistent has just left the opera hall after delivering his stunning lectures called "Seven Easy Steps to the Deeper Life."

⁷ Now Christiana Hausfrau is in Philippi. For only seven denarii a Christian receives three full seminars and a box lunch. She is popular throughout the empire. ⁸ Her big seminars are entitled "How to Dry-Mop Your Atrium While You Deepen Your Prayer Life" and "How Christ Can Help You Become a Better Mother and Lover." Her supporters say she is strictly Dunamis!

⁹ Next week the evangelist Silas Scorchem will be holding a crusade in the coliseum while the lions rest. ¹⁰ His most famous treatise is entitled: "Severus Maximus—the Antichrist." Those who have heard it are sure that the Roman Senate is the Great Harlot of the Apocalypse. ¹¹ One of the good things about Scorchem is that his ministry is supported entirely by freewill offerings. ¹² They do ask the slaves to try to be sacrificial for the sake of Scorchem's love offering. After all, it does cost something to buy fuel for the flambeaus.

¹³ Besides the many speakers who hold seminars, there have been lots of musical groups as well. The "Happy Romans" will be holding a concert on the thirteenth, and the "New Plebians" will be in Philippi on the twentieth. Best of all, "Lucas New Life and the Third Chapter of Zephaniah" will be here on the twenty-third.

¹⁴ I can at last understand what St. Paul meant when he chastised our brothers in Corinth. So many are made neurotic by the fans and supporters of each of these renowned lecturers and entertainers.

¹⁵ "I am of Christiana," say some. Others say, "I am of Silas," while others say, "I am of Lucas New Life." Right now the "Lucas New Life" supporters are trying to organize a group outing to the concert. ¹⁶ They are, of course, able to get a better rate at the coliseum if they travel in

large oxcarts and sit together as a group. [17] Lucas has a special rate for those who sign up to go with the church.

[18] Clement, why must the church ever be the pool where all the touring authorities seek to draw the net? [19] The church, called to fish for men, finds herself in the mindless support of a score of special interest groups.

[20] One of the brothers was most intolerant because I would not sit in our special section at the "Lucas New Life Concert." "Why would you want to pay the higher rate?" he asked. "Our Lord always wants us to be good stewards. [21] Ask yourself, 'How can I draw closer to Lucas New Life at the best savings possible?'" he challenged me.

[22] Who shall deliver our age from this fever? How are we to seek the church's independence and preserve the integrity of its people?

[23] The lions may help! These artists and lecturers seem to dwindle when the authorities begin to scour the countryside for victims to use at the games.

[24] The days sometimes grow serious and force the church to a focus on Christ it cannot have while her separate heroes flourish.

How a Partisan Group Limits the Work of the Local Church

8 Last week Alexander of Alexandria sent me an epistle asking permission for the use of our meeting hall on a Tuesday night. Alexander is one of the Born-Again Gladiators. [2] It seems a worthy organization, but I am yet suspicious of those organizations that serve Christ and other themes.

[3] Clement, I must ask your opinion. Is it in the best interest of our dear Lord's love that we support all who wear his name?

[4] These born-again gladiators are a case in point. One year ago upon the Lupercal, Bruto the Bludgeon gave his heart to our dear Lord and was, as all said, "a convert to Christianity."

[5] Bruto stood in the arena and said before all of Rome that never again would he bash any brother except he would give all the glory of his victory to God. [6] From this beginning he has been crushing opponents for Christ, and is always faithful to say that it is only because of his Lord that he is able to be a winner in the arena.

[7] He is truly an excellent athlete. He is to share his testimony before thousands in the Roma Bowl on Ben Hur Causeway. [8] The problem is

that he is charging five denarii per seat for those who will hear how truly selfless he has become since embracing Christianity. [9] In this sermon it is believed he will tell how he vanquished Nicholas the Nubian by piercing him with his own trident and crying, "Ah, Nicholas, see how unbelief can be hazardous to your health."

[10] These Born-Again Gladiators certainly seem to capture the imagination of the young. But is it right, most excellent Clement, that they charge so much for their testimonies? [11] They say that Bruto has bought a gilded chariot and rides the streets in pomp since his fee to "share the Word" is adequate to all his needs. [12] He certainly has a powerful testimony, and being such as he is, no one has the courage to suggest that this testimony fee may be out of character with his calling. [13] At all costs we must be careful not to make him angry lest he forget his state of grace. [14] I've never been much for gladiatorial combat. But I realize that all Christians must take up the cross and follow our Lord. [15] Such following requires self-denial. Woe to all who use the cause of Christ to gild their own chariots! [16] No, Clement, we are not to follow him for five denarii per seat, nor for the golden chariot our famous repentance may bring.

[17] I marvel that Bruto can sing the hymns of martyrs. Yet he does have a lovely voice which, like his trident and net, he uses for Jesus. [18] Oh, how our heroes cause us to stumble. I passed a line of truants waiting to get into his rally. They all want Bruto to autograph their broadswords. [19] Who knows but what one of these little tykes will someday have a great testimony worth thousands of denarii.

[20] Still, I would rather somehow that we give our Lord such glory as comes from free testimonies and sermons steeped in the cauldron of study. [21] In case there is not a Christian gladiator in Ephesus, I beg of you, consider my words, "Heroes of faith are those who follow Christ to his passion." [22] Let us, therefore, remember: The way to Calvary was not strewn with posters telling how our Lord sprinted the Golgotha Marathon for so much a seat.

[23] One of the great athletes of Philippi was converted to Christ following Bruto's dynamic testimony. [24] He had been injured by an atheistic Gaul who is now popular in the empire. [25] I asked the convalescing gladiator if he would like to share his conversion experience among our congregations. [26] "Sure," he said, "how much does it pay?" When I reminded him that grace was free, he simply replied that free grace was God's problem and not his. Unlike God, he had a fee.

The Acting of Compassion

9 Clement, I committed an unpardonable sin. I have angered the Constable Coriolanus. [2] It has marked an unfortunate turn of events for me. My preaching has fallen on hard times. To Coriolanus, at least, it is no longer acceptable. [3] My struggle with Coriolanus came to an apex this past Lord's Day.

[4] Publius the Paralytic was not expected to live through the morning. Publius asked to see me at the hour of his death, and I felt it was my obligation to go to him and "to pray him across," as he phrased it. He had such a high fever that it seemed he could not live through the morning.

[5] I prayed for him as I have prayed for few men. God was gracious! Publius was completely healed. [6] How shall I say complete? He is still a paralytic, but his fever is gone.

[7] Back at the church there was consternation that the pastor wasn't there. While waiting for me, they sang through thirty-one hymns before they gratefully pronounced the benediction and left the service. [8] Most of them had a blessed hoarseness that they referred to as "doxoma," a condition which results from singing too many hymns in a row. [9] Naturally I felt bad. My emotions were mixed having seen Publius the Paralytic gloriously healed of a fever.

[10] Coriolanus asked me to stay after all of the others had left the church.

[11] "In my thirty years as a member of this church, it is the first time that the blessed, holy Word of God has not been preached!" he thundered. "What do you have to say for yourself, Reverend Eusebius?"

[12] "Well," I replied, "I felt that the ninety and nine were safe in the fold. Publius was about to die."

[13] "Reverend Eusebius, do you feel called to shepherd this flock?"

[14] "I do."

[15] "Yet you let the sheep come and go without fodder. A good shepherd would love and feed the sheep. But you have sent them away empty."

[16] "But Publius was healed."

[17] "Can he walk because you missed your obligation to the sheep?"

[18] "Well, not that . . . his legs were not healed. But his fever is gone. He will live, Brother Coriolanus! He will live!"

[19] I can assure you, Clement, that while Publius will live, I am not

sure that I can survive the new hostility I have engendered by missing church merely to pray for a dying man.

²⁰ I was foolish to assume that the church would see the glory of my ministry to Publius and excuse the absence of my sermon. ²¹ Through pain I have learned that it is still wrong to heal on the sabbath—at least during the eleventh hour.

²² Is a paralytic worth widespread congregational doxoma? Is the yet-paralyzed Publius worth the cancellation of my morning sermon? I have betrayed a tradition to furnish forth a single act of compassion. ²³ Oh, the institutional cankers that do fester when traditions are unserved! If I go on missing church merely to perform miracles, I must endure the wrath not only of Coriolanus but the whole congregation.

²⁴ It is time for the evening vigil now, and I have just received word that one of the lepers is at death's door and has called for me to come. Shall I go to tend the dying, or shall I go to church and keep my place? ²⁵ I had planned to talk tonight about how we must minister to our world before we seek each other's consolation. I am still unforgiven by most for healing the paralytic. Now I must go to the leper and seal my fate. ²⁶ Grief is seldom convenient to our scheduled worship.

²⁷ I had a dear mentor, Constantinus, who was shepherd of the congregation in Antioch. His church's meeting house was near a busy road. One day, five minutes before his well-packed service was to begin, a Roman chariot ran over a beggar and left him dying before the church house. ²⁸ How grieved was the pastor that most of his members stepped over the bleeding man to carry their prayer scrolls on into the sanctuary.

²⁹ Constantinus was a gentle pastor and full of the love of Christ. He scooped up the emaciated old man and carried him to his grieving widow. In the process of his ministry to this victim of Roman traffic, his hands and toga were fouled with blood. ³⁰ There was no time to go home and change clothes, so he entered his pulpit besmirched by the gore of his own compassion.

³¹ Clement, many in that congregation never forgave Constantinus his bloody toga. Ministry must ever be willing to face tradition. Somewhere a leper is dying. Tonight I shall act out a sermon. I can preach next week when human suffering is more remote.

The Second Letter of Eusebius of Philippi to His Beloved Friend Clement

A Visit to the Monastery of St. Thaddeus

1 A year has now passed since I wrote my last epistle to you. It has been a year of quiet for the church. We have not lost a single member to martyrdom, and we heard that the authorities were thinking of shipping the big cats to Rome where the persecution seems to be really getting underway. 2 I cannot believe that in the economy of the kingdom, God would rather have the cats eating Romans than Philippians. I can say the atmosphere here is not so tense, and we are breathing deeply.

3 I only wish I could say that I was feeling the same freedom in the assembly. For the last year Coriolanus has repeatedly explained to me God's will for my life. He believes I should leave this pulpit. 4 He offered me a stipend of many shekels if I would take an empty pulpit just outside of Rome. I told him that I had heard that the Romans were receiving the Philippian lions to be ready for a new wave of persecution. 5 He informed me that a true man of faith would never turn from lions to sidestep the will of God in cowardly self-interest.

6 I am afraid, Most Excellent Clement, that Coriolanus will not be content until I am no longer shepherd of this flock. 7 Last week he invited every elder of the church to his home for squab and honey, but neglected to add me to his invitation list. He is applying a kind of ostracism. 8 It is possible to face it, but it does keep me busy praying that I may not reciprocate his hostility with hostility of my own.

9 I have learned a little more about the sad case of one of my predecessors whom we have called Tertius. It seems that on the day he entered the marketplace singing hymns he had had a long discussion with Coriolanus who explained to him the will of God. 10 According to Coriolanus it was the will of the Father that Tertius join the order of St. Thaddeus. You will recall that these monks live high on a rocky pinnacle north of Atticus. 11 They all submit to having their tongues torn out so that they never again will be tempted to utter a single syllable that might break

the silence of their lifelong vigil of prayer. [12] While Tertius had always been known as a man of prayer, the idea that his tongue would be tenderly removed as part of the sweet will of God had not been revealed to him so clearly as it had been revealed to Coriolanus.

[13] Last week I visited the monastery at St. Thaddeus. It is all true. It is a silent settlement manned by thirty tongueless monks. But, my dear Clement, here was the startling impact of my discovery—twenty-two of them had once been the shepherds of local congregations before entering their tongueless lifestyles.

[14] Can you imagine that? I could but ponder what had taken those tongues once given to sermonizing and subjected them to amputation and the life of prayer and silence that it produced.

[15] I must admit that mine was a silent sojourn among these brothers! They wheezed and breathed, occasionally sneezed, and I found out that many even snored, but year after year they passed without ever saying so much as "Good day!" [16] Cicero Chrysostom and I became as good friends as we might with my talking and his nodding or writing monosyllable phrases on the scratch parchment.

[17] Cicero had once preached in the suburbs of Philadelphia. By his own immodest testimony he was a popular preacher and large crowds attended him whenever and wherever he spoke the gospel. [18] You are probably moving ahead of me in this tale, but he had his own Coriolanus who knew God's will for his life and, thus, the inner persecution began.

[19] "Do you like the silent life?" I asked him.

[20] He dipped his quill in the berry juice and scratched on the parchment. "I like preach!" he wrote, living up to his monkish vows to write no more words than absolutely necessary to communicate what had to be said.

[21] "How are the accommodations here?" I asked.

[22] "Bed hard!" he wrote.

[23] "And the food? Is it well prepared?" I asked.

[24] "Bad cook! Food awful!" he complained with his quill and parchment.

[25] "Do you miss preaching?" I asked.

[26] Tears came to his eyes, and he dipped his quill and wrote for fully five minutes, "I like preach. I like feel God power. I like see people's faces when they hear sermon. I like power of spoken gospel. [27] I used to feel like God moved inside my life to form every word of sermon and people

were powerless to resist. Once wrote sermon on repentance. Thirty-four Philippians heard sermon and came out of sin to Christ . . ."

²⁸ He stopped writing. He buried his head in the sleeve of his robe and convulsed.

²⁹ When he stopped convulsing, I spoke softly. "I am a preacher in Philippi, but I have been having second thoughts. I may come here and become your silent brother. You see, things aren't going well for me in the congregation, and I felt it may be God trying to tell me to . . ."

³⁰ Cicero Chrysostom jumped up and shoved me onto the rough-carved bench. He dipped his quill into the ink and scrawled in large, angry letters across the parchment:

³¹ "NO! NO! NO! KEEP TONGUE! 'Faith comes by hearing and hearing by the Word of God.' How shall they hear without a preacher?"

³² He stopped writing the giant letters and opened his mouth and faced me. There was an odd and powerless cavity. ³³ Nothing was behind his teeth, Clement. ³⁴ For the first time in my life I realized that silence cannot truly serve our dear Lord best. Only sound may serve. The sound must be trumpeted in faith. ³⁵ It must not quail before those who would seek to put to silence that speech of integrity that has something to say and has to say something; that sound that must trumpet a warning because it has seen the distant chasm and knows the pitfalls that the adversary has dug in the path of humankind.

³⁶ Now I am back in Philippi. I am determined to preach the gospel.

³⁷ Coriolanus may divert the flock from my affection, but he will not silence my tongue. ³⁸ It may be foolhardy to preach in the face of my current alienation, but by the foolishness of preaching I hope to fill my world with saving sound.

³⁹ Clement, remember the monks of St. Thaddeus! Twenty-two of them would give their lives if they could just stand one more time in the marketplace and cry out above the hostile unbelievers, "Jesus Saves!"

The Conversion of Croonus Swoonus

2 It is certain now that all of the lions are gone. The first wave of persecution is over, and we are enjoying a new period of peace and security. ² But security is never the friend of faith. It is peril that produces steadfastness. When the church is secure, she gains too many freedoms. She enjoys the freedom to doubt, the freedom to major on minor issues, and the freedom to indulge herself in community acceptance.

³ The most ghastly freedom of all is the freedom from the utter dependency she must have to weather the crisis. Since the lions are gone, the people are speaking openly of being born again.

⁴ Even the mayor of Philippi is speaking unguardedly of being born again, and while these pagans have no idea what the term really means, they are sure that it has some connection with Christianity.

⁵ Others in our community are printing the words "Born Again" and "Try God" on their togas. ⁶ I tell you, Clement, it all started when they took the lions to Rome. You may be sure that when they bring them back, there will be much less open talk and toga signs.

⁷ But now we are into it. It is almost a fad.

⁸ Some of the local actors are also saying that they have been born again. One of the tragedians in the local theater says he will never again do Greek tragedy, his joy is so great. ⁹ He is going to become a joyous comedian and act in a thousand theaters to the joy of the Christ who has saved him. He is born again!

¹⁰ But the most notable conversion has been that of Croonus Swoonus. Yes, that is right; he, too, is born again. ¹¹ It all happened when his hairdresser who is a member of our church stuck a Scripture parchment in his shining toga telling him how to be born again. And thus it happened.

¹² He was famous before for his homespun ballads like "Back Homa in Roma" and "Nighty, Nighty, Aphroditey." But he is through crooning that he "found his thrill on Palatine Hill." ¹³ Now he is born again, and he intends to give his entire life to singing songs in the traditions of the church. He has a stunning new composition called, "Pleeze Jesus, Just Seize Us and Heal Our Diseases."

¹⁴ Well, that is how it goes when one is born again.

¹⁵ How authentic Brother Swoonus is would be difficult to say. I know he means well, but there were numerous rumors that his singing career was about over when he had the good fortune to be born again. ¹⁶ There is something about his deportment that suggests that the good fortune was really all God's and that the Almighty was certainly lucky that the golden throat once "given to the world" is now "committed unto God." ¹⁷ I suppose it was God's lucky day all right. At least the amphitheater is being packed night after night to hear Croonus "lay 'em in the aisle for Jesus."

[18] A single verse from his big-hit musical testimony will tell you more than I can:

> *I've been set completely free*
> *Since the man of Galilee*
> *Died upon the cross for me.*
> *Yeah, Yeah, Yeah.*

> *Deaf and mute I had no sight.*
> *Life for me was just a fright,*
> *Till I stumbled into light.*
> *Yeah, Yeah, Yeah.*

> *Now I'm giving up my sin;*
> *Love commandments one through ten.*
> *Praise the Lamb, I'm born again.*
> *Yeah, Yeah, Yeah.*

[19] As you can see, Clement, this song is not quite up to the one the beasts and elders sing in the Apocalypse.

[20] In the interest of Christian art it might be better to have the lions back. [21] Pray for us that the faith that has such surface popularity may grow deep. Pray for Swoonus that his lyrics may improve even if his commitment does not.

Of the State of Things in Philippi Regarding Christian Ministry, and
Why Eusebius Felt It Necessary to Correspond with Clement at All

3 The Lord is faithful in a turbulent time when the very pinions of faith seem grounded. [2] Much more in these days of joy have my thoughts been turned most naturally to you whose endurance is in a more southern pulpit.

[3] Yes, to you, Clement, for while I have often heard you criticized by the brethren for your unconventional views, I still think that your own walk of faith is a triumph of honesty.

[4] But let us consider our ministry in these latter days. [5] Parchment is expensive, and I cannot write all I would about the degeneration of the faith. [6] I am not overlooking the basic nature of Christianity. I know

Christians are just people with their worldview under renovation. ⁷ But, beloved Clement, how shall the faith endure when there are so many blemishes on sanctity?

⁸ Do you remember when the emperor ordered the last purge? Some of those here in Philippi escaped arrest by joining the flight into the wilderness. ⁹ They went into the forest of Berea to win souls just as the authorities were locking up their less fortunate brothers who couldn't afford their timely excursions. ¹⁰ Are these wilderness witnesses for real? I believe not. They have found a way to minister that has alleviated all sense of personal risk.

¹¹ Here, however, are born most of my reservations about a kind of faith that serves one's own safety before it serves God's will. ¹² I do not mean to be burdensome to our friendship, but I must ask if it is right for any preacher to build his own empire, replacing God's kingdom with his. ¹³ Many seem to determine God's will for their lives by first measuring exactly what each venture of faith will hold for themselves. ¹⁴ One of my most ardent members tells us that the one inviolable test for demonstrating whether something is the will of God or not is to say with openness, "This must be the will of God because it does so much for me."

¹⁵ There are many examples of this decaying Christian ministry in our day. I want to relate some primary examples and ask you to help me find a simple way to harmonize God's plan for his world and the attempt of so many Christians to use his purpose to further their own ends.

Christian Ministry Is Always under Threat by Church Business

4 There is something official and evil that always lurks around the board meetings of our church. ² When it is most blatant it disrupts the work of feeding the hungry or visiting the prisons. ³ In fact, when our church's civil struggle gets fierce enough, all ministry comes to a stop.

⁴ You have, no doubt, heard by now of the fate of our most elect brother, Dubious, usually called Doob by the brethren in church. ⁵ Doob has caused great consternation among his brothers because he has not been able to let his "yeas" be "yea" nor his "nays" be "nay." His "yeas" are usually "nay," and his "nays" are always "never." ⁶ He wears a certain grieved look as though he has just discovered the gospel is bad news.

He scowls over the communion cup and has a certain dyspeptic leer as though he had just won a dare with the Almighty.

⁷ Some say he wears his corset too tight, and hence, must live with his pinched expression. Others feel that he needs to mix his communion wine with the milk of human kindness. ⁸ Some think it is essentially a liver problem.

⁹ At the last church conference, Doob slinked in, dragging his toga in defeat, and rose to make a motion that the youth of the church be censored for playing their lyricons in the meeting house. ¹⁰ He denounced the "Boom-booms," the "Bangos," and the "Scotty-Wotty Jesus Four" as perverters of the great hymns of the church.

¹¹ Elder Hector has a son in the "Scotty-Wotty Jesus Four," so in a moment there was a small explosion in the church meeting. ¹² Doob finally walked out only three votes short of a stoning.

¹³ It was a terrible scene, my dear Clement. Doob is back on goat's milk to quiet his three-ulcered faith. ¹⁴ The Elder Hector is trying to get the three necessary votes for Doob's stoning and the "Scotty-Wotty Jesus Four" say they are going to open their act in Ephesus where lyricons are welcome in the meeting houses.

¹⁵ I remember the words of our brother Paul who warned us that, if we bite and devour one another, we must be careful we are not consumed by one another. ¹⁶ The quarrel itself is not the chief transgression but rather that it replaces the good ministry.

The Marathon Team

5 The times are free! Dear Clement, our church here at Philippi is fielding a marathon team which will participate in the Delphic Open Olympics. It is a five-man team of rugged, well-muscled men who in their preconversion lives were men of athletic reknown.

² Each of them can run at least from Athens to Corinth and probably much farther. We are optimistic that they may, indeed, win this great set of games.

³ Last month Delos threw his discus with such force that the judges gasped at the record-setter, and were all the more amazed to find out he was a Christian. ⁴ He looks like Zeus and yet charges onto the field like an unbound Prometheus and immediately defeats all other discus throwers.

⁵ The times are free . . . free . . . FREE! Only a year ago we were afraid to go into the streets for fear of being arrested. Now we have our own

athletic teams that are doing very well in the competition. ⁶ They are athletes who love the feel of pebbled track against their bare feet. They love the raw wind—the wafty air of the Aegean Sea—full in their face. They love the brisk air coming full against their nude superiority as they fling the torch to the morning. They love the strain of their own competition set against the pagan athletes of the empire. ⁷ They love all.

⁸ Perhaps not all. I am often concerned that they may not love our dear Savior as much as they love the game itself. ⁹ They train for months on end to have a go for the bronze laurels of the games, but they are all too remiss at training for the approval they may someday need at the judgment seat of Christ. ¹⁰ How shall we build athletes who have learned the secret of the life struggle against the tempter himself?

¹¹ We wrestle not against the wrestlers of Smyrna and Thyatira. ¹² Do we seek the laurel, display our trophy, claim our sweet victory, and never see him who won his race in the bleak light of Good Friday? ¹³ Our Christ entered the arena and wrestled with principalities and powers and left to us that same legacy. If there be a fault in the athletes of our church, it is that they take their smaller contests too seriously.

¹⁴ Menelaeus is our best miler. He rarely makes church on Sunday morning since he needs his sleep for his afternoon training sessions. ¹⁵ He rarely says grace before he downs his yeast and beef. Of his own admission a great athlete is too busy on the track to spend much time studying the great scrolls of Scripture. ¹⁶ But at least in the games he calls himself by the name "Christian," and having prayed for the laurel, he usually sees his prayer answered.

¹⁷ I found a certain athlete who declined to be a part of the church team. He was a slave of the emperor until he was made a free man only last year. ¹⁸ He was called in the city of Rome the Italian Zephyr, for he was a sprinter of so fleet a foot that it was said that none could match him. He was a snow courier. ¹⁹ He ran snow from the top of the Apennines down to the palace so that Caesar could have his ice cream in late spring. He came to our church in the spirit of the victory that heralded his own vital walk with Christ.

²⁰ When the other athletes were putting the team together just before the games at Athens, naturally they asked the Italian Zephyr to be a part of the team. He only sat and shook his head sadly. ²¹ He would not join. He remembered his fellow slaves who had died in the dreadful attempt

to bring the unthawed snow to the palace kitchen. For nothing more than a simple dish of ice cream for the Caesar, their own lives were forfeit.

²² "No," he said to those who sought to make him part of the team. "There is but one contest worth the running. There is but one crown worth the struggle. There is but one course that shall have my stamina."

²³ "Which set of games? Which course?" they persisted. "The track at Delphi or the stadium at Athens?"

²⁴ Most of those who heard his answer did not realize that he was quoting the letter to the Hebrews, since most athletes are better at running than reading, but the Italian Zephyr simply lowered his eyes and told them of the big race: ²⁵ "Wherefore seeing we also are compassed about with so great a cloud of witnesses, let us lay aside every weight, and the sin which doth so easily beset us, and let us run with patience the race that is set before us, Looking unto Jesus the author and finisher of our faith; who for the joy that was set before him endured the cross, despising the shame, and is set down at the right hand of the throne of God."

²⁶ "Some race you just described," said Menelaeus. "Who was the fellow that managed that sort of marathon?"

²⁷ "If he lives here in Philippi," added Delos, "let's get him on the team."

²⁸ The Italian Zephyr shook his head.

²⁹ After a moment he started to answer; then he clutched his chest and died instantly. The athletes looked on dumbfounded.

³⁰ "He's dead!" said Menelaeus.

³¹ "Dead?" Delos was puzzled. "Athletes don't die."

³² "Probably all those years of running snow to the palace," said Menelaeus checking his pulse and confirming the diagnosis.

³³ "Probably," Delos nodded. "I wonder who that fellow was he was talking about who could run when the stands were filled with hecklers turning their thumbs down."

³⁴ "I dunno," answered Menelaeus. "I'll tell you what, men. Let's get out there on the track and win this one for the old Zephyr."

³⁵ And so they did!

How Ministry in the Church at Philippi
Is Being Destroyed by Theological Controversy

6 The church knows only two kinds of business. ² There is good business, which keeps the congregation pointed in the direction of ministry and looking out to its world.

³ And there is bad business, which, congenial or not, diverts the church from its true course.

⁴ Our Savior himself once took the basin and towel and washed feet. ⁵ How far we transgress when we slam the basin down, throw in the towel and stomp off in angry sandals!

⁶ But, Clement, theology too is sometimes set against ministry. How I wish we might remember that Jesus was a practical rabbi. ⁷ His compassion was such an urgent preoccupation with him that he rarely took time to debate.

⁸ An incident happened in scroll study this week that will illustrate how far we have moved from him who encourages us to give a cup of cold water in his name. ⁹ Phoebe came to the women's scroll study with a most unusual question: "Will Jesus come before the great tribulation or after it?"

¹⁰ The question seemed innocent, but a great controversy soon broke out. ¹¹ Thirty-two women voted *pre* and thirty-two voted *post*.

¹² In this ghastly deadlock Phoebe was undecided. She felt the uncomfortable strain of both groups wanting her to cast the deciding vote for their philosophy. ¹³ She wanted more time to think about it. She was burdened, she said, by having the weight of our Lord's second coming fall squarely on her shoulders.

¹⁴ At this moment she is still undecided. She is studying furiously, realizing that so much of the planet's destiny rests on her decision. ¹⁵ She thinks the recent destruction of the Jewish state by the hated Romans means that we have little time to get ready for the event. ¹⁶ On the other hand, she feels that we are definitely in the last days, and she cannot tell if the great persecution now is the great tribulation or just one of the many inhumanities of man.

¹⁷ Some are saying that she is wishy-washy, and some say for the sake of harmony in the church she should make up her mind. One thing is sure: She is popular among all the women. ¹⁸ After she casts the deciding vote, she will be popular with only half of them.

¹⁹ How dedicated are these who study? They meet every week to have dessert and discuss the end of the world. They show each other the latest interpretations of the scholars and bring their parchment charts on the final signs of the times.

²⁰ I passed Phoebe late this afternoon on the way to the leper colony.

I was surprised to see she was not attending the second coming scroll study which was anxiously awaiting her decision at that very time.

²¹ "Don't you care about the end of the world, Phoebe?" I asked.

²² "A little," she replied, "but I decided to go and help the lepers today."

²³ "Alone?" I asked, for there was clearly no one with her.

²⁴ "I must go alone," she said, "for there is so much need, and most of the women are at the second coming study."

²⁵ "But what if they get the date all set and your charts are unmarked?" I asked her.

²⁶ She seemed not to hear. She was carrying a large basket of bandages for the lepers. ²⁷ I couldn't bear to see her carrying such a large basket alone. I took the basket from her and walked along with her.

²⁸ We walked in silence toward the leprosarium. I could not repress a kind jibe. "Phoebe," I blurted out. "Don't you care? Is our Lord coming back before or after the tribulation? When he comes back, where do you want to be found—in this state of indecision or at the second coming study?"

²⁹ "There is where I want to be found," she said, pointing to a circle of low, thatched huts.

³⁰ A little boy came running up to us from the compound. His face was badly blighted and part of his hand was gone.

³¹ "When do you think the Lord is coming back, my child?" asked Phoebe. A single tear ran down across his cheek.

³² I handed her a bandage and couldn't remember why I thought the question was so important.

³³ I can tell you this, Clement, I did not find among all the lepers a single chart of these dreadful last days. ³⁴ It was as if the lepers had lost interest in the whole issue of the second coming. ³⁵ We spent the afternoon binding lesions.

How Worship in the City of Philippi Interrupted the Church's Ministry

7 I have long believed that worship is the business of the church collected. ² Adoration and praise are important among all of God's people. ³ I have also believed that it should be done creatively. ⁴ Too often the worship of the church just happens; it isn't well planned.

⁵ Boredom in the church is the evidence that neither sermons nor worship services have been well planned. ⁶ Remember Eutychus who

fell asleep during Paul's sermon and fell out the window? ⁷ Could planning worship save nodding slaves from broken necks?

⁸ Our problem is different. Services here at Philippi suffer from too much planning. They are a production. ⁹ Those who worship here are leaving the service with great applause for the actors, almost demanding encores. ¹⁰ But who remembers him in whose honor we are gathered?

¹¹ And it is the planning itself that stirs up dissension. ¹² Consider our annual Easter pageant, a remarkable performance on our Lord's resurrection. You may have seen it—it is always a cold show with frost on the sepulchre.

¹³ One of the deacons stands behind a clump of bushes at sunrise and reads the scroll while Mary Magdalene approaches, weeping her way up to the grave. ¹⁴ Then a deep voice thunders out above the tomb, "Weep not, Maria. He is not here for he is risen!"

¹⁵ At this point the choir, which has been shivering in the Easter air booms out the anthem, "No Room in the Tomb for Gloom." ¹⁶ Then everyone shakes hands and hurries to the Hall of Tyrannus to have hot nectar and resurrection bread.

¹⁷ Last year there was a great crowd, the annuciation angel appeared with his trumpet on schedule, but the director was horrified that he was wearing a turban to cover his ears. An angel in a turban?

¹⁸ Now the church is locked in a great controversy whether or not angels should be allowed to wear fleeces and shawls, and most of all, whether the annunciation role should be given to anyone who had disturbed the performance last year. ¹⁹ Two people have already quit the choir, and the actors are incensed by the criticism. ²⁰ Sister Syntyche says she will not come back to the tomb until someone makes apologies to her dear friend, Erastus, who played the resurrection angel.

²¹ Never since our dear Savior walked out of the tomb has his resurrection caused such a stir. ²² Should not we, Brother Clement, emphasize the life of the church as that dear, kind quality of life that our Savior brought back from the grave? There is something anti-Christ about an Easter quarrel!

²³ Sentrus the Seer says that this is to be another cold resurrection morning. ²⁴ The Oracle at Delphi agrees that Michael could be back in a turban. What's a poor resurrection angel to do with such a frigid forecast?

²⁵ If you should see a red glow in the northern sky on Easter morn-

ing, you will know that a quarrel in Philippi has erupted and that Easter has finally destroyed what it was born to create.

²⁶ And once again the ministry of the church will have ceased while we quarrel over the Prince of Peace.

The Berean Wagon Ministry and Its Shortcomings

8 Hylus, the pastor of the church in Berea, is trying to get me to begin a new children's ministry which he says will double the attendance at our children's service. ² Berea began the ministry only last month, and they have had unparalleled success. ³ I have been resisting the pressure in our little congregation to begin a wagon ministry here in Philippi. ⁴ Is the competition of nearby congregations to build the biggest attendance at scroll study an exercise in one-upmanship?

⁵ Here is how it works. ⁶ On the Lord's Day a huge harvest wagon travels out the Athenian Way as far as West Berea. It picks up children and brings them back to scroll study in Berea. ⁷ Last month thirty-three *puellae* and thirty-four *pueri* rode the wagon. Each of the children received a cluster of grapes and a little squab just for riding the wagon to church.

⁸ It worked so well that a second wagon is being sent to the neighborhoods at East Berea this Sunday, and this week every child who brings an *amicus* gets an autographed parchment from Evangelist Octavius. ⁹ Every child who brings more than ten *amici* gets a hub bolt from a Roman chariot. ¹⁰ They are expecting more than a hundred children in the wagon ministry this week. ¹¹ The pastor told me that if it works they plan to tape a lucky denarius under the wagon box for the child who brings the most *amici*.

¹² I have heard of a church south of Athens that has twenty-seven wagons in their ministry now, and the adult winner of last month's contest got an all-expenses-paid trip to Antioch. ¹³ They had a motto: Believe in the Rock and go to Antioch. The winning child received a Shetland pony—a real *equus minimus*! They had over four hundred in scroll study.

¹⁴ The future of wagon ministry, however, may not be bright. Many of the Romans, it is believed, are only letting their children ride the wagons to get them out of the atrium for a quiet Sunday morning.

¹⁵ Rumor says the Christians and the lions may soon be at it again. Probably the Romans will keep their children in till the season of hate is over. ¹⁶ It can be dangerous to be baptized during the games, and most

Romans will not run the risk of letting their children get on a church wagon for fear they may get thrown to the lions.

[17] Clement, I must be honest; I am afraid we may communicate an easy gospel where children come to church only for squab and grapes. [18] There has been some disaster in the church. Some of the older members in Berea said that the little Romans are sticky and greasy, and they leave the wagons full of seeds and bones.

[19] I suppose if children are led to know Christ, there is some merit to the ministry, but does it not create wagon-ride Christians? [20] Is there a way to win children without spending so much money on squabs and grapes? [21] Wouldn't our Lord, who consistently taught self-denial, see this as evangelism by indulgence? [22] I could use a restful week in Antioch, but I think I will pay my own way.

[23] It is so hard to know how our Lord would have us minister to children. I remember the tender picture of him cuddling them in his arms and telling the quarreling apostles that the kingdom would be composed of the childlike. [24] I just can't picture him loading them in wagons and giving them prizes.

The Abominable Monster of Bythinia

9 Are young people in Coos dropping out of church? [2] The pastors in this area aren't sure what to make of it. [3] Some feel that the youth are not seeing credible Christian elders in the church. [4] I call to witness Hezekiah, the abominable monster of Bythinia.

[5] Hezekiah was found wandering in the forests of Cenchrea. [6] It would be impossible to tell you all of my impressions of this young man, although I might describe for you his symptoms. [7] He is stooped and haggard far beyond his years. He is unshaven. He prefers sitting quietly in a corner and ignoring the world. [8] Ever and anon he will pick up a Scripture scroll and growl and begin chewing on it.

[9] When I first saw him growling and chewing, I thought that he must be an incorrigible youth who had spent a great deal of his life chewing on sacred Scripture. [10] We all know some worldly-wise young man who cannot bear to be told anything, "lest having eyes he see, and having ears he hear."

[11] But this proved to be a false assumption. He came into the assembly growling and chewing and making a frightful noise while the rest of us tried in vain to sing the psalms of which we have grown so fond.

¹² During the singing of "Blest Be the Bonds of Jesus' Love" his growling became ever more intense. ¹³ And when a brother prayed for the "sweet, sweet fellowship" of the church, he nearly gnawed the spindle from the scroll.

¹⁴ It was only yesterday that I learned the truth about poor, mad Hezekiah. He was at the business meeting in the congregation in Cenchrea where a brother was dismissed for his views on baptism. ¹⁵ Well, there was a very narrow vote to release him—some feeling his views were sound and others feeling his views were *only* sound. ¹⁶ A quarrel broke loose and half the congregation led by True-to-the-Word Marcus promptly denounced those who had denounced the brother and left the meeting hall. ¹⁷ A third group denounced everyone, having already taken a stand against denunciations in the church.

¹⁸ Hezekiah is an impressionable young man, and he had only recently become a disciple. ¹⁹ He became distraught, not knowing whether to follow the major position, the minor position or the antidenunciationists. ²⁰ It put such a strain on his own need to be secure he began weeping and then, of course, chewing scrolls.

²¹ I have seen one other case. This young person on seeing Christians set against each other went off to study philosophy in Athens. I regret to say he has become an atheist lecturer and is trying to get "In Deus We Trust" taken off every last denarius in circulation.

²² Oh, the harm that is done when our convictions supersede our compassion! ²³ It is especially the young who suffer. They can't seem to love Jesus and a fighting church at the same time. ²⁴ Did not our brother Paul encourage us to "Be kind one to another, tenderhearted, forgiving one another, even as God for Christ's sake has forgiven us"? It is certainly spiritual wisdom.

²⁵ It looks as though we may have to put poor Hezekiah in chains lest he chew more scrolls than he has the stomach to digest. ²⁶ I cannot say his madness is terminal. ²⁷ I am told there is a certain hairy creature in the outer forests of Galatia who lurks outside empty churches on the dark of the moon and pounces on old elders as they wind past their empty meeting halls. ²⁸ Some say the Ghoul of Galatia is a wolf who once wore sheep's clothing until he saw the sheep devouring each other. ²⁹ They are trying to trap him now, but I have the feeling that when they

do they will only have discovered a night fiend created in a vicious church business meeting.

³⁰ Clement, you see why it is so important for me to accompany Phoebe when she goes to the leper colony. ³¹ There is a leper there named Simon. He cannot live much longer, but he has a rich baritone voice that will be with him to the last of his life. ³² I heard him singing the ninetieth psalm the other day, and I knew again how important it was that each of us number our days, and thus, apply our hearts unto wisdom.

³³ I remember that the psalmist also said, "He that winneth souls is wise." Our Lord once drove the money changers from the temple. ³⁴ Perhaps he did it so that the temple would not be the place where men use God's good ground to grow their own rank reputations. ³⁵ Temples create either monsters or ministers. ³⁶ May Christ so tower above our assemblies that we shall meet only to worship God and to roll bandages for the broken world.

The Return of the Lions

10 Three crates of lions were unloaded today at the seaport of Neapolis. In our prayer group this afternoon one of our members prayed that they were for the city zoo. ² But on the way home from church I saw the great cages being towed along the causeway to the stadium. ³ Clement, we are very much in for it, I fear.

⁴ I was one of the four men who helped carry Publius the Paralytic home after our prayer meeting.

⁵ "Have you ever been in prison for the faith?" I asked Publius.

⁶ "No," he laughed, "and I never will be!"

⁷ "Why? How can you be so certain?" I asked.

⁸ "What jailer wants to be bothered with a paralytic? Only Christians can tolerate such creatures as myself. No pagan jailer wants to be bothered with someone who requires bedpans and spoon-feeding. ⁹ I couldn't commit a crime had I the will to. And it would have to be a magnificent crime before any jailer would lock me up."

¹⁰ "You're jailproof," laughed one of the other litter carriers.

¹¹ We joined him in laughter before we all turned the corner and were suddenly brought face to face with the caged beasts that had just been unloaded. Their size caused each of us to shudder as we passed. ¹² We

tried not to imagine the confrontation that might be ours if the persecution does indeed come.

¹³ We had walked a mile before any of us could break the silence. I finally spoke, "What would you do, Publius, if you were thrown to the lions?"

¹⁴ "Do?" he answered with a weak chuckle. "What do paralytics always 'do'? The only thing I could do would be to spit in his eye. It wouldn't be much of a defense. ¹⁵ 'Do'? I'd just lie there and try to taste as bad as I possibly could."

¹⁶ We laughed at the thought of it. ¹⁷ "Perhaps we should start praying that God would make every Christian in Philippi taste so bad that no beast of wholesome palate would ever consider us tasty," said a man on the other side of the litter as he changed hands on the stretcher pole.

¹⁸ "Still," said Publius, "they never throw paralytics to the lions. There's no show in that for these overfed Romans. ¹⁹ Think how you'd feel if you had paid thirty shekels for a season ticket to watch Christians scream and run and then be forced to watch them eaten, immobile and paralyzed. Why, you would demand your money back and reinvest it in Gladiatorial Combat. ²⁰ So far they have yet to throw one paralytic to the lions. I've checked the casualty lists in all the arenas. They don't even throw in the seriously crippled. ²¹ Take it from me, if you want to be lionproof when the heat is on, you just get a good friend to detach your spinal cord at the thirteenth vertebra and you'll be safe forever. Still, you'd best be sure that you've got four fine Christians such as yourselves who'll carry you to services the rest of your life."

²² Soon we arrived at Publius's hut and deposited him safely inside.

²³ "Publius, have you prayed for healing?" asked one of the men.

²⁴ "I once prayed for nothing else," he replied, "but only my head continued to move to exert my will. I have cried myself to sleep many nights. ²⁵ I do not even have the muscles which would give my mind enough obedience to commit suicide. But I will one day meet the Master just beyond the threshold of death. Then you who have carried me to a thousand prayer meetings will see me spring upright, and I shall leap in the healing light of heaven. I will dance—and run a thousand tireless furlongs. ²⁶ Sometimes I cannot tell if I would like to see Jesus first and then run and leap or to leap first and then see Jesus. But my agenda for heaven is as simple as these two items."

²⁷ "But what of the future? Do you not fear it?" asked another.

²⁸ "No, for in the future I shall meet God. It is the *now* that seems most wearisome. I have presumed upon your eight good arms and legs to keep my dead frame from taking root. Oh, dear brothers, you must face the lions. I must face only my daily unwillingness to be a burden to the church of Christ. ²⁹ I am confident that you will tend to me until the threshold of eternity. ³⁰ The first lion I must face is the Lion of Judah, and I shall be free to run the golden fields with the lion of St. Mark. Forgive my heavy, dead existence until that day shall dawn."

³¹ A tear crossed his cheek.

³² In the distance we heard the lions roar.

³³ We all knew that there was shortly to be an edict that might affect the entire life of the church—perhaps its very existence.

³⁴ Still, we all felt a kind of victory in the presence of a man who did not have to fear lions. Even so we didn't really want to pray.

³⁵ I took a flask of wine and poured the contents into five cups. We broke a loaf of bread and passed the pieces to the others in the small hut.

³⁶ "This is his body!" said Publius as I held the bread to his mouth and he ate.

³⁷ "This is his blood—the blood of the new covenant, in force beyond the threshold," I said as I held my small tin cup to his lips.

³⁸ Again we heard across the silent night the roaring beasts. One of the men held his cup toward the ceiling.

³⁹ "To the great lion," he said, "the Lion of Judah, the lion of St. Mark." We all brought our cups together in the thin clanging that tin can make on tin. We drank. "This is the blood of the New Testament!" said Publius.

⁴⁰ We smiled at the distant roaring.

The Third Letter of Eusebius of Philippi to His Beloved Friend Clement

Mock Cheer

1 I am in prison.
² Coriolanus is still free, and he came to my cell today to bring greetings from the flock. I have been concerned about their welfare in my absence, so his visit was welcome. ³ But there was little cheer in his cheer. As a matter of fact, his cheer left me depressed for five hours.

⁴ He feels that it would be a glorious honor for me to be thrown to the lions should my imprisonment end in the arena. Oh, Clement, that is easy for him to say! ⁵ One should not turn from glory or take it lightly. But the prospect of my martyrdom did not afford me the honest joy that it supplied him. ⁶ Then he asked me if I would let him have my tunic if my name became posted for the honor of this ultimate witness. "No use getting it all torn and spotted," he said. "We must be practical. A good tunic is hard to come by these days."

⁷ "How about my sandals?" I asked, with much less buoyance than characterized his attitude.

⁸ "Do you mind going barefoot?" he asked.

⁹ "The afternoon sand can be awfully hot," I replied.

¹⁰ "But not for long," he said, "and some of our flock would appreciate your kindness at the hour of such a gallant and selfless witness. It would be a glorious example to the whole church."

¹¹ "Well, I'm all for exemplary living . . . or dying," I said. ¹² I was eager to change the subject. "Maybe I'll be released."

¹³ "Don't count on it," he counseled. "Just keep your eyes on Jesus!"

¹⁴ "All right," I said, "but if I am released I can hardly wait to get back to the assembly and preach again."

¹⁵ "Well, I don't know if you should go directly to the church from prison. Many of our people don't like the idea of having an ex-convict in the pulpit."

¹⁶ "I see."

¹⁷ "It doesn't set a good example for the children. I must be honest,

Brother Eusebius, you've lost a lot of credibility with the flock. ¹⁸ While we don't want you to become discouraged and we wish you Christian cheer, it has come to our attention that there is a little chapel in Konos that needs a new pastor."

¹⁹ "But Konos is nearly a ghost town!"

²⁰ "Ah, but God loves those people."

²¹ "What people?"

²² "The people of Konos. There are a few people in that congregation, and God loves them just as much as he loves those of Philippi. To minister to the few is as important as to the many."

²³ I meditated a good long time. Just as Coriolanus was standing to leave, I finally asked the question, "So it is either the lions or the pulpit at Konos?"

²⁴ He nodded his head and smiled.

²⁵ "Be of good cheer and look to Jesus!"

²⁶ After he left I found myself even more morose than before. How am I to pray, my dear Clement? Should one desire to be devoured or to pastor in a ghost town? ²⁷ I am riddled by resentment. How can I be charitable and cheerful, thinking about being devoured while Coriolanus wears my robe and sandals to my execution? ²⁸ It is death or the dust of Konos, I suppose. ²⁹ More than my uncertain future, I am troubled about the cheer I received from Coriolanus. ³⁰ Such Christians make lions look kind.

³¹ They say our brother from Atticus has such a deacon. The day he was to be devoured, his adversary came to observe. I can barely stand the idea that Coriolanus might be there on my fateful day should it come. ³² I am frozen by the cold image of a deacon grinning above my martyrdom and cheering the beasts.

³³ Compassion is of Christ. A Christian with mock cheer is probably a mock Christian. And those who grin at martyrs must be like those who once thronged the cross with dice and vinegar. ³⁴ I once heard there was a Pharisee who stood in the Good Friday crowd. While our Lord cried, "Eloi, Eloi, lama sabachthani?" he was crunching bread and pomegranates. It is a bleak heart that packs sandwiches for crucifixions. ³⁵ Animosity cloaked in piety is a demon even if it sits in church praising the Creator.

³⁶ Oh, I am alone. "Eloi, Eloi, lama sabachthani?"

The Encroachment of Mt. Olympus

2 Clement, time drags slowly in a cell. The days are drudgerous. "Tempus fugit" is a lie. I have filled up some of the empty hours by a new concern about syncretism.

² I am increasingly disturbed that Romans seem to be quite subtle in blending their worship of Zeus with our immortal Jehovah. ³ I hope you will tell me that I am being oversensitive. Generations yet unborn will suffer unless we recognize the possibilities of syncretism. ⁴ Those who are converted to Christianity from their pagan shrines often come into our fellowship wagging their polytheism behind them.

⁵ Take their enthusiasm for Vesta, the goddess of home. We have actually had a suggestion that we in the Christian church try to adopt a hearth emphasis. ⁶ They do not want to call it the day of the Vestal Virgins, only Mater Dies. Should we have a mother's day? ⁷ There does seem to be something noble in the idea, but buried in it is the idea of Vesta, goddess of the hearth.

⁸ Clement, I know you're an orphan, so you may not understand this desire to start a day when all families who love our dear Lord will be able to honor their mothers as well.

⁹ So there you are, Clement—Mater's Day! On such a day we could honor our mothers and write poems about them, pin roses on their togas and generally do nice things for them.

¹⁰ I mentioned the idea to Publius the Paralytic who was brought to the jail yesterday to visit us, but he was not enthusiastic either. "Sheer syncretism," he said. ¹¹ "What about all the mothers who practice infanticide or abortion?" he queried. ¹² "What will they wear on their togas? A thistle or a spray of thorns? And what about Cressia the Creepie, who burned her poor babies with faggots just to hear them scream!" Publius became as animated as his paralysis would allow. ¹³ "Yes, Eusebius, what about these child abusers—Mater Horribilis? What shall they wear on their togas?

¹⁴ "Besides, you start to honor them, and they'll form groups and clubs and soon they'll want to vote in the proconsul elections! ¹⁵ Then you'll have anarchy. ¹⁶ Mark my word, Eusebius, give a mater a pace and she'll take a furlong! They might even form groups that will say that if a mater does the work of a pater, she should get the same pay. ¹⁷ That could erode confidence in the denarius. Then you'll have inflation and a storm of

liberated maters marching on Rome; it'll make Spartacus look like Via Sesemia. [18] Before you know it they'll be calling snowmen 'snowpersons,' and girls will be training as gladiators.

[19] "Is that what you want—women teaching in the church and men washing dishes? Legionnettes, not legionnaires? Equal rights for feminae? [20] Then some radical mater will stand in the forum and pray to her 'Mother in heaven,' and it will all be over. [21] If they pin roses on their togas, it could change the whole sexual philosophy of Rome itself!"

[22] By this time Publius the Paralytic was so excited by the power of his own oratory I thought that he might jump up at any moment.

[23] "No, by heaven. I'll not pin a flower for the reign of feminine terror and oppression it might spur." [24] After he was gone, I thought of the priority most people placed on motherhood.

[25] I suppose it does have its risks, but I think I may go ahead and try to get Mater's Day going. What can it hurt? It's not for Vesta but for Jesus. [26] Here's to roses on togas.

More on the Fear of Syncretism

3 I can endorse Mater's Day more easily than the new emphasis on romance. [2] I'm speaking of Valentinus. While he is not Bishop of Philippi, the accusation against him could bring trouble for all of us. [3] And to what end are his romantic notions?

[4] Valentinus wants to see the institution of Christian marriage. This is in direct contradiction to the Roman civil law. [5] Who knows where this whole thing might lead? [6] It is exactly in this way that traditions begin. [7] Right now unless he burns incense to the emperor, he is slated to be shot by archers.

[8] Some in the church are saying that Val has his values scrambled, that he has unwittingly confused Cupid with Christ. [9] Some say he is ever the romanticist humming "Hearts and Flowers" when he should be studying the Book of Romans or helping his church understand the perplexing issues of the second coming.

[10] In truth, Clement, there is not one biblical text in support of his madness. Our dear Lord never once taught that people should be married by the Book. [11] Nor is there a single injunction in the letters of Paul that teach what Valentinus calls the "Christian marriage."

[12] The bishops disagree with one another, but all of them are asking, "Where will it all end?" [13] During these ceremonies Val's disciples are

standing up before young brides and grooms and "calling down Cupid."
[14] They say, "Beloved in Christ, we gather here and these two people come to pledge their love." [15] Then they sing, if you please, various sorts of romantic ditties, light candles, and kiss right in the house of God! On the mouth, too! [16] Mind you, I'm open to new ideas, but I think Valentinus may have gone too far. If you start with Christian marriages, someone could suggest Christian prayer in the Roman Senate and invocations at athletic events. [17] You could actually develop a whole lifestyle under the name of Christ.

[18] I'm insecure. I think we should keep Christ for the Christians and Cupid for the Olympians. Pastor Valentinus is sure to be executed by the archers, and who for? [19] He will be the first martyr to have lived for Christ and be shot for Cupid.

[20] There are too many new ideas bombarding the church at once. Pray for me, Clement, that I can handle them all with some sense of balance. [21] In prison the issues are more difficult to understand than they might be if I were free.

[22] I am bewildered. Think of the mess the world will be in with everybody falling in love and sending each other poetry.

Concern about the Festival of Demons

4 Here in the north of Greece we have a custom that has grown increasingly more popular.

[2] It must have come originally from Circe the Sorceress. [3] Lamentably, the custom celebrates the realm our Lord so much abhorred: the kingdom of the demons. [4] Ordinarily if one finds a demon on his doorstep he drives it out or calls for the village exorcist. [5] But at the autumn festival of the damned we actually celebrate the dark kingdom. [6] Since you do not have this custom in the South, you may find the idea untenable. [7] But here we are celebrants at this festival. [8] The day is almost here. [9] Soon the little ones will be tripping the streets of Philippi dressed as goblins and crying out at every door for sweetmeats.

[10] These little village demons are too much like ourselves. We are at once ugly and beautiful, holy and sinister, good and ghoulish. How shall we ever learn to deal with the two sides of our nature? [11] How often, my dear Clement, have I wished vengeance on people who mistreated me. [12] The children are like us in one other way. They hide behind faces that are not theirs. [13] Ah, that we might take away our demon faces and let

our real countenance shine through. ¹⁴ But alas, it is easier to wear a mask. An ugly face is sometimes better than a real one. Thus are we afraid to show each other who we really are. ¹⁵ All of us endure the goblinhood that masks our fear of being known.

¹⁶ Those who wear a pretense sometimes end up all that they pretend. ¹⁷ Has all our bloody history come from faces molded by the masks they wore? ¹⁸ Dear Christ, make one that which we are and that which we appear to be. Be Lord of naked faces.

How Traditions Get Started

5 I have had the feeling that traditions are often the result of happenstance and sentimentality. We must be careful. Have you heard of the Figgy Ghost? ² He passes through the city every night. Those children who have lost a tooth may put it on the window ledge, and he will pass in the darkness and exchange the tooth for a fig.

³ The myth is perpetuated by the parents who teach it to their children and do themselves the work they attribute to the Figgy Ghost. ⁴ What in the name of Pluto would the ghost want with a million Greek teeth? Where would he keep them? How much of the poor ghost's life is dedicated to fig picking? Where does a pure spirit find the muscles to lug around a basket of goodies and teeth?

⁵ Behind traditions are the ashes of logic.

⁶ Some say it all began in a tale of Aesop several centuries ago. Some say the old Greek storyteller himself is the Figgy Ghost, leaving his grave every night to delight the Aegeans. ⁷ But it likely all started when the governor's wife realized that a fig was good for the healing of her children's gums, or when a clever cook lost a tooth in a green fig and contrived the story for the procurator's children.

⁸ But I am most worried about some of the Christian traditions I have observed getting started. For the last two years we have had Sandal-Egging. ⁹ Phoebe detests the tradition and despises the notion that she herself started this one because she lent two eggs to her neighbor.

¹⁰ Can she be blamed? Ah, Clement, no one loves Christ or despises shallow traditions more than Phoebe, but she did lend her neighbor eggs. ¹¹ And as luck would have it, when her neighbor came to return the eggs, Phoebe wasn't home. The neighbor noticed that Phoebe had hung her sandals on a branch to dry after she had washed them. ¹² With-

out thinking, Phoebe's friend just put the eggs in the toe of the sandals and went home.

¹³ When Phoebe returned, she was hungry and couldn't find a thing in the house to eat. Our economy being what it is, she didn't have even a single denarius to go to market. So she decided to go on a prayer fast.

¹⁴ After she had finished fasting and praying that God might provide something for her to eat, she went out to the branch to retrieve her sandals and, lo, she discovered the eggs. ¹⁵ She was so struck by the eggs that she fell down before the bush and thanked our God for the miracle. Then she looked at the particular bush on which she had hung her sandals. It was a sandalwood tree.

¹⁶ The leaves of the sandalwood shrub are egg-shaped with a tiny crossvein in the center of the leaf. ¹⁷ As Phoebe thought about the miracle of the ova and saw the little crosses in the center of the leaves, she could not help but think of Christ and his sacrifice.

¹⁸ She shared the experience with the women's scroll study. Some were so moved that they wept. Thus the sandal-egging tradition was born. ¹⁹ For the last two years the women of Philippi have decorated their homes with boughs of sandalwood and left eggs in the toes of each other's sandals to represent the message of the cross and the fertility of the gospel among the heathen.

²⁰ It sounds absurd. But the custom is spreading and some churches in the remotest provinces are celebrating the miracle by the customs I have just suggested. Clement, be careful where you hang your toga or your sandals or your tunic. ²¹ Human sentiment issues from a sweet insanity that can build a lovely idea from things base. ²² If we continue to clutter the simplicity of the gospel, we could lose its power altogether.

²³ Phoebe feels responsible for this digression. She said during the season just past she could not find a single woman in Philippi who would come to scroll study. They all had to do some last-minute shopping for eggs or new sandals or they were off to the woods to collect boughs of sandalwood.

²⁴ She confessed her grief to me. "Eggs are better scrambled than worshiped. Sandals are better worn than adored," she said. "Could I borrow your axe?" she asked me. ²⁵ "Sure," I said, "but why?"

²⁶ "I'm going home to cut down my sandalwood shrub."

²⁷ "It's no use, Phoebe. You can't call back a tradition once you create it."

²⁸ "Not even if I hang my sandals inside to dry from now on?"

[29] "It is too late. Straight thinking is the only way to combat the sentimentality that smothers truth in heaping sweetness."

[30] Clement, it is here that honesty is saved. We cannot chop down the shrines of sentiment, but we do not have to stop and worship. [31] Pray for Phoebe. Imagine how you would feel if sandal-egging were laid at your feet.

[32] Traditions must be strangled as infants.

[33] They say over in Berea that last Lord's Day a surprised child found a new toy in his father's leggings. There was also a note that the toy was given to help the child remember that the holy wise men once gave presents to the baby Jesus. [34] It could be nothing, but we had better keep our eye on this one.

Of Rules and Freedom

6 Brother James came to my cell today. He wanted my counsel on holding the annual Cupid Banquet in the Hall of Bacchus. [2] I felt there were several things wrong with the idea. First, the persecution being what it is, if a careless young Christian drew a fish on the washroom walls, our entire youth department could be incarcerated. [3] But there was a more immediate consideration for the church.

[4] Coriolanus and the elder Scrubjoy believe that it is impossible for a Christian to drink and go to heaven. Not that there would be any of that at the dinner, but its mere association with the sinful Hall of Bacchus leaves the whole event in question. [5] Do we not all know that the Hall of Bacchus in Philippi is the epicenter of all debauchery in northern Greece?

[6] Brother James does occasionally take a little wine for his frequent infirmity, and Coriolanus strongly disapproves. [7] Scrubjoy went so far as to say that his infirmities would be less frequent if his tippling were less frequent.

[8] Brother James is in for trouble. [9] Scrubjoy was once the chief customer at the Hall of Bacchus, staggering home night after night. One night his bleary eyes misled him and he stumbled into the back of our church entirely by mistake. [10] Flavius the Flame was holding special services, and at the conclusion, Scrubjoy swaggered forward and laid his flask on the altar. [11] He came to love our Lord as much as he hated the "filthy, dirty, rotten liquor," as he put it.

[12] He constantly told the youth to stay away from all appearance of evil. He warned them about compromising their convictions. [13] "You cannot serve God and Bacchus," he used to say. "You will never find drinking lips and a praying tongue in the same mouth, just as you will never find a dancing foot and a praying knee on the same leg."

[14] Yes, Clement, Scrubjoy became incensed when he heard of a church member having a drink or going to a dance. And whenever he heard that anyone both danced and drank, he would move to the other side of the street and trace the sign of the cross in the air.

[15] Gradually Scrubjoy came to emphasize personal purity as the ideal of the believer. [16] Under his spell many in the church have become disciples by "notting." [17] If you do *not* drink and you do *not* dance and you do *not* leer at the hemlines of short tunics, then you may go to heaven where presumably everybody will get together for celebrating an eternity of Scrubjoy's discipline.

[18] So Brother James has agreed not to hold the dinner in the Hall of Bacchus. They can all have a picnic in the park and have just as good a time. [19] He could remember when Brother Timothy came to our church to lecture on Christian sexuality. Scrubjoy rose erect and dry and scowled at the congregation.

[20] "Christian sexuality, my brothers, for shame! Did not our Lord tell us that we are to have his mind? [21] Should the church ever focus on smut and bless it with the name of Christian? We must take a stand against this wicked doctrine," he cried.

[22] Several older brothers shouted, "Amen!"

[23] "You will never find drinking lips and a praying tongue in the same mouth! You will never find a dancing foot and a praying knee on the same leg! And my brothers and sisters, you will never find Christian thoughts and a lusty mind in the same brain!" cried Scrubjoy.

[24] "Amen!" cried the others.

[25] Scrubjoy is, indeed, keeping himself unspotted from the world and his countenance is stern. [26] Clement, it is not God's commandments but our own that become so grievous. We make the world miserable in measuring each other by our own moral maxims. [27] The youth of Philippi are tired of being inspected for such blemishes as Scrubjoy delights to find.

[28] Rules blunt the appetite for Christ.

[29] Joy intrigues.

[30] I can tell you it has been many a season since Scrubjoy has bubbled anyone into the kingdom.

[31] One Saturday night they threw into my cell Cassius the Crock. He reeked of brew so strongly that the rats all left, but by morning his stupor had thawed. [32] Who can admire his habit? Still, it has blessed him with a sort of wisdom. [33] He was in no immediate danger. They don't throw drunks to the lions, only Christians. He knew he'd be out by noon. When he found out that I had already been in prison for all these months, he looked downcast.

[34] "I used to have a good drinking pal who became a Christian," he said. "A fellow named Scrubjoy, the riot of the ale halls. Ever hear of him?"

[35] "Maybe," I said cautiously.

[36] "Well, he was one funny man. We used to laugh and sing half the night. He knew more funny stories than the god of wine himself. But he became a Christian and I haven't seen him smile since. [37] Tell me, Reverend, why would a man want to believe in Christ so much that he'd be willing to give up smiling and risk the lions, too?"

[38] "Hmm!" I said as the jailer came. He took the keys, gestured to Cassius and unlocked the door.

[39] Cassius staggered upward, still talking. "You see, Reverend, drunks get out on Sunday and they have a lot better time than Christians. You sure you don't know Scrubjoy?"

[40] "Maybe," I repeated.

[41] "Well, it wouldn't do any good to throw Scrubjoy to the lions. Even the beasts aren't all that anxious to devour a bland life," he said.

[42] He started out the door, then turned back for a last comment. "I'll tell you this. You'll never find a happy man and a Christian in the same tunic."

[43] The door clanged shut.

Praise and Earthquakes

7 Coriolanus has been arrested and has now become my cell mate. At first I protested to God that there was no justice in the universe. Coriolanus now and my own possible martyrdom in the future! Gradually I am adjusting.

[2] We have lived together without resentment. [3] Tuesday night Coriolanus made a magnificent discovery. Near the base of the wall he found

the Latin names Paul and Silas etched in the stone at the end of a prayer. [4] We noticed that the cell wall was crossed by fissures that could have been caused by a great earthquake. [5] Suddenly it dawned on us that perhaps this was the very cell where the apostle Paul was once a prisoner.

[6] Remembering how Paul and Silas sang at midnight as God sent an earthquake to open the doors of the jail, we took courage. [7] "Do it again, God!" cried Coriolanus near midnight. He began to sing a hymn in monotone, and I joined in. We praised God at full volume with some of the great songs of the faith. [8] Ever and anon we stopped to see if we could hear even the faintest rumblings of a quake. By three in the morning we still had not raised a tremor and decided to give it up. There seemed so little to rejoice about. [9] Suddenly a jailer who had heard us singing sprang into the cell.

[10] "Sirs, what must I do to be saved?" he asked.

[11] We told him in great joy.

[12] "I can't do that," he said. "It's too risky."

[13] As he left, he yelled over his shoulder, "Would you cut out the noise! It's three in the morning."

[14] Still, I felt better for simply having praised him. Praise clears the heart and dusts the mind of selfishness. It lifts the spirit and transforms the prison to an altar where we may behold the buoyant love of Christ. [15] It is not jailers who make convicts. It is the self-pitying mind that makes a man a captive. Praise frees us. The jail cannot contain the heart that turns itself to attend the excellency of Christ. [16] "Gloria in excelsis!" deals with stone walls and iron bars in its own way.

[17] When morning finally came, I was elated. I found a flint rock in the cell and scratched our own names above the etching of Paul and Silas: [18] "Eusebius and Coriolanus—We sang at midnight and felt much better the next morning."

[19] Was it foolish, Clement? [20] It is always right to praise God, and maybe my inscription will help the next prisoners who occupy this cell to remember the principle, earthquake or not.

The Fourth Letter of Eusebius of Philippi to His Beloved Friend Clement

On the Necessity of Prayer

1 I am still in prison and disturbed by what goes on in Christianity. The God of the martyrs has gone sweet. ² There are some who are now teaching that God is a cosmic grandfather who gives to his children anything that they ask for if only they believe. ³ Those who espouse it do not call it by the name I have chosen. They call it the Intercessory Prayer Movement. ⁴ I cannot tell how many categories of prayer are being emphasized in the church now, but that is the popular one.

⁵ Prayer was not given to people to make them master over God. ⁶ Yet, Clement, that is exactly what many in the congregation assume. If they pray, then God has to answer since they have asked him in utter sincerity. ⁷ It leaves God a dispensary attending his give-me communicants.

⁸ How in this egotistical school of thinking shall we ever have people who will seek God for the pleasure of his company alone? ⁹ What an honor to find him in a lonely moment and feast on the pleasure of our relationship, which begs nothing because it has everything.

¹⁰ God is our friend. Who can keep a friend who seeks only favors? ¹¹ This leads to what I would call the Our-Father-who-art-in-heaven-gimme-gimme-gimme syndrome. ¹² It becomes a kind of celestial wishing before the throne of grace, ordaining Jehovah, our fairy godfather.

¹³ I barely can stand this insult that leaves God a baggage boy. ¹⁴ Our Lord did not approach his Father requesting a list of gifts. ¹⁵ He did not even seek bread after he had fasted for weeks. He sought the Father because he was God and there is no higher communion than that.

¹⁶ Shall we not seek as he sought? ¹⁷ Shall we not shut the door against earthly noise and find that, once the noise is gone, God will roar all about us? ¹⁸ It's the silent communication of the closet that best declares his reality.

¹⁹ The secret language of the heart never heard by anyone else is the language of heaven. ²⁰ But in the noise of life we can never hear God.

²¹ Earth is so blatant that heaven does not interrupt the noise with her music.

²² When we pray in public we speak so much to others that God remains remote. It is the nearer audience to whom we pray. ²³ He only overhears our public prayers.

²⁴ Once I heard a priest of Zeus read a prayer before a public sacrifice. He read it well, but not for Zeus. ²⁵ When you consider the object of the reading, you may be sure that if Zeus can hear he can also read. ²⁶ The Savior has reminded us that our heavenly Father knows our needs before we ask. As soon as the stylus scratches the paper, he knows what the prayer will say.

²⁷ There are many admirable things about praying in public. But it is not the best kind of prayer.

²⁸ It is closet praying which addresses God alone. ²⁹ Such prayer is itself a discipline, unattended by lesser ears or human compliment. ³⁰ May we meet him in our loneliness to serve him before the watching, listening world.

The Prayer of Coriolanus

2 These are strange days of martyrdom and miracle. Our beloved Portia has gone to be with the Lord. She was facing the arena day by day, and while I do believe she would have been victorious at the final hour, it never came. ² Fearing the arena, she prayed to be delivered from the beasts and died of smallpox in her cell. So far the contagion has not spread, so we are rejoicing that Portia has been delivered.

³ While numbers have perished in the arena, there are victories from time to time. ⁴ Urbanus wrestled the taurus, Apollyon, and survived. Actually he broke the bull's neck, and the crowd was so impressed, they turned thumbs up. So he is back witnessing in the streets.

⁵ Urbanus is so popular that he has not been afraid to return to the jail. Best of all, he has taken over my work in the leper colony. He is so strong that he can carry Publius the Paralytic to church all by himself.

⁶ Phoebe is not afraid and visits the jail with news of the flock. She brings me the necessary parchment to continue my epistles. She really is a saint, and it is a miracle that she has not yet been arrested.

⁷ Circumstances are not so gracious for Brother James. He is down the lower corridor in a cell that has been called "The Swamp." It abounds with lizards and such cell partners as few can endure. ⁸ The guards have

given him a small club to defend himself. And as we hear from time to time, he sings cheerfully in the cell and does not complain about his rather bountiful bedfellows.

[9] There is a somber tone in the prison.

[10] Last week the "event list" was handed through the bars. Coriolanus's name was one of the main events for the spectators at the matinee games. He was to be trampled to death by wildebeests. [11] My poor adversary and current cell mate was clearly disturbed by the announcement. I wanted to suggest that we try to save his toga and sandals if he didn't mind going barefoot, but I took the course of compassion.

[12] "We must pray, Brother Eusebius," he said.

[13] "Amen, we must," I replied.

[14] So we set our hearts to prayer. Daily he prayed for God to deliver him from the wildebeests. [15] I suggested that he pray only for strength to face the deadly stampede, but he insisted on being delivered from the wild herd. So we prayed as he desired.

[16] When the day came for his final witness to the faith, we were handed a note saying that he had been temporarily excused from martyrdom as the wildebeests had been smitten with hoof-and-mouth disease and were in no shape to trample Christians.

[17] Coriolanus was ecstatic! "Glory! I have been delivered!" he cried.

[18] Clement, he was snatched from the fire at the eleventh hour.

[19] His near miss with martyrdom seems to have softened his arrogance. He owns, at least for the moment, a new humility. [20] I know he must be growing in his piety for I asked him if he knew God's will for my life, and he had no idea.

[21] He no longer speaks for God but is content to seek him.

[22] "When we are released, Brother Eusebius, I am going with you to take communion to the lepers," said Coriolanus.

[23] "Excuse me," I said, unable to believe my ears, "what did you say?"

[24] "The lepers . . . Christ died for them too. All are welcome at the table of the Lord."

[25] "Coriolanus, you have not seen Lucia. Her hands and face are so eroded that the cup of our Lord's blood will come back as cankered and unclean as her bandages."

[26] "Brother Eusebius! They are all God's children. What he has cleansed you must not call common or unclean. Lucia is our sister."

²⁷ At that moment Phoebe entered the dungeon. The guard walked her to our cell and then went back to his post.

²⁸ "Coriolanus, you are still here," she said in amazement. "I don't understand. What of your sentence and the wildebeests?"

²⁹ "They all have hoof-and-mouth disease," he replied.

³⁰ "The saints be praised. I have brought you communion," she said, unwrapping a little tin cup of wine and half a loaf of bread. She extended the bread to me and Coriolanus took the cup.

³¹ "It is his body," she said to me. "It is his blood," she said to Coriolanus.

³² "It is his body!" I repeated, tearing off a piece of bread and putting it in my mouth.

³³ "It is his blood!" said Coriolanus lifting the cup to his lips and beginning to drink.

³⁴ As we took the blessed meal, Phoebe went on. "The lepers were kind. Lucia only drank a little from this cup. She left this much wine and bread to share with you and your cell mate, Coriolanus . . ."

³⁵ Her sentence ended with the eruption of wine in the air all about us. Coriolanus spat, it seemed a thousand times, to get the wine from his mouth.

³⁶ "You mean you took this very cup to the colony?" he asked.

³⁷ "Yes, they are God's children."

³⁸ "But they are diseased," he protested.

³⁹ "Coriolanus, what God hath cleansed you must not call unclean."

⁴⁰ There was a strange silence. I took the cup from Coriolanus and drank.

⁴¹ "It is his blood," I said.

⁴² It is strange how I believed Coriolanus. But it is even stranger that he believed himself free of the curse of fear and death. ⁴³ How often we make our greatest commitments only to be foiled by little adversaries! We will face the devil himself with courage and be bested by a crippled demon. We will face the wildebeests and quail before a communion cup.

⁴⁴ Phoebe took the little bread and wine that was left and went to share the last portions with Publius the Paralytic. ⁴⁵ In the remaining wine he will taste neither the leprosy of Lucia nor the hypocrisy of Coriolanus. ⁴⁶ He will taste only the remembrance of a great deed long gone and feel good that consenting lips have been on that very cup before his own.

⁴⁷ Thus is the church made one.

And of Intercession

3 There has been victory throughout the church. Victor the Veterinarian was thrown to the lions only one week ago. Nothing like this has ever happened in the history of the martyrs. [2] Victor prayed for God to stop the mouths of the lions. [3] When the great tawny beasts entered the arena, they advanced to Victor and circled him as though they would attack but then lay down, apparently uninterested.

[4] Victor was happy about his deliverance. But not the spectators!

[5] When you pay three denarii for a seat, you expect to see someone eaten. The crowd booed and hissed, I can assure you. [6] Finally they sent out thirty-two Asian lions who had been starved for a week. They ran up to Victor, sniffed all around him and then joined the others lying in the sun.

[7] The emperor was infuriated.

[8] Twice more they released the big cats and twice more Victor's prayer tamed the huge beasts. [9] Finally the crowd became so enraged they stormed the box office, determined to throw the ticket merchants to the lions.

[10] It was a bad afternoon.

[11] Sometimes you pay to see a game and there really isn't much going on. At least that is how the Romans have viewed the whole event.

[12] But it has introduced a new question to the church. Consider the lone image of Victor the Veterinarian standing silently in the sea of big cats with his head bowed in prayer.

[13] Victor has always had a lot of confidence in the power of prayer, and yet one cannot explain it all on this basis.

[14] I remember Thecla of Thyatira who prayed to God to heal a little crippled boy from Bythinia. God did it, too. The little boy could walk and run ever after without the slightest limp. [15] She was clearly a great woman of prayer, but her prayers, so often effective for others, could not finally avail for herself.

[16] Thecla was arrested and sentenced to be thrown to the lions. Like Victor, she prayed to God to stop the mouths of the lions. [17] The entire church joined her in the prayer. Nevertheless she was devoured before fifty thousand spectators.

[18] She was truly a saint . . . as much as Victor, I think.

¹⁹ Why, then, would God honor one prayer but not another of the same kind? Who can say?

²⁰ Victor stands as proof to the entire church that God can answer any prayer for such is the power he has at his disposal for his people. ²¹ Thecla is proof that God does not choose to answer every prayer.

²² I have always heard it said that God may answer a prayer with either a "yea," a "nay," or a "one moment, please." Victor was back in the services this past week. Everyone there was glad to see him.

²³ "What did you learn that day praying in an open field of big cats?" I asked him when he came to see me in prison.

²⁴ "I learned," he said, "that God may be gracious to us and that he has all power to do everything that we ask."

²⁵ As I turned away, he tugged at the sleeve of my tunic.

²⁶ "One more thing," he said. "I learned one more thing!"

²⁷ "Yes?"

²⁸ "It is always right to ask."

²⁹ Clement, we may all come on hard times. We may all face terror of the beasts. But Victor is the proof that no matter how impossible the crisis may appear, "It is always right to ask."

Prayer in the Senatus

4 I am sure that you are aware that many martyrs in recent years have been arrested because a legionnaire discovered them praying in public. ² Now I have some disturbing news to report. I, too, once committed the blunder of spiritual indiscretion.

³ When I was pastor in Bythinia I was once arrested—for saying grace in a public park. I will never forget the sense of humiliation I felt. ⁴ There I was praying for the fish and cheese and honey, and when I raised my head there was a centurion saying, "In the name of Caesar, come along with me."

⁵ "What is the charge?" I asked.

⁶ "Praying in a Roman municipal recreation area," he said curtly. It was years ago, but it was my first arrest and I have not forgotten the sting of it.

⁷ I was released in a couple of fortnights. ⁸ But it has led me to a lifelong examination of public praying.

⁹ Should Christians do it?

¹⁰ We are saturated with prayer as our way of life. There is a children's prayer that is now popular in Ephesus that goes:

> ¹¹*God is great,*
> *He made the trees.*
> *Thank him for the figs and cheese.*
> *Bless Mater, and Pater,*
> *and Soror and Frater.*

¹² We must be careful not to let the children pray where they might be caught. On the other hand, is it a coward's way out? ¹³ If the empire has ruled against public prayer, should Christians continue to practice it or not? ¹⁴ Our Lord encouraged us to "render unto Caesar that which is Caesar's and unto God that which is God's." ¹⁵ But the Caesars don't believe that anything belongs to God. ¹⁶ One emperor defamed the doctrine by proclaiming his mount a proconsul and ordering Romans to offer prayers to his horse. ¹⁷ The world is certainly confused when it is ordered to pray to a horse and arrested for praying to the true God.

¹⁸ But we must protect the children and at the same time encourage the church to be more in prayer than ever. ¹⁹ The times are vicious and the consequences of our way of life must be considered. ²⁰ I agree with our brother, Paul, who said, "I would that men everywhere pray"—whatever the consequences.

The Church at Praise and Prayer

5 Clement, my entire parish is now convicts, or rather I should say, ex-convicts. The committee and all except the lepers and paralytics are finally in jail. ² The good Urbanus brought Publius to the jail yesterday afternoon to see us. The old man was much more frail than I remembered. ³ His paralysis has been most unkind. But he is still a person of exceptional power in prayer. ⁴ When we came together, Publius repeated what I had already surmised to be true.

⁵ "The church is empty for the jail is filled with believers," he said, and then asked, "Where is our sister Phoebe?"

⁶ "Cell thirty-two," I replied.

⁷ "And Dubious and Brother James?"

[8] "Cell seventy and The Swamp respectively," I replied.

[9] "Tonight at midnight I pray," he said.

[10] "For an earthquake?" I asked.

[11] Publius looked hurt at the cynicism in my voice. "I'm sorry, Publius, but we tried that last month. We couldn't even crack the plaster."

[12] "Tonight it will be different," he prophesied before he and Urbanus took their leave.

[13] We all endeavored to keep faith with Publius, and so at midnight we began to pray. We linked hands from cell to cell and just repeated the words, "Jesus, the Son of God, is Savior of the church." [14] As we repeated the phrases over and over, we felt a strange oneness.

[15] Finally we shouted together, "JESUS, THE SON OF GOD, IS SAVIOR OF THE CHURCH!"

[16] The floor began to move, then ripple. The ceiling began to fall and the bars twisted in the stone. Soon the whole place roared. [17] The noise was horrendous; the splintering of stone and steel tore at our eardrums. The door of every cell swung open.

[18] We all ran out into the corridors and then began to sing as we left through the stone arches at the end. The jailer was asleep. [19] He may have been in a state of shock, but he appeared not to see us at all. We were all completely outside when I remembered the old inscription.

[20] I tore myself from the group and reentered the prison. In the midst of the debris I found my cell and went quickly to the stones near the floor. [21] I picked up a flint rock, and found the other etchings: "Paul and Silas" and then above that: "Eusebius and Coriolanus—we sang at midnight and felt much better the next morning."

[22] I had to do it. Other Christians who might one day have the cell needed to know. I scratched my name and date just above the other two inscriptions and drew a crude arrow from my name to the names of Paul and Silas. [23] I scratched a simple phrase beside the crude arrow: "GOD DELIVERED US. KEEP THE FAITH."

[24] I stepped over broken stones and rushed out into the starlight. Urbanus came out of the night carrying Publius who shouted through the darkness, "Did it work?"

[25] "The jail is empty," I replied.

[26] "The church is full," he cheered.

The Arrest of Scrubjoy the Pure

6 Coriolanus seems to have returned to his former manner of life. His generosity toward me has seriously ebbed since we were cell mates. Still, the common ordeal of the church has generally freed us all from the dominion of any man. ² Coriolanus suggested to me that while the pulpit at Konos no longer needed a pastor, there was a small church in Arabia. He now feels that God is leading me to pastor there.

³ The church has erupted with joy. ⁴ Publius has just gone to be with the Lord, and we have buried him in a sunny field on the way to the leper colony. ⁵ One must never be sentimental over the whereabouts of graves since to be absent from the body is to be in the presence of the Savior. ⁶ Still, could he know it, he would love the field and the sun.

⁷ Urbanus has left the church and gone to Asia Minor to help with the work there. Phoebe and Lucia are working together among the lepers to extend the gospel among those who are not welcome in the city.

⁸ What can I say, Clement? The church services are marked by joy. ⁹ It is so good to be preaching in my own church and to know that the peace of Christ that accompanied me to prison will now go before me.

¹⁰ Did I ever tell you what happened to Scrubjoy? He was far too open in his crusade against all sin. He built one of his famous "purity fires" and was burning some "dirty scrolls." An old and scruffy tippler noticed the fire and wandered over to warm his hands.

¹¹ "Scrubjoy, you old viper, how have you been?"

¹² "Cassius! I'm fine. I'm a Christian now. I'm serving my sweet Jesus and taking my stand against all sin."

¹³ "At once? Wouldn't it be better if you tackled one or two at a time?"

¹⁴ "No. God hates *all* sin and so do I." Scrubjoy threw a few more scrolls on the fire and watched them flame without smiling. "No, Cassius, my values have all changed.

¹⁵ "The ax is laid to the root of human folly. The time has come for all iniquity to be judged. The chaff is in the fire. ¹⁶ All connivers, fools, adulterers, and dancers will be thrown into the pit. Those who have made their tunics enticing and their evil habits an abomination will be judged."

¹⁷ Cassius looked at Scrubjoy through his bleary eyes. He hiccuped.

¹⁸ "You might as well know it, Cassius, your drunkenness is an abomination, too."

¹⁹ Cassius accepted his judgment in silence. Scrubjoy threw a few

more scrolls into the flames and Cassius coughed as an unexpected puff of smoke came his way.

[20] "Scrubby, what is Jesus like?"

[21] "He is a great judge throwing sinners in the pit. He is the flame of the harvest that burns the evil chaff of this world. He despises low men and low morals. [22] He sets on fire the course of nature till justice prevails and all men leave their evil wine and filthy minds in the devil's pit where they came from."

[23] By this time Scrubjoy was preaching so loudly and his purifying flames had grown so high that a group of centurions noticed the light, heard the commotion and came to investigate.

[24] "Wouldn't you know it, boys, another fanatic," said the centurion.

[25] "Shall we arrest both of them?" asked a second soldier.

[26] "No, just arrest the Christian. Leave the drunk alone. Drunks are pleasant people."

[27] Well, Clement, Scrubjoy is the only member I have in jail at the moment. [28] If he would just build smaller fires and fight a few sins at once, we might be able to keep him out of trouble.

[29] Bear greetings to all in your parish who know me.

[30] I commend you to Christ.

The Fifth Letter of Eusebius of Philippi to His Beloved Friend Clement

The First of Four Souls—Atticus

1 Atticus of Ephesus—no, Philippi—no, of Thessalonica—no, of Berea, has died. It makes little difference where he was from. ² He is in heaven now, or so we may hope. ³ Let us be positive and pronounce him to be there.

⁴ He died at the Sunday morning games while most of us were at worship. He did not face the lions as a martyr. ⁵ In fact, he had not gone to the games under persecution for his faith. He never openly declared himself a Christian, and that Sunday morning he cheered with the pagans the passing of his brothers.

⁶ For the last several years he had been overeating and overdrinking, and as you have already surmised, skipping worship for various amusements.

⁷ This particular Sunday he had gone to the games quite drunk and staggered awkwardly up the ramp during the main event where the Asian lions were loosed upon the African Christians. ⁸ The Christians, as usual, were faring badly and Atticus turned to have a look near the top arena rail. ⁹ He was bumped by a plebeian who was dashing for his seat and began to sway comically before he fell over the edge. ¹⁰ The lions were on him in no time at all, and thus, against his good pleasure, he died in the faith.

¹¹ So we may say our brother has gone to meet the Lord. Let us assume that when he got there the Lord was not too upset about his untimely arrival. ¹² He was a member here in Philippi, but when I reported his passing to the rest of the fellowship, many of them asked me, "Atticus who?" ¹³ It was then that I stammered the list of cities and empirewide addresses where the young man had from time to time been a member.

¹⁴ "Atticus who?" That is the question. I must admit that even I had to search my memory when the bereaved family requested his burial. ¹⁵ "After all," they reasoned, "he began his Christian commitment in this

church, so it is only natural that he finish up his Christian life at the same place."

[16] During the next few days I attempted to reconstruct the life of Atticus from the time he disappeared from our church. [17] I found that Atticus was visited many times because he was rarely in church on Sunday and avoided all mention of committing himself to anything. According to an old elder, the reason for his last departure was that he was asked to serve as an usher.

[18] Atticus moved to Thessalonica where there was a large congregation. There it was easier to stay unnoticed. [19] One of the Thessalonian deacons informed me that our late friend left in anger one Sunday morning when the pastor could not immediately recall his name.

[20] From there Atticus went to Berea where he attended a service. [21] But his visit came on a Sunday when the sermon was on commitment and he never went back.

[22] Some months later Atticus began attending the church in Apollonia, and it was there that he seemed most at home. [23] At least he remained long enough for nearly everyone to become acquainted with him. [24] In fact, he even organized a marathon team for the boys of the church. One of the charter members, Sister Penelope, accused him of poor spiritual leadership for the boys, and the phantasmic Atticus vanished again.

[25] Two months later he reemerged at Berea where he lived for years before he died as a Christian incognito. His nearly devoured remains will be delivered here tomorrow for burial. After all, is it not natural that one should end his earthly sojourn at the place it began?

[26] I suppose his entry into heaven is a testament of grace. While I realize that nobody is ever worthy to enter those celestial halls, probably Atticus is less so than others. [27] Still, we must not be too hard on him. The lions, they say, had been starved to madness. The poor beasts were desperate. [28] The hapless Atticus was likely the first square meal they had eaten in a month. [29] While the committed martyrs may have tasted better, I suppose we must grudgingly admit that from the lions' point of view, what Atticus did for their hunger was a ministry of sorts.

The Second of Four Souls—Sapphire of Cyprus

2 Sapphire of Cyprus is getting ready to take her annual fair-weather leave. She has been polishing and oiling the wheels of the sporty new chariot she hopes to drive to her beach house on the Mediterranean.

189

[2] She loves the summer and, while the weather is fair enough to permit witnessing along the Roman Road, she prefers to use the time for herself. [3] She will arrive home in the fall with an excellent suntan and offer our Lord a lovelier complexion for her ministry among her paler sisters of this inland church. [4] Her tribe is becoming manifold. I grieve their absence in the fellowship. There are so many things that need doing for God, and so few available for the doing at certain seasons of the year.

[5] But the Ides of May have come! Things go ill then that never go awry in the Ides of March during the winter solstice. [6] I am tempted to be depressed by the coming of summer. [7] Soon the trees will bloom and the birds throb with song. [8] And what will the Christians do then? [9] Many will join the coming exodus into hedonism. Their flight is on the heels of a winter which has lasted too long.

[10] So they pitch their tents in the foothills of pleasure. By heaven, Clement, one must preach against this seasonal allegiance to faith. I'll not have it!

[11] Shall we envy our brothers who soak in the sun and the sea? [12] No. Let those who worship the sun burn in it! [13] Woe to all whose leisure makes havoc of love! [14] Woe to those for whom God is only a three-season deity! [15] Woe to those who sun in glee, too stiff of knee to pray!

[16] It is not that I would have men languish in the guilt of sacred summers. [17] I cry to those who must withhold themselves from God and offer their bronzed bodies on the beaches of each lost Lord's Day. [18] The voices of their Sunday infidelity rise from open-air indulgence crying their denial in the streets.

[19] Woe upon our generation! [20] Woe to the August of this heated infamy! [21] Return, you rebels, from the sea lest God smite the shores on which you play!

[22] Know this, O perverse generation, he who worships a nine-month God does not understand his unfailing foreverness. Autumn gods are absent gods. [23] Clement, you may feel that I am harsh to these summer truants.

[24] But I burn in the heat of this issue, and it is more than the Grecian humidity that makes me swelter. [25] It is the seasonal apathy of the redeemed. [26] Was our Lord's commitment to his Father's unflagging love only a seasonal affair? [27] Sapphire of Cyprus and all the others of her ilk race to the beaches and leave behind them their ministry.

²⁸ May hurricanes destroy summer! May the wheels break from their chariots. May their horses go lame! May vermin infect their figs and cheese! ²⁹ May they know only rain for the summer! But more than all else, may I learn to accept them and love them despite their sunny pilgrimages!

³⁰ Enough! I am out of breath. ³¹ Still, I am torn. Must Calvary's love be lost in sunsets and botany? ³² One wonders what the Galileans were doing that April Friday when the cross was raised. Were they picnicking in Galilee on the shores of Tiberias?

³³ That's the rub! We must learn to serve the whole year and worship the Christ of all seasons.

Bacchus and the Problem of Too Much Commitment

3 Occasionally I find a person who gives more to Christ than Christ wants. Some of these give more credit to our dear Lord than he would prefer. ² I remember a sister who read the poems of Ovid and felt that she herself was a great Christian poet. ³ In her zeal she would read selection after selection of her work in the assembly and after each reading, she would demurely say, "The Holy Spirit gave me this poem; I take no credit for it myself." ⁴ There was a widespread belief in the fellowship that the Holy Spirit didn't want the credit for it either.

⁵ It was not that she didn't mean well. Of course, she did. What is a Christian pastor to do to help those whose gifts are more limited than their zeal to use them? ⁶ They have a humility that is willing for God to have all the glory that their small talent may yield. ⁷ On the other hand, they have just enough arrogance to push their not-overly-sought-after talent on the undeserving.

⁸ My latest problem is Bacchus the Basso. He recently came to our assembly choir from the country chapel of Bythinia. ⁹ He boasted of being the best bass in the Bythinian brotherhood, having bested all other bassos in the back country.

¹⁰ How shall I liken his control and delivery? He is loud and deafening, like a clap of thunder in a stone tomb. He pumps too much of his melody through his nostrils. ¹¹ His softness isn't soft, his vibrato doesn't vibrate, and his precision is imprecise.

¹² All these qualities are not as disturbing as his main affliction—his dedication. ¹³ He testified in the assembly that he just "had to sing for

Jesus." By heaven, Clement, he'll have the Almighty with his fingers in his ears! And all the while he feels that he is doing heaven a service.

[14] I have tried to dissuade him from using his gift. One elder suggested that he try ushering. Some are praying that the Lord heal him with laryngitis. [15] Others are coping by arriving after the music is over, just in time for the sermon. [16] If Bacchus continues, worship is done for in Philippi. The rodents left the building three solos ago, and soon the congregation will join the race of the rats.

[17] You are far more skilled at diplomacy than I, dear Clement. [18] How does one tell a brother that his talent isn't, or that the gift he had laid on the altar of the Lord should have been laid to rest?

[19] Willingness is an important quality in the life of a believer. It speaks against those who have gifts but are too stingy to make them usable. [20] Have you noticed that the greatest gifts often sit silent in a church while the poorest are exercised often and—as in the case at hand—in extreme.

[21] I remember a certain alto sister who had been kicked by a taurus in the adenoids. She loved our dear Lord and sang violently to his glory. It may seem incredible, but she also was from the back country of Bythinia. [22] She would have perished in the first wave of persecution, but singing as she did at the hour of her death the lions would not go near her. [23] We were finally able to divert her talents into charity work among the earless lepers of Cenchrea where she is at the present time.

[24] But of Bacchus I am not so optimistic. He is to sing again on the Lord's Day. Fortunately, I feel a flu coming on.

Petrus—the Last of Four Souls

4 I want to get this letter to the courier on the southern sprint, so I must bring it to a close. But I would also like to ask your prayers for our church as it currently is. [2] My problems began some time ago, actually, but there have been certain deficiencies in our church programming since our latest stroke of ill luck.

[3] Two years ago a certain Petrus was thrown to the lions and the church at Philippi suffered terribly. It was not merely the grief that left our fellowship disconsolate. [4] The truth is that Petrus was busy, and his passing left a lot of holes in our church administration. [5] Whatever do you do when your best committeemen are devoured?

[6] Petrus not only taught a Scripture class, but he was the keeper of the sacred purse, deacon widow tender, worship leader, and church

greeter. [7] I know it sounds crass, but wouldn't it be nice if the lions devoured only the mediocre and nonactive members? [8] The beasts are chewing holes in our church structure.

[9] I realize that the issue has not so much to do with the appetites of the lions as it does the current misunderstanding of discipleship. It raises all sorts of questions. [10] Did the late Petrus take upon himself much that other Christians might have done? Has the Archenemy arranged it so that church workers who are unpalatable to God do not whet the appetites of lions either? [11] Should only a few of the people do all the work? Can the problem be reversed? [12] It is almost like the very arena in which poor Petrus perished. There were thousands of spectators looking down on a few people doing all the struggling. So it is from week to week in the churches.

[13] And those who do all the work are often bitter because there is so little help. [14] Take Petrus's widow. She died of nervous exhaustion only a couple of weeks ago. She too was an athletic Christian. [15] She sang in the choir and played the lyricon for cherubs when they sang. She was janitress, deaconess, babysitter, and collected old togas for the poor. [16] She ran atrium sales and baked squab for the visiting evangelists. It is hard to know whether it would be better to be eaten by lions or just collapse from the schedule.

[17] It is said that when Petrus died he stared at the lion and said, "Passio meus in Christi est." (My suffering is in Christ.) It was all so lovely and noble. [18] Petrus's widow on the other hand, just collapsed baking a pan of figgy bread for the women's group. Her last words were not directly translatable, although some thought it sounded rather like a grateful gasp.

[19] Something must be done, Clement. There must be a better way to balance the work. [20] Some say there is a new wave of persecution coming, and the lions are hungry. [21] I'm worried because so much of the work of the church is now being done by Julius. Were he to be devoured upon the Lupercal, we would be hamstrung at the church until the Ides of Janus when the new nominating committee meets for the first time.

[22] Pray for us that more Christians here in Philippi will see their divine responsibility to become committed. [23] Pray that Julius will not be arrested for the Emperor's sport. We cannot stand the loss if we are to succeed in the current growth campaign.

[24] The lions make it hard to keep our attendance where it should be.

[25] Think of us at Lupercal.

The Sixth Letter of Eusebius of Philippi to His Beloved Friend Clement

The World Is Coming to an End Along with Patience

1 Who can deny that the world is coming to an end—soon and abruptly? [2] There are many indicators, "signs of the times," as they are all prone to say in the streets. [3] This is truly a time of transition, the worst time, I think, that the world shall ever see. [4] Never has there been a time so short of time as our own. These are the last wretched days of the putrid planet earth.

[5] Am I overdoing this, Clement? Keep in mind that there is the hint of universal winter in the air. The night is upon us. [6] The Gauls have marched into Germania and are holding the natives at swordpoint. [7] Here at the very height of the Iron Age the Britons are raising the price of ore again. We shall soon not be able to afford rims for our chariot wheels. [8] Complicating the peace is the Nubian protest. The orb is restless.

[9] Is this the last dark hour? Some are saying the world will not long endure and that our very Caesar is the Antichrist. [10] They say that Gaul is the Great Gog of Ezekiel, and that the conflict over iron will lead us at last to the battle of Armageddon. [11] Some are saying that the century will never see its close before doomsday dawns.

[12] What do believers do when they are confronted with perilous times? All ages are ages of transition and soon give way to the next.

[13] We Christians are frustrated by these times. We have forgotten our birthright. We are citizens of the world to come. [14] Should the planet itself come to an end, we could get by without it.

[15] The other day I passed a little man carrying a sign that read: "The World Is Coming to an End!" I thought to pass on down the street when I heard a sickening thud on the cobblestones behind me. [16] A runaway chariot had skidded into the sign bearer and crushed him. [17] They picked up his frail, old bones and threw him into a cart and then tossed the sign on top of him.

[18] It was somehow symbolic. Do not most messages end with their messengers? [19] We should check our own pulse and respiration every time we

diagnose the terminal diseases of our planet. And we should not stand when we are sick with a high fever to talk about the death of the age.

[20] The world itself may be old, but the prospect for the life of the believer is joyous and new. Forgive me if I am not as morose as others seem these days. [21] God seems well enough. [22] I shall post this small epistle, believing it will safely reach you before the end of all flesh shall come.

The Urgent Ministry of Quintus Quick

2 My own concern about these desperate days has been sparked by the furor around these itinerant preachers of Christian doom. [2] They are not entirely gloomy, of course. They feel all believers will escape without a scratch in the glorious rapture of the church before the battle of Armageddon begins. [3] I should like thinking that Philippi will not shortly go up in smoke, but if it does, it's nice to know that the millennium dare not begin until I am snuggled in at the throne.

[4] Quintus Quick is in town and says that the day of the Lord is upon us. [5] "Get ready! Get ready!" he thunders out over the heads of the hearers. [6] "The great beast is about to make his mark on every forehead in northern Greece. Woe to those who receive the mark!"

[7] How are we to adjust to his desperate urgency?

[8] The day of the Lord is surely nigh. The signs of the times are all about us. [9] Our blessed King is coming again soon. MARANATHA! We are eager to see him. Each morning I find myself looking east and asking the question, "Why not today?" [10] But I always feel a certain uneasiness in this immediacy. [11] The preaching of Quintus Quick has caused no little stir among the believers here. [12] He has written a devastating scroll called *The Late Great Date of Human Fate!* He has drawn a great number of historical parallels between the Book of Daniel and the current time. [13] He feels that the Roman Empire is the great ten-horned beast of the Apocalypse and that the angel has already begun to pour her golden vial on the sun and that the age is shortly to end.

[14] Last night an ardent brother asked if the Lord could come back before all the Jews returned to Jerusalem. [15] While Brother Quick felt that this was not possible, he did feel that the great whore, drunk with the blood of nations, would probably prevent the two witnesses from sharing their midtribulation testimony. [16] "This," he said, "could cause a kind of satanic infection in the third toe of the great beast, and some

of the ten horns would then decline in size as the scarlet rider begins her charge across the world with her pillaging and death."

[17] Several were alarmed at Brother Quick's message that the Abomination of Desolation was already becoming obvious. [18] He said that the livid horseman of Revelation was none other than the current grain shortage in Thyatira. [19] This famine would be used by the new satanic trinity to draw men and women to commit adultery with the golden idol of time, symbolized by the great statue of Nebuchadnezzar in the Book of Daniel.

[20] His lecture tonight is entitled, "Who is Gog?" [21] He has promised to reveal the mysterious identity of old Six-Sixty-Six. [22] I guess it will be nice to get a little inside information on the Antichrist, but somehow I am insecure about Quintus Quick. [23] His crusade in Philippi and other cities has made him a lot of denarii. He can now dress in the best togas. When the rapture comes he will surely float upward in the best of threads, leaving the planet in class.

[24] But he does seem consistent. The sticker on the bumper of his chariot reads clearly, "In Case of Rapture, This Chariot May Become a Runaway." [25] I suppose if the second coming occurs tonight, Quintus will be whooshed away with the rest of us. He will probably be a little sad, however, to have to end his dynamic series on the subject.

[26] It is always hard to wait for the second coming, Clement. I'll write more later; right now I'll go and plant an apple tree. If Quintus Quick is wrong, I may someday enjoy its fruit.

On the Problem of Relics

3 It has not been more than a few decades since our Lord walked the planet, and there are now hundreds of souls making trips to the Holy Land in search of relics of one kind or another. [2] Last year Zelpha of Iconium found a board that was supposed to be a part of the cradle where Christ slept as a baby. Being somewhat of a devotionalist, Zelpha kisses the wood each morning; then holds it up toward Nazareth and prays in the name of the Infant King. [3] She is certain God hears her prayers and even if he doesn't, the board sure brings her good luck.

[4] Last year between Easter and Whitsun several relic peddlers came through selling everything from a martyr's tooth to a feather from Gabriel's left wing. [5] I ask you, how can they tell it was his left wing? What shall we say to these things? [6] When does the worship of holy things at last supplant the worship of a Holy God?

⁷ But here is the grand problem. Lavinia came on the Lupercal displaying the holy cloth. She says this sacred cloth is the very towel used by our Lord to dry his hands on the way to the cross. ⁸ If you look, you can still see the imprint of his blessed hands on the towel, she says.

⁹ When she came to church last Sunday, she was followed by a crowd of pilgrims, singing and swaying in adoration for the "Holy Hand Towel." ¹⁰ The towel had once been in the possession of Barbara of Berea, who was barren and whose barrenness was the bane of her dear Brutus, who always wanted children. ¹¹ Well, Barbara laid the towel across her barren body, and behold, she conceived in her womb. ¹² She and Brutus have been blessed with a baby boy whom they have named "Bartus of the Holy Hand Towel." ¹³ Not only that, but Barbara washed the holy cloth and hung it on a dead tree limb to dry, and when she went to bring it in again, lo, the dead tree had brought forth leaves and flowers.

¹⁴ She gave it to Lavinia who once was plagued with warts, but since the holy cloth has been in her keeping, her skin has become clean and pure without a blemish.

¹⁵ Should Lavinia come to Coos, she will let you see it for three mites or touch it for a shekel. This is the way she has chosen to finance her holy ministry. ¹⁶ This slight charge has allowed her to trade in her old chariot for a new one, and she plans to build a prayer tower down by Rhodes financed by the proceeds from the pilgrims.

¹⁷ Soon Lavinia wants to take the towel on a healing tour of lower Greece.

¹⁸ Clement, do you think the towel could have any real powers? It does seem strange that since Lavinia has owned it, she has rarely spoken of our dear Lord. ¹⁹ Wherever she goes, they fall down before the cloth, but few are coming to faith. ²⁰ Christians who used to praise God now only say, "Wow!" "Wow" is a new word I hadn't heard before. Its meaning is unsure, but I think it expresses more wonder than praise.

²¹ Let us beware of such shallow adoration that the world may turn from relics to reality.

A New Discovery and Its Effect on the Fellowship

4 We are in such a quandary here in the church to know exactly how to deal with those who from time to time receive the gift. ² I must

confess, dear Clement, that I myself have prayed to receive the gift, ardently and long. But so far it has never come.

³ The problem is that those who have received it wonder at my lack of excellence. ⁴ It is hard, indeed, for a pastor to live with such a reputation when others have received it. ⁵ The latest in the congregation to reach this plateau of spiritual excellence is Dolores of Delphos.

⁶ Dolores has received the gift. She has been praising God often and loud, sometimes standing in the middle of my sermon and shouting syllables of joy. ⁷ She smiles constantly, weeps much, and in general has many wishing her gift was still wrapped.

⁸ Dolores went to a women's gleam group depressed and came back smiling. She has been smiling ever since. ⁹ Even when she had a fever, she smiled, praised God and raised her hands till all her bracelets fell to her elbows.

¹⁰ Her experience has been a little difficult to understand. It is her praise phrases that seem to nettle the less emotional brothers in the fellowship. ¹¹ She "blesses God" regularly. ¹² For instance, she was introduced to a new member of the church, and when it would have been entirely appropriate to say, "Hello," she "blessed God!" ¹³ When she was told of the death of Hyrum of Pisidia, she once again "blessed God."

¹⁴ But "blessing God" is not her only idiosyncrasy. ¹⁵ She abounds in "praise phrases." "When you're distressed, seek to be blessed!" Or several have heard her remark, "Precious Jesus, heal our diseases." "Lift up holy hands, brother!" is another of her phrases.

¹⁶ Now it seems that her affectation is shortly to become an infection. She has been trying to organize spiritual gleam groups in the church. ¹⁷ For a while some were glowing. Sister Priscilla thought she had the gift, but after three days of smiling she had to sit down and rest. ¹⁸ Aphia of Antioch also smiled for a day and a half, but an early elbow injury kept her from holding her hands up for very long; she is dropping out of her gleam group and joining a Christian discussion club. ¹⁹ Patience is threadbare. We cannot force ourselves into the irreverent position of telling Dolores that her gift is grating on our group. Never has the quiet love of God been so blatantly obvious in the church.

²⁰ What are we to do? Since Dolores got interested in her new joy, she has scarcely had time to minister to the sick and the lost. All her energy is expended on blessing God and starting gleam groups. ²¹ Her happi-

ness seems all right for her, but it is clearly driving the church up the arbor insectus.

²² And who gets all the credit for her eternal smile? The Holy Spirit. ²³ Can this be the same Holy Spirit sent to comfort us in times of grief?

²⁴ There's the rub. Grieving is as much a part of life as gleaming. How can we give the giddy, ever giggling Dolores a balanced view?

²⁵ Jesus was serious at times. Four times the scrolls say that he actually wept. We showed Dolores the very passage that said, "Jesus wept," but she only smiled and blessed God and handed us an invitation to the next gleam group. ²⁶ We are at an impasse.

²⁷ Some other epistle I might close by saying, "Bless God," but things being what they are, I think I'll just say, "Have a pleasant day."

The Lepers

5 I am in need. Three of our wealthiest members had their homes and goods confiscated by the authorities, and thus, the church income has declined. ² Before my conversion in Asia Minor I used to make sandals and leather boots for the legionnaires. Well, I have gone back into the work again. ³ My hands have suffered terribly. The leather is often hot and the huge needles have cut savagely into my palms. ⁴ I am sure that they will toughen and that before long I will be able to work faster.

⁵ I had enough scraps left from my first four pair of sandals to make a left thong for Lucia the Leper. ⁶ How I suffer in knowing that the dear woman, even if she could afford to do otherwise, must always buy her sandals one at a time! I cannot tell you the joy on her face when I took her the new shoe. ⁷ She has been a leper for twenty years, and the disease has not been kind to her. She has a wealthy daughter in Philippi who could take her all she needs to ease her stay in the colony of the damned. But she hasn't heard from her daughter in three years.

⁸ "Tell me, Brother Eusebius, would you cross the Neapolis Road and see if you might inadvertently catch a glimpse of my daughter in the garden?" she asked when she had finished lacing up the thong on her left sandal. ⁹ "If I could know my daughter was still alive and in good health, I could go to my grave in peace. She just never could tear herself away from the comforts of Olympian society to face the risk in being a Christian.

¹⁰ "The last time I saw her," the old woman went on, "was the year I lost my right foot. She had just been to the games during the high per-

secution and was thrilled that so many of our brethren were being destroyed. ¹¹ How much it hurt me, Brother Eusebius, to hear her so critical of the martyrs. She told me then that the sooner the whole Grecian Peninsula was cleared of our heresy, the sooner the gods would bless the land with rain and new crops."

¹² She hesitated and turned away. At length she spoke. "Come!"

¹³ She hobbled off on her right crutch and new left sandal. "I have been selfish," she said over her shoulder as I followed. ¹⁴ When we reached the back of the hut she pointed to a bronze box hidden by the foliage. She sat down suddenly and drew out the box with her gnarled hand.

¹⁵ "Will God forgive our selfishness?" she said.

¹⁶ "He forgives all," I answered.

¹⁷ "I have kept this far too long. It is all I have owned of any value. I have kept it for no reason except it was mine and it is new. I will not be guilty of storing up trifles. Do you know Delia who lives in the mud thatch near the cemetery?"

¹⁸ "Yes. I have heard that she is considering becoming a Christian."

¹⁹ "Then you have not heard!" she exclaimed, overjoyed about the news she was to impart. Her face was alive with spiritual radiance. I no longer saw the contagion that scarred her face.

²⁰ "Delia *is* a Christian now!"

²¹ I smiled as a kind of weak mirror to the radiant joy of Lucia.

²² "Here, you open it!" She handed me the bronze cask. Her malformed hands throbbed with excitement.

²³ I hesitated a moment to reflect on this episode of joy and the mystery of the box.

²⁴ "Well, go on," she insisted.

²⁵ I opened the box. In it lay a single sandal.

²⁶ "I put it here when my condition became so bad that I could no longer walk. Then I lost my right foot. This box since that time has been a shrine of self-pity. ²⁷ When my daughter ceased to care about me, I came only to dote on my desolation. But when you gave me this sandal just now, all that changed. ²⁸ Leprosy is but an earthly category. Delia says that in all the anthems of the crystal city they have never heard the word 'unclean.'"

²⁹ "It is true," I said.

³⁰ She ran her hand across her face, "Then the only scars in the new eternity are those which mark the hands of Christ."

³¹ We sat for a moment; then I put the sandal back in the case and started to leave.

³² "No, No!" she protested. "Take it to Delia. It is a small token for our hope. Do you know where her hut is?"

³³ "I can find it!" I said.

³⁴ I made my way through the brush feeling the new joy my old occupation was providing. Back in the sandal business after all these years! How can we ever know that Christ himself may hide in so simple a thing as a sandal.

³⁵ I was lost in thought. Still swinging the simple gift, I saw Delia's hut. Lucia's strange token held a meaning I did not understand.

³⁶ I caught sight of Delia squatting outside. When she saw me, she rose up and leaned against a leafless tree.

³⁷ Then I knew. Delia was standing on her right foot. It was bare. ³⁸ Her left was gone.

³⁹ The love of one leper may sometimes keep thorns from the foot of another. And in a world where two amputees are required to make a single set of footprints, eternity is a welcome word.

On Nicholas the Liberal

6 You will pardon the smudges on the parchment, but I have been getting some oil together for the big burning.

² Nicholas the Liberal is to be ignited at the seventh watch today.
³ Nicholas has been teaching doctrines unfriendly to the faith, so I'm afraid he must be burned.

⁴ Burnings are not what they used to be since oil is in such short supply.

⁵ Clement, I do not like these burnings. They are no witness to the love of Christ. ⁶ Nicholas has denied the key doctrines, and the faith can scarcely exist if his kind of heresy is tolerated. ⁷ Yet I feel uneasy in these events. ⁸ I cannot believe that God is altogether pleased.

⁹ I remember last year when we burned Brutus Dubitus. ¹⁰ His wife and children were crying so you could hardly hear the choir singing "Love Divine." It took much of the dignity out of the occasion. ¹¹ Brutus preached in the Chapel of Errors before he was arrested by two of the

Fiery Faithful. [12] They said his views of Scripture were unsound. [13] As they lit the oil, Brutus began to sing the praise of Christ. [14] Now I have a feeling that he may have been burned by mistake.

[15] I believe every word of Scripture, and I hate to hear it maligned, but I am nervous. [16] A certain narrow saint heard me preach only a fortnight ago and told the Fiery Faithful that I was strong on the incarnation but never once referred to transcendent holiness. [17] Clement, could we be burning tomorrow's heroes before the facts are in? [18] Now there are rumors about me all over Asia. [19] Should you be asked to bring the oil to my burning, I would have you understand I do not doubt the Word. [20] We have to stop burning each other or we shall leave our finest witnesses in the ashes. [21] It does no good to sing of love while we grind our teeth. [22] Nor is it easy to whip the error-ridden into hell while we try to preach the way to heaven.

[23] It is a mad world where Romans burn Christians who, in the pursuit of good doctrine, burn each other.

[24] Hark! I hear a knock at the door. Good doctrine be forever! It is the Fiery Faithful crying for my blood, "Where truth is spurned, men must be burned." [25] I must bury this letter under the floor before I answer. The stake may await me.

[26] Should I never see you again, Clement, we shall meet in greater light.

Four to Three

7 Clement, wonder of wonders, I have been acquitted at my heresy trial. The Fiery Faithful were somewhat divided in their assessment of my theology. I was acquitted by a vote of four to three. [2] After the trial we all sang, "We are One in the Bonds of Jesus' Love." It's a beautiful hymn, but all the time I was singing, I just kept thinking, "Four to three!"

[3] After Nicholas was found guilty, they sang the same hymn before the burning. Again the vote was four to three.

[4] I believe, however, that the Fiery Faithful will soon cease their witch-hunting, for the persecution is gaining in intensity. One of them was thrown to the lions only yesterday, in fact, to seven lions at once. [5] Three of them showed no interest in devouring him, but four tore him to pieces.

[6] May all the lions vote in my favor if my time should come. Clement, pray for me as I do for you, in these perilous times.

The Unfinished Epistle, the Last Known Letter of Eusebius to Clement

[1] Clement, the time of my departure is at hand. [2] Even now through the iron grating of my arena cell I hear the hungry snarling of the big cats. [3] I am slated to fight it out with the African lions. Fight it out? What real chance is there—the lions always win.

[4] Clement, how much over all these years have I enjoyed our friendship! Although we were forced to communicate across so many miles of desert, mountains, and open sea, how surprising it has been to find all of the things that we have had in common! Our tastes, our petty grievances, our fondness for integrity, our admiration of the ideal. [5] How shall I ever thank you for your letters? And now, dear amicus, the lions shall stop our correspondence.

[6] For me our letters have been a useful outlet. Knowing that you read and sometimes shared my troubled experiences has made it easy for me to be open and honest. [7] Brother, though I have sought to be, I am not that brave in the pulpit.

[8] I am not a brave man—not even a man who finds it easy to talk of the supernatural, faraway, spiritual realm you find so near and natural. [9] I am just a doomed commoner who, given a fondness for the here and now, nonetheless believes all he can. I always feel the crunch of being trapped between what I was and what I would rather have been.

[10] The truth is, the times were too desperate for the luxury of orderly and logical thinking. But I struggled for it. [11] I faced my own weaknesses and found that I tried to love God with a faith that was often too practical to be deep and too timorous to be courageous. [12] I am frightened to the depths.

[13] I have not experienced the martyr's syndrome. I have gone through shock, anger and acceptance. [14] I was shocked when I first was notified. "Why me?" I protested to the Almighty. [15] A voice spoke out of the dark-

ness: "Eusebius, it's just your lucky day! Think of the joy it will be to beat all the nonmartyrs to the fullness of heaven!"

[16] Then I went directly into anger. "Look God," I said, "you've got the wrong man! I'm not that dedicated!"

[17] Clement, they say that your namesake, Clement of Alexandria, at his arrest looked steadfastly into heaven and said, "I go now to Rome to become the bread of God, made from meal, ground between the teeth of lions." How sweet and how beautiful! [18] How pleased the Almighty must have been with this lovely, poetic anticipation of a noble death.

[19] I am never going to be one of those little sugary, prayer-filled martyrs who sings hymns as he is torn to pieces. [20] I will embarrass God running and crying before the lions. It's going to be a bad show. I love God but am afraid of animals. [21] I remember when Antipas was devoured, he cried, "Sola Christus vita mea est!" How spiritual compared to my "Let me out of here!"

[22] Clement, my anger has turned to bitterness. It just isn't fair! I have dealt with Coriolanus and the deacons. I have carried bread to the lepers. I have preached in prison. [23] And what do I get for all this? Nothing. The lions are the winners. All of my dedication to the ministry ends as a meager serving of fodder.

[24] I could have been a success if I had worked for Jupiter. His priests pronounce the invocation at the very games where we are devoured. [25] These pagan priests laugh in the streets that their invocations are really a kind of table grace for the beasts. [26] In truth I cannot think of the lions and pray, "Lord, bless my body to their body."

[27] Oh, Clement, this is my last letter. It is all over! [28] Your final vision of me will not be as you have always thought of me. No, no, no! You will see your dear friend running pellmell from the animals and crying in terror. Where's the dignity in Christian death?

[29] I am praying moment by moment for the second coming. It would be the best way out for both God and myself. [30] Then the lions could go back to eating whatever they ate before Christ came and hapless martyrs believed.

[31] I have been very tense lately, Clement, with a lot of chest pains. It could be my heart. This morning I experienced a massive pain that stopped my breath and seemed for a moment to paralyze my vision. [32] It could be serious . . .

To Clement of Coos:

I found this letter addressed to you lying by the body of Eusebius who was discovered dead in his cell. Had he lived one more day, he might have been a gallant witness to your God. He spoke constantly of Jesus, and rarely in his last week of life did the jailers pass his cell without hearing him at prayer. Even in the face of martyrdom his disposition to his keepers was congenial and his faith was intriguing to us all. He believed with such force that we who kept his cell were almost convinced to join him in faith. If he was right in his visions, he has now joined a hope we Romans have tried in vain to challenge with lions. If he was wrong, I yet envy the joy his faith provided.

Sincerely,
Lucilius
Arena Warden

Afterword:
Who is Helmut Niedegger?

In February 1970 I was invited to a three-day colloquium of archaeologists held in Baltimore. My interest in this particular conference was immense because several papers were to be read on the gnostic gospel of St. Thaddeus which had been found the previous year in a wine cellar in Beirut. The manuscript was clearly a forgery, but it was a third-century document composed near the end of Diocletian's reign of terror.

When I arrived on Monday, I was disappointed to discover that the first paper on the gnostic gospel would not be read till Tuesday. I might have stayed away from the opening symposium altogether except for the title of the Monday night seminar: "Egyptology, Assyriology, and Coosiology in Perspective." It was the word *Coosiology* which arrested my attention. I had never heard of the discipline. I ran my finger down the list of lecturers and was surprised to find not just one paper but three on the subject, and all were to be read by Helmut Niedegger of Leipzig Library. Dr. Niedegger was to read his first paper at the close of the Monday night session.

Fatigued though I was, I went to the opening of the symposium. The first two papers addressed Egyptology and Assyriology respectively. They were plodding. Besides, I was familiar with these disciplines. But Coosiology was such a new field that most of those in attendance were locked in rapport with the small German scholar as he delivered his paper. I was fascinated to discover that Coos, which Dr. Niedegger always pronounced "Ko-os" in two syllables, while the rest of us continued to rhyme it with "moose," was in more modern times called Stanchio, an island with many pigeons. It was once a major island in the Aegean. The apostle Paul, legend has it, had weighed anchor there on one of his missionary journeys.

Dr. Niedegger explained that he had come to believe that there existed somewhere on the island near the monastery of St. Thaddeus a second-century manuscript written by Eusebius of Philippi during a horrible wave of empirewide persecutions. He himself had searched for this manuscript for more than thirty years but had never been able to find it. He believed that it was hidden somewhere in the vaulted archives of that monastery. He mentioned that the monks of St. Thaddeus not only took an oath of silence like Trappists but actually consented to having their tongues torn out. This assured them that they would never be tempted to break their holy vows. Since this was a small Eastern Orthodox monastery, they wrote only in Greek and never spoke at all. Dr. Niedegger believed that the lost manuscript might have been easier to find if the communication barrier had not been so great.

After the delivery of his outstanding paper, "Coosiology and the Lost Documents of Philippi," I, like thirty or forty others, had an overwhelming desire to touch the eminent scholar. For reasons that I now believe may have been uniquely inspired, I had the good fortune to be staying at the very same hotel as Dr. Niedegger. In a city the size of Baltimore this can hardly have been a mere coincidence. Thus our fellowship tightened into esteem during our three days together. Dr. Niedegger filled me with a growing appetite to visit Coos and to obtain, if I could, any information at all about the lost Philippian document. While I knew that the manuscript would not be directly related to the New Testament era, I began to believe that it was a key to understanding the general era of the early church fathers.

I took Dr. Niedegger to the airport in Baltimore. He had to deliver The Eastern Research Lectures at the Smithsonian foundation before he returned to Germany. "Good-bye, Calvin!" he yelled back in a broken German accent as he walked down the Jetway, "If you need me, you can write me at the library of Leipzig!" he said, melting into the queue of passengers.

"Auf Wiedersehen, Helmut!" I yelled after him. Standing a moment, looking wistfully away, I turned on my heel and walked out of the airport. Dr. Niedegger had awakened an idea within me that would not sleep.

I arrived in Coos (please forgive me for not using the modern name of the island) six weeks later. The island was much as Dr. Niedegger had explained it. I had flown in on a sea plane from the harbor at Rhodes and, after taxiing on the dockside, hired a cab for my trip to the base of Mt. Arphaxad. Once I reached the base of the mountain, I began the steep ascent to the monastery of St. Thaddeus that could only be reached by foot.

When I was finally inside the compound, two monks showed a look of panic and rushed upon me as though I was standing on forbidden holy ground. They seized me and began shoving me toward the stone gate by which I had entered. "Unhand me, brothers!" I shouted to the silent and brutish holy men. They continued shoving me until I cried out, "I am a personal friend of Helmut Niedegger!" At the name of Niedegger they fell backward as if they had seen an angel. They bowed before me and rose again. With kinder faces they led me back into the compound.

There were now only twenty-four monks at the monastery, all committed in silence to their years of ministry. A novice showed me the library, kitchen, and wine cellar. Another showed me to a small, crudely furnished room. It was apparently the guest room, for as I stepped inside, they made mute gestures of welcome as though they wanted me to stay there.

Only two items hung from the walls—an ivory crucifix and a photograph of none other than Helmut Niedegger of Leipzig Library. As they bowed to leave the room, they genuflected not before the crucifix but before the portrait of Helmut.

I will not detail how my next two months there were spent. Among the silent brothers of St. Thaddeus I became the close friend of the Abbot Androcles. After some time he encouraged me through the unique sign language that had developed at Mt. Arphaxad to search for the missing manuscript that Dr. Niedegger had mentioned at the colloquium in Baltimore. Even if it were important to tell of this search, it would not be expedient. It is sufficient to say that every niche and cranny of the dusty monastery was searched. Everywhere I looked I well imagined that the Librarian of Leipzig had already been there. I was disappointed and was soon convinced that my search could not avail. I made preparations to return to my parish in the Midwest since I knew my congregation would soon be wondering what had become of their pastor.

On the day I was to leave the most fortuitous event of my life occurred. The Abbot Androcles had ordered the wine vat enlarged in the third-century enclosure directly beneath the stone larder that had been built in the twelfth century. During the removal of the stones, a large leather bag was discovered. In the bag was a scroll which the Abbot Androcles gave to me.

While the scroll was attached only to one spindle, it was obviously substantial. The uncial Greek characters ran together in a manner typical of second-century manuscripts. I was delirious! Across the opening vertical column of faded black letters ran the words *To Clement of Coos from Eusebius of Philippi.*

I assured the Abbot that I would give proper credit to the brothers of St. Thaddeus for the discovery of the piece if only he would let me take it to Leipzig and share the joy of its discovery with Helmut Niedegger. At the mention of the Coosiologist the Abbot released the scroll to me.

I changed my travel plans and flew directly to Leipzig, having wired the council of the church I pastor, telling them that they must wait two more weeks for my return. I knew that they would understand when they learned of my discovery and of the importance of my consultation with Dr. Niedegger.

Once in Leipzig I took a taxi to the university and went directly to the library. After I reached the small, neat German campus, I entered the library and asked the receptionist for directions to the study of Herr Professor Doktor Helmut Niedegger.

"Niedegger?" she asked.

"Helmut Niedegger?" I repeated my question. "He is here, of course," I added, impatient with the Fräulein.

"I'm sorry, sir, we have no Niedegger on this faculty. There's a Mr. Neidenstein who cleans up the place. . . ."

"I'm sorry, miss. I'm speaking of Helmut Niedegger, the eminent Coosiologist," I said in my broken German.

"The Coosiologist?" she repeated the word as though we were playing some sort of game and then winked at what she obviously considered to be our little secret. "Why don't you try the Coosiology lab, my good fellow."

I was furious. But in an entire afternoon of searching, I found no mention of Helmut Niedegger in any part of the School of Antiquities or any other faculty. No one had ever heard of him. Could I have been crazy? Did he not deliver the key papers at a great American symposium on archaeology? Did not twenty-four monks in the Aegean worship his picture? A man of this stature simply does not drop out of the intellectual circles that sired his reputation. Yet no one in the university knew anything about Niedegger nor, indeed, of the discipline of Coosiology.

Disheartened I returned to America where I set to work translating what I came to call *The Philippian Fragment.* It was clearly a partial scroll and I needed the rest. I knew that somewhere sometime there had existed another spindle with more of the precious document wound around it. When I submitted the manuscript to the Department of Antiquities at the Smithsonian Institute, they declared it a forgery and surmised it had been scripted by a calligraphy student in the art department at Baltimore Metrotech. When I talked to the curator on the phone, he assured me that it was a bogus document. I felt ashamed and then cautiously asked him if he was familiar either with Dr. Helmut Niedegger or Coosiology.

"Coosi-what?" he asked.

"Never mind!" I said, hanging up the receiver.

A week later I received a list of criticisms of the manuscript. Most scholars had rejected it on the basis that the existence of a coliseum in Philippi was highly dubious and that the monastery of St. Thaddeus mentioned in 2 Clement 1:13 could not have existed in the second century since monasteries were produced in a much later day. Besides, the critics said, no monks in Christian history were ever known to tear their tongues out to enforce silence.

I returned to Coos for the proof I needed to establish both the reputation of *The Philippian Fragment* and of my mentor, Helmut Niedegger. I arrived at Mt. Arphaxad in June 1974. The monks were glad to see me. They wanted to know how Helmut Niedegger was faring in Leipzig. I couldn't bear to offend them, so I assured them that he was just as alive and well as a man of such renown and age could expect to be. They were pleased.

The Abbot Androcles, who seemed much older than before, motioned me to the back room and gave me a towel in which was wrapped the other spindle and the rest of *The Philippian Fragment.* I could hardly contain my joy. Then he took me to the chapel of St. Thaddeus and we had a special mass of thanksgiving for the discovery of the other half of the uncial scroll. I photographed the Abbot Androcles and his twenty-three brothers to use as proof of the existence in Christian history of tongueless monks. I also photographed the picture of Helmut Niedegger that hung across from the crucifix in my room. I intended to staple this to the old program that I had still retained of the Baltimore colloquium so that Coosiology and the Coosiologist could be restored to their rightful prominence in the world of archaeology.

Who can know the reason for all that befalls us? My last night on Coos I decided to stay in a beachfront guest house. I had packed early in the afternoon, taken the other half of the manuscript and left. That very night Mt. Arphaxad was destroyed by an earthquake. The monks were all buried in the rubble. The portrait of Dr. Niedegger was destroyed. In the aftermath of looting and confusion, my hotel room was burglarized and my camera and all the exposed film were lost.

When I returned home, I translated the remainder of *The Philippian Fragment*. Now that it is published, I suppose it will become a laughingstock in archaeology. During the past five years I have sought to locate any mention of Helmut Niedegger in the world of scholarship, all to no avail. I deeply regret the lack of esteem that exists for my work and especially the life work of my missing mentor.

Now that I have finally found a publisher who believes in my work (the editor smiled when he told me that), I only plead that you, dear reader, will see the intrinsic merit of this magnificent document. If after your study of this volume you still believe it to be bogus scholarship, I ask you to answer one question for me: Who is Helmut Niedegger?

Calvin Miller